Molly O'Neal

Witches, Fairies, and Saddle Oxfords

Book One

MOLLY O'NEAL

Witches, Fairies, and Saddle Oxfords

Pamela Gillette

LUMINARE PRESS
WWW.LUMINAREPRESS.COM

Molly O'Neal: Witches, Fairies, and Saddle Oxfords
Copyright © 2019 Pamela Gillette

All rights reserved. This book or any portion thereof may not be reproduced or used in any manner whatsoever without the express written permission of the publisher, except for the use of brief quotations in a book review.

Molly O'Neal, Witches Fairies and Saddle Oxfords is a work of fiction. Names, characters, places, and incidents either are the product of the author's imagination or are used fictitiously. Any resemblance to actual persons, living or dead, events, or locales is entirely coincidental.

Printed in the United States of America

Cover Design: Melissa K. Thomas

Luminare Press
442 Charnelton
Eugene, OR 97401
www.luminarepress.com

LCCN: 2019911940
ISBN: 978-1-64388-201-7

Many thanks to Patty for all her support, suggestions, and inspiration

Chapter One

Molly's childhood was carefree and almost normal, until the summer of 1961. She was born in 1952, in Stanton: the fourth child of Charles and Anna O'Neal. Her mom noticed that Molly was, as her family from the old country would explain it, sensitive to the spirits around her. As a baby in her crib or playpen, Molly could entertain herself for hours: cooing and babbling to the air. When she began to speak in full sentences, she had conversations with her *imaginary friends*. Mom didn't let Molly's siblings make fun of her, because Mom understood the *gifts* she had inherited from her Grandma Giba. Mom grew up being aware that some women in her family had a heightened sense of intuition. Mom's sister Veronica was sensitive to the spirit world as a child, but like most people with the *gift*, as she grew older, she ceased to be open to it. Grandma Giba never lost her understanding of the spirit world. Grandma counseled Anna on how to raise Molly as normally as possible, and to protect her from evil spirits that might seek her out.

When Molly was about a year old, the O'Neals moved to Kansas. They rented a little stone house, and her father worked as a gas station attendant. Molly was too young to remember anything about living in Kansas, but Mom remembered that Molly cried a lot in the middle of the night.

Mom thought the house was haunted, when she learned its history. She heard from a neighbor, that a couple rented the house before them, and the husband had killed his wife and her sister and then he killed himself. Mom thought some spirits were upsetting Molly. She was afraid to live in the house and wanted to move back home to Stanton.

Mom got her wish, and they moved back to Stanton a year and a half later, just in time for Mary to be born. Grandma found a house for them, and she visited them often. A railroad track ran right down the middle of the street and just a few yards from their front door. Molly was terrified of the railroad tracks and the loud trains. When they went by, they shook the house. One vivid memory Molly had, was standing up in the backseat of the car watching a train headlight coming their way and her father straddling the track. He wasn't worried at all that the train was coming, but Molly remembers being terrified. Another memory, although not a scary one, was of when she, and her older sister Maggie, painted the neighbors white picket fence with mud, and they got in trouble.

A FEW MONTHS AFTER MARY WAS BORN, THEY MOVED AGAIN, because Dad had gotten a job at a finance company in the town of Laton. This time they moved to a white, clapboard house on Bellum Street. The town was fairly large and spread out over several miles. Right after they moved to Bellum Street, Mom opened a little beauty shop in the front room of the house. She practiced on her girls, curling and styling Molly and Maggie's hair. Mom was happy on Bellum Street.

During the two and a half years the O'Neals lived on Bellum Street, all the older children walked to St. Patrick's Catholic School about four blocks away. Maggie always complained that Adam and Nathan wouldn't walk with her, and she didn't like crossing the two very busy streets all by herself. She was only seven and eight years old at that time.

Molly had to entertain herself when the older children were at school. Mom was busy inside with baby Mary and the occasional customer at the beauty shop, so Molly played outside alone when the weather was good. As she sat on the back-porch steps, she could see into her next-door neighbors' yards. An old couple lived right next door on the left. They had lots of pretty flowers, and the old man worked in the yard all the time. He always had a big wad of tobacco in his mouth, and he spit a lot. The house on the right was blocked by the O'Neal's garage and driveway. Behind the garage was the backyard of a nice lady who sunbathed almost every day in the summer. Molly wandered over to talk to her all the time. Molly was amazed at how tan and shiny the lady was. She never stayed long, because the sun was too hot. One day, Mom finally realized that Molly was leaving the yard, so she called her back home and told her not to bother the nice lady anymore.

Months went by, and one day Molly went outside and walked to the back of the property. She saw a small dog pen full of weeds, but since it was winter, all of the greenery was gone and nothing but dried stalks remained.

Molly O'Neal

Over to one side, she saw a gate, so she opened it and went in. In one corner, she saw a little doghouse with a sign above the door. She heard whimpering coming from the doghouse, so she looked inside and saw a little beagle. She coaxed him to come out. As she held him, she looked into his big brown eyes, and she could tell he needed a friend. He was very sweet and lovable but seemed very sad.

"Come on. I'll take you to show my Mom," Molly said.

Molly stood at the back door holding the dog and called for Mom to come outside.

"It's freezing out here. What do you want, Molly?"

"Look what I found in the pen back there," Molly said excitedly.

"What is it dear, an imaginary friend?" Mom asked. She couldn't see the dog, so she was humoring Molly.

"It's a little dog. He has a doghouse in the pen with his name on it. Will you read it for me?"

Mom was curious, so she put on a coat and went to the dog pen. She read the name above the opening of the doghouse. "His name is Chester."

"Can I have him, Mom?"

"Well, I can't see him and I won't have to feed and clean up after him, so sure, you can have him."

Molly was so excited to have a dog of her own.

ONE SPRING DAY, MOLLY WAS OUTSIDE WITH CHESTER, MOM was hanging out wet clothes, and Mary was inside taking a nap in her crib. The old man who lived next door was working with his flowers and walked over to talk to Mom.

Pamela Gillette

"I noticed the dog gate in the back there is open," he said as he pointed to the pen.

"Molly wandered back there a few months ago," Mom said.

"Sad story about the pup who lived here," said the old man.

"Will you tell us the story?" Mom asked.

"Well, about twenty years ago, a family lived in your house. They had a little girl, and when she was very young, her parents gave her a beagle puppy she named Chester. They grew up together, and he followed her everywhere she went. When she walked to the candy store, he would wait outside on the sidewalk for her. When she went to school, he sat on the back porch all day and waited for her. He slept in her room, right upstairs in your house. One day, I came home from work, and the neighbor was building the dog pen. He lovingly built the doghouse and carved Chester's name in a piece of wood. I walked over and asked him if I could help, and he told me that Bridget, his little girl, had polio and was in the hospital. Her father was crying as he built the pen. A few months later, Chester died. I think he died of a broken heart. Bridget's father buried him right by the little doghouse."

"Oh my, what a sad story. Do you know if Bridget lived?" Mom asked.

"They brought Bridget home a month or so after Chester died. Her father came over and told me they were moving away, and I never saw them again. Lots of families have rented this house, but no one has had a dog since Bridget had Chester."

"I'll take good care of you, Chester," Molly whispered to her dog. "I like the name Chester."

When Molly stood up, Chester tugged at her shirt. Molly turned and said, "No, no."

The neighbor was watching Molly, and he noticed that it looked like something was pulling on her clothes. He

Molly O'Neal

stared at her while she ran around the yard as though she were playing with someone or something.

Mom noticed him staring and said, "My Molly has a wild imagination, and she has a dog for an imaginary friend."

"Oh, that explains it. Well, I'll see you ladies around. Bye now," said the old man as he went in his back door.

As Mom was going inside, she saw the neighbor and his wife looking out a window and staring at Molly.

"Come on in, Molly, and watch some television."

"Okay, Mom. Come on, Chester."

THE NEXT FALL, MOLLY STARTED HALF-DAY KINDERGARten. Mary was old enough now to play with Chester while Molly was at school. Molly and Mary were the only members of the family who could see sweet Chester.

Molly walked to kindergarten by herself most of the time. The public elementary school was only six houses down and on the next block. Crossing guards helped all the children cross the streets, so it was safe.

THE NEXT SCHOOL YEAR, MOLLY STARTED FIRST GRADE at St. Patrick's. Molly and Maggie walked to school alone, because Adam wouldn't walk with them and either would Nathan. The girls walked up Bellum Street, a couple of blocks, to Laton Road. The intersection was very busy, and the girls always had a hard time crossing. When they finally got across Laton, they cut through a parking lot and then an alley. They came out of the alley across the street from a shopping plaza on Linden Avenue. They walked down Linden another block to St. Patrick's Drive, and crossed the busy street at a school crosswalk.

St. Patrick's needed more room, so they were building a new church and school farther down the road, across the highway, and next to the cemetery. Molly's classroom was in the old school. The sixth, seventh, and eighth grade classrooms were the only ones finished in the new building. The new church and school would be combined in one building when the construction was finished. The old school and church were also connected. The old school had double doors at one end of the long hallway leading into the church, so the children could enter the church without having to go outside. It would take years to complete the new school and church, because work was done in stages as the money came in.

CHRISTMAS WAS SPARSE THAT YEAR. THE FAMILY TRADItion was to open their gifts on Christmas Eve. They had an aluminum Christmas tree with hardly any ornaments. Dad was late getting home, so the family didn't open their gifts until close to bedtime. Molly's only gifts were cut out dolls and a tiny baby doll wearing only a diaper. Christmas day was always spent at Grandma and Grandpa Giba's house.

During Christmas vacation the family moved again. This time they moved to a house that the girls actually walked past on their way to school. The house was on Linden which was only a couple blocks away from Bellum Street and just around the corner from St. Patrick's School.

Molly was so sad to move, because she had to leave Chester. Mary had grown attached to him too. Molly was

Molly O'Neal

devastated. At the very last minute, when the family was leaving for the new house, Molly and Mary took Chester back to the pen, and Molly coaxed him in the little doghouse. The girls were bawling all the way to the car. They could hear him howling from the pen. Molly cried for days. She felt like she had abandoned her little friend. Molly's only solace was school. She loved St. Patrick's and the nuns, but Chester was always on her mind.

Chapter Two

Two years later, the O'Neals were still living on Linden. Molly got used to her new home. The house was on a busy street and only two doors down from a plaza with a grocery store, drug store, laundromat, and Molly's favorite place, the dime store. If Molly ever had a spare dime, she would walk over to the plaza and ride on the automated horse in front of the grocery store. Many times, she pushed the coin return, and she would get her dime back and use it to ride the horse again. Other times, she used the dime to buy ten pieces of penny candy or two candy bars from the dime store. Two times a week, in good weather, Molly walked with her mother and sisters to do their laundry at the laundromat. Molly carried a small bundle of clothes. Maggie carried a bundle of clothes and held little Mary's hand. Mom pulled a small cart full of clothes and a box of soap. There was no sidewalk between their house and the plaza. The side of the very busy street was nothing but rocks and dirt, which made it very hard to pull the cart. Molly's mother never learned to drive, so the plaza was very convenient for grocery shopping and washing clothes.

Molly's mother, Anna, was born in Czechoslovakia, so her family spoke Slovak, but they understood Hungarian also. Anna's father and mother, Stefan and Joanna Giba, were Roman Catholic. Molly's father Charles, on the other hand, was of Irish descent and came from a long line of Protestants. When Charles and Anna got married, a person's religious affiliation was very important when choosing a match. Anna was one of the first known Catholics in the O'Neal ancestry.

Molly was very close to her grandparents on her mother's side. She never had a chance to get to know her grandparents on her father's side. Her Grandpa O'Neal died when she was four years old, so she barely remembered him. Her Grandmother, Ruby O'Neal, died in 1936, long before Molly was born. Molly's father had six siblings, but Molly only knew three of them. Her mother only had two sisters, and Molly saw them all the time. Molly was especially close to Grandma Giba, because she understood Molly so well.

Molly's best friend, since first grade, was Paula. She and Paula sat together at Mass every morning, and Molly always tried to make her laugh or talk, but she never could. They usually got to sit next to each other in class, and they were inseparable at recess. Paula's house was right across the street from Molly's, but they never got to play outside of school very much, because neither of them could cross the busy street alone.

Molly continued to go to St. Patrick's Catholic School. It was just around the corner and on the next street. Paula always walked to school with her sister and brother, and

Molly usually walked alone through her backyard and down a path by a small creek. The path led to the back of the church. Molly's school didn't have a playground, so the children played on the church parking lot. Even though they didn't have any swings or monkey bars, the children had fun playing games like four-square ball, jumping rope, kick ball, hopscotch, and red rover.

Molly loved school and always felt very secure there, but unfortunately her third-grade school year was coming to an end. When the final bell rang, she walked out of the school with her best friend, Paula. They had already talked about how Molly and her sister Maggie were going to their grandmother's house for most of the summer, so Molly wouldn't be able to see Paula again until August. As they walked out of the school, Paula broke the news to Molly that her family was going to move to another house in a couple of weeks, so when Molly got back from her grandma's, they would be gone. One consolation was that Paula would still be going to St. Patrick's next school year. Molly felt sad, because Paula was her only friend who lived close by.

Molly didn't like playing with her sister Maggie, and she certainly didn't like taking care of Mary. Life seemed a little bleak, as sadly she said goodbye to Paula and watched as Paula, and her brother and sister walked off. Molly walked to the back of the school and down the dirt path toward home. She walked through the carport in the back of the house and up the steep driveway to the front porch.

She walked in and yelled, "I'm home!"

Her two older brothers, Adam and Nathan, were never home. Maggie was on her bed reading a book, and Mom was talking on the phone to one of her sisters. Little sister Mary was the only one who ran up and gave Molly a big hug. Molly had a closer bond with Mary. They had more in common and liked to share some of their *imaginary friends*. Of course, to them they weren't imaginary, they were real.

"Change out of your uniform, and put on your play clothes," said Mom as she hung up the phone.

Molly went into the girls' room to change her clothes. Molly, Maggie, and Mary shared a big bedroom in the back of the house. The house had a walk-out basement with a garage, so their bedroom was above the garage. A door from the bedroom led to a small landing and a set of stairs, which was a side entrance to the house. No one ever used the side entrance, so a dresser was pushed up against the door. The room looked like a girls' dormitory with three twin beds. Mary and Molly's beds were pushed together, because Mary would get scared in the night. Molly had a sage and lavender bouquet tied to her headboard that Grandma Giba had made for her. She told Molly the herbs would help chase away her bad dreams.

The boys' bedroom was at the back of the house next to the kitchen. They shared a bathroom with their father, so it was called the boys' bathroom. All the girls shared the pink bathroom: pink for girls.

Mom peeked around the corner of the girls' room and said, "Maggie, your father is going to drop you and Molly off at your Grandma's on Saturday, so I told your brother Nathan to take you girls to the swim club tomorrow."

"I didn't know the pool was open yet," Maggie said.

"Tomorrow's the first day of the season, so it should be pretty crowded," Mom said. "I would really appreciate it if you girls would take Mary and watch her closely."

"Oh, Mom, why do we have to take her? She's too little, and she can't keep up with us," moaned Maggie.

"Let me put it this way, just like I told your brother, either she goes or nobody goes," Mom said sternly. "I've got ironing to do, so go watch television."

"Okay," Molly said as she went to the living room.

"Just think, Molly, no work at Grandma's for two whole months," Maggie said.

"I can't wait to go to Grandma's," Molly answered. "I wonder if we'll have to go to confession while we're there."

"I don't think we have to go to confession while we're on vacation," Maggie said.

"I don't want to confess to a strange priest," Molly said.

"Me either. I wonder if they have a candle stand in Grandma's church. You know, like our church has with all the candles and the coin box."

"Remember the time you lit all the candles and only put in a dime?" Molly said.

"It wasn't me, but it was pretty. There must have been at least twenty lit. I think you did it, Molly," Maggie said smugly.

"It wasn't me, but I think the guy who came out from the back of the altar and snuffed them all out, thought we did it. He should have left one burning, because you did put in a dime." The girls had a good laugh.

"It was you, Maggie."

"No, it was you."

"Quiet!" Mom shouted from the kitchen.

THE NEXT MORNING MOLLY AND MAGGIE HAD TO GO with their mother to the laundromat, and then after lunch they were able to go to the swim club. The girls' normal route to the swim club was to walk past their school and

Molly O'Neal 13

down the road to a busy highway. They had to cross the highway in front of the big cemetery. They had a choice of going through the cemetery, to cut off about a block, or walk along the side of the highway in the rocks and grass.

"Hurry up you guys, I'm leaving," Nathan said as he walked out the front door.

"Okay, we're coming," said Maggie. She and the girls ran out the door to try and keep up with Nathan.

Molly thought it was too scary to go through the cemetery, even in the daytime, but since Nathan was fourteen years old, she thought it would be safer. The girls could tell that Nathan wasn't happy to be walking with them. He wouldn't help with Mary, and he kept running ahead of the girls. He didn't help them cross the highway, and as soon as he got to the cemetery gate, he went in and started running through the tombstones.

"He's stepping on people!" cried Mary.

"He's a brat," said Maggie, "We'll stay on the cemetery road. Who needs him anyway? I'm still going to tell Mom."

It was a bright sunny day, so the girls weren't too afraid, and Maggie knew the way. They walked through the cemetery and exited through the side gate on the same road as the swim club.

The girls finally made it to the clubhouse. Before entering the pool, the children had to change in the clubhouse locker room. The boys' locker room was on the right side of the building, and the girls' locker room was on the left. Each girl was assigned a small locker to hold their clothes and money. After the girls changed into their bathing suits, they walked out to the pool.

"Some of my friends are over there. I'll see you guys later." Maggie yelled as she trotted off.

"You're supposed to help me take care of Mary!" Molly yelled.

"Go to the kiddie pool," Maggie yelled back.

"Come on, Mary. Let's go to the shallow end. The kiddie pool is for babies," Molly said as she took hold of Mary's hand.

Molly found some of her friends from school, and they all played together in the pool. The swim club also had a playground, shuffle board, and tether balls. The girls had plenty to do, so the time flew by. Molly and Mary bought some hot dogs and soda for supper and ate at a picnic table with some of Molly's friends and their moms. It was a good day, but soon the sun was starting to go down, and the pool lights came on. One last jump off the low diving board and Molly was ready to go home. The lifeguards were packing up and blew their whistles for everyone to get out of the pool. Molly and Mary headed for the lockers, changed, and went out to look for Maggie and Nathan. They found Maggie in the parking lot saying goodbye to her friends, but Nathan was nowhere to be found. Maggie started looking for Nathan. She ran in and asked the locker room attendant if she had seen him. The attendant said she saw him leave with some friends about a half an hour earlier. Maggie was furious. Cars were leaving the parking lot and kids were walking home.

She turned to Molly and Mary and said, "Come on you guys, we have to walk home alone, so let's walk fast. That creep left us!"

The girls walked through the parking lot and down the street toward the cemetery. They came to the side entrance, and had to decide whether to cut through the cemetery or go the long way around.

"We have to cut through to make better time. I'm so mad at Nathan for leaving us," Maggie said.

"I don't want to go through the cemetery!" cried Mary.

"It'll be okay. We'll all three hold hands and walk as fast as we can," Molly said as she reached for Mary's hand, and in they went.

The girls kept their eyes straight ahead. It was almost dark, and the road through the cemetery looked hazy. A large light came on in the middle of the cemetery, and there was a small light above the door of the mausoleum, and the girls could see the street lights from the highway. The lights helped them see their way through the cemetery. They tried not to look at the tombstones. When they walked past the mausoleum, the girls started hearing moaning. The moaning was soft at first and then it got louder.

"It sounds like it's coming from the mausoleum. Why is the door cracked open?" asked Molly.

"I see a hand on the door!" cried Maggie.

The girls started screaming and running toward the gates to get out. Mary was crying and fell down, so Molly stopped to help her up. Maggie kept running.

Then Nathan yelled, "Hey you guys, it's me, don't be so dumb!"

Nathan stepped out of the mausoleum, and the door slammed shut behind him. "Oh well," he said as he shrugged his shoulders and started running to catch up with the girls.

Maggie was already running down the side of the highway trying to find a good time to cross.

"Boy, you're going to get in trouble with Dad when we get home!" cried Molly.

Nathan was still laughing and said, "Can't you take a joke? You guys are hilarious."

"You're horrible! I hate you!" cried Mary.

At least Nathan was there to help Molly and Mary cross the highway.

Maggie was waiting by the school building, and when she saw Molly and Mary, and Nathan, she yelled, "Nathan, you're so stupid! I'm telling Dad!"

"It was just a joke, Maggie."

No one thought it was funny but Nathan. When they got home, Nathan didn't get in any trouble. Mom was too busy to listen, and Dad was involved in a television show.

"No one's hurt, no one's dead, everything's fine," Dad said as he continued to watch his show.

Chapter Three

Saturday morning came and Molly and Maggie were finishing their packing. They were a little apprehensive about going to Grandma's house.

"I'll miss going swimming," Molly said.

"Yeah, me too, but Grandma is such a good cook, and we won't have to take care of Mary," said Maggie.

"Come on girls, let's load the station wagon and get going. Nathan's coming along for the ride," Dad said.

"Are you going to see your sister today?" Mom asked Dad.

"I'm going to drop the girls off at your Mom's and then Nathan and I are going over to Evie's house."

"I wish I could go to Aunt Evie's," Maggie said.

"Next time," Dad said.

Before they left, Mom hugged the girls and gave them some orders. She said, "Help Grandma around the house. Pick up after yourselves, and stay close to the house, and for heaven's sake, don't get into any trouble. Love you. Bye."

Molly ran to the car and yelled, "I call the back seat on Mom's side."

"Sorry, already here and not moving," said Maggie. "You know how Dad flicks his cigarette ashes out the window while he drives, and the ashes fly in through the back-seat window. I don't want them in my eyes. I'm never going to sit behind him in the car again."

"I'll sit in the third seat then," Molly said as she climbed over the back seat.

On the long car ride to Grandma's, Maggie was trying to read a book, but Molly kept talking to her.

"I had a really weird dream last night," Molly said.

"What's new, you always have weird dreams. I'm trying to read."

"I was walking in some woods, and it was getting dark. I saw fairies flitting around."

"Oh brother," Maggie said.

"One little fairy got up close to my face and said, 'Molly, you have to stop the witch called, Sarah. She comes out here to our waterfall and looks for us. She carries an iron rod. Make her leave.' I've had other dreams kind of like it before, but no fairy ever talked to me."

"I'm reading," Maggie said as she tried to ignore Molly.

"Oh well," Molly sighed as she scrunched down in the seat and closed her eyes.

GRANDMA AND GRANDPA GIBA LIVED IN COALTOWN, the same little town and the same house where Molly's mother grew up. Her mother was the middle child of three girls. Grandma had lots of pictures of her girls as children, and she always marveled at how Molly was the spitting image of her mother. They had the same green eyes, both had dimples, and the same big smile. The only real difference was that Anna had brown hair and Molly was a blonde.

Grandma Joanna, Grandpa Stefan, Veronica, and baby Anna immigrated to the United States from Czechoslovakia. Soon they learned to speak English and settled into the

Molly O'Neal 19

community. After a few years, the Depression hit the area pretty hard, so they moved into an apartment in the city, so Grandpa could get a job in a factory. By that time, Joanna had another girl they named Julie. She was too young to go to school, but Anna and her sister Veronica went to a Slovak Catholic school. The nuns taught the children in the Slovak language. Anna attended first through third grade there. The church was only a block from their apartment, and the school was right next door to the church. Anna remembered her time in the city fondly. Grandma and Grandpa never learned to drive a car, so they walked everywhere, except for the rare occasions when they asked a friend for a ride. Everything they needed in the city and back in Coaltown, was within walking distance.

Grandpa, Stefan Giba, was born in Austria-Hungary. Molly always thought Grandpa was a big man. He worked hard in the coal mine outside of town, until he suffered a severe electrical shock from a loose wire, so he had to retire early. He kept busy puttering around the house fixing things. He chopped wood for the kitchen stove, and he gardened and mowed the grass with an old-fashioned push mower. He made lawn furniture for their yard and for other people: like the two-seater swing in the backyard and the bench by the door. He was very social and loved to have a beer with friends at the local saloon.

Grandpa loved when his grandchildren visited. He always called them *monkey kids*, probably because he couldn't keep all their names straight. Occasionally, he reached into his pocket and pulled out his black leather coin purse and gave each grandchild a nickel or a dime. He would always give the children wise advice, like how to wipe their mouths at the dinner table, or "Don't be hungry like home." Molly's favorite advice from Grandpa was how to wipe your nose with both sleeves, which was very similar to how to wipe your mouth at the table. He smoked a pipe, so the house always had a sweet smell of cherry tobacco. He was a good grandpa.

Grandma, Joanna Giba, was born in Austria-Hungary also. She was very religious. She always had a rosary in her pocket and never missed Sunday Mass or a Holy Day of Obligation. She had a picture of the Pope hanging on the wall and a piece of palm, from Palm Sunday, hanging over the calendar in the kitchen. She had a beautiful orthodox style crucifix in her bedroom, and a fairly plain crucifix hung in the kitchen.

Grandma was also very industrious. She was the best cook in the world, and all the Slovak dishes she made were very delicious. She made sweet breads, poppyseed bread and nut bread, fantastic chicken noodle soup, and fried donuts, just to name a few of her specialties. She canned all her fruits and vegetables and dried several varieties of herbs. She washed all their clothes using a wringer washer, and hung the clothes outside to dry in nice weather and inside in the winter. No one could say that Grandma was afraid of hard work. She also made rag rugs on a big loom in the back shed. Neighbors all knew Grandma made rugs, so they saved all their old material, curtains, and bedspreads for her. She tore all the material into long strips and wound them into large balls similar to balls of yarn. She used the strips to weave into rugs using her loom. She was very proud of her loom and the work she did. She also made wonderful handstitched quilts, and she made all of her own dresses using a treadle sewing machine. She was pretty, in a Grandma sort of way, with her beautiful white hair always pulled into a loose bun. She wore an apron around the house, but when she had company, she would dress up and wear earrings and a matching necklace. She was very social, and loved friends and family to drop by. She too, like Grandpa, had a thick accent and old country ways. Grandma kept it quiet that she had special insight into the spirit world, because she didn't want to be called names or be misunderstood.

Coaltown was only a little over a square mile. The streets were tar and asphalt with huge pot holes in some areas. The tar on the streets would bubble up and be very sticky in the hot sun. The sidewalks lining the streets were very narrow and cracked up. Most of the houses were small but very neat and tidy. It was a nice little town with a high school and elementary school, but the best thing about Coaltown, was that it was a safe place to live. It was a close-knit community, so most everyone knew each other, and they knew each other's business.

Grandma's house was about a forty-minute drive from the O'Neal's house. When they reached Coaltown, Dad pulled up on the road in back of Grandma's house and parked next to her back gate. Grandma's backyard was small but every bit of it was put to good use. Grandma had a shed for her loom and another shed for Grandpa's tools. They even had a brick outhouse that Grandpa still used, but everyone else used the bathroom in the house.

"Everyone, grab something and carry it in," Dad said as they got out of the station wagon.

The girls brought two small suitcases full of clothes and some grocery bags filled with games, books, jacks, chalk, and crayons and practically everything they owned. They didn't want to run out of things to do. Molly carried her suitcase and led the single file line from the car down the narrow sidewalk and into Grandma's backdoor.

Molly yelled, "We're here!"

The girls ran up to Grandma, and she gave them big hugs. "I'm so glad to see you, come in, come in!"

After they carried everything in the house, Dad said, "You girls be good now. Have a fun vacation, and have fun at the Homecoming, and be careful."

"Bye, love you. We'll be careful," Molly and Maggie said.

"Bye, you guys," said Nathan as he jumped in the front seat of the station wagon.

Grandma and Grandpa and the girls waved until the station wagon was out of sight.

Molly and Maggie were just in time for one of Grandma's sumptuous lunches. She had carved thin pieces off a fabulous ham and cut thick slices of her homemade sweet bread for sandwiches. Everything she made was heavenly.

Grandma had made up the cozy spare bedroom for the girls. The bedroom was just big enough for a double bed and a small closet and a chifforobe with drawers and a place to hang a small amount of clothes. Grandma had made the bed with one of her beautiful patchwork quilts. All the linen smelled like sunshine, because Grandma hung all her laundry outside to dry. The room had one big window at the foot of the bed. The window was always open to allow a breeze to flow in. Molly and

Molly O'Neal

Maggie put their clothes away in the chifforobe and went outside to play before supper.

Grandma's one-story house was sided with gray asphalt shingles. It was small but comfortable, with an eat-in kitchen, dining room, living room, one bath, and two bedrooms. The small enclosed back porch, off the kitchen, was where Grandpa kicked off his dirty boots, and Grandma kept her broom, mop, bucket, washtubs, and bunches of dried herbs and flowers. There was only a screen door to the porch with a flimsy hook lock on the outside of the door, not the inside. Molly asked Grandma why the hook lock was on the outside of the screen door. Grandma was surprised by the question, and she told Molly that was how she locked the door when she left the house. Molly thought that was odd. The back door leading into the kitchen was made of heavy wood and covered with layers of paint. There was a window in the door with cotton curtains and a large old lock, which took a skeleton key. The key was always in the keyhole so it wouldn't get lost.

Right off the back-porch step was a sidewalk that wound around to the front of the house in one direction, and through the backyard in the other direction. The sidewalk in the backyard cut right through the middle of the small yard and led to the back gate. On both sides of the sidewalk was a small patch of grass to accommodate the clothes lines. The rest of the backyard was an herb and vegetable garden. Grandpa helped Grandma with the garden, but Grandma was the one with the green thumbs. She grew a huge bounty of herbs and vegetables in a small space. She also grew lots of flowers. Molly loved all of Grandma's flowers, but she especially loved the moon flowers, because they bloomed at night.

Grandma had two big trees in her front yard and a pine tree in her flowerbed near the bedroom window. Next to the bedroom window was a small front porch. Grandma had a set of chimes hanging on the porch and a welcome mat.

In the next block was Livingood's grocery store. A bell was hung at the top of the screen door, so when the door was opened, the bell rang. The door made a friendly banging noise as it closed. The front steps and the floor of the store were made of wood, so shoes always made a nice clumping sound. It was a great little store. The owner, Mr. Livingood, waited on all the customers with a friendly smile. He sold everything from iced bottled sodas and candy, to vegetables and meat. The girls always loved to walk to Livingood's with Grandma.

Grandma's house was three blocks from Main Street or, uptown, as she called it. On Main Street there was another small grocery store, dime store, hardware store, a couple of taverns, and the post office. The railroad tracks bordered the town and ran right by the post office. A few old houses and the coal mine were on the other side of the tracks.

Every day, except Sunday and weather permitting, Grandma walked to the post office to check the mail. No one delivered mail to the houses, so everyone had a post office box. The friendly clerk knew everyone in town by name, and he was always ready with some town gossip when Grandma came in to get her mail.

AFTER SUPPER, THE GIRLS WATCHED TELEVISION FOR A while and went to bed.

Molly O'Neal   25

"We can walk around town tomorrow and see if there's anything to do," Maggie said.

"I sure hope there is. Good night," Molly said. Soon both girls were fast asleep.

"Breakfast," Grandma called, waking up the girls.

Molly and Maggie were anxious to check out the children in the neighborhood. After breakfast, they got dressed and asked Grandma if they could go outside.

"Wait for me girls, I promised the neighbor I would introduce you to her girls."

They walked through the backyard to the Riker's back porch and knocked. A very nice-looking lady came to the door and greeted Grandma calling her Mrs. Giba. She seemed very excited to meet the girls.

"I see all of you O'Neal children sometimes when you come on weekends to visit your Grandmother," said Mrs. Riker. "Doris, Gail, the girls are here."

The girls came running to meet Molly and Maggie. Doris and Gail were very friendly. Gail was tall, and she had brown hair and freckles. She was the athletic type and very outgoing. She was Maggie's age. Doris was Molly's age. She had a great smile, brown hair, dimples, and a very sweet disposition.

The girls spent the rest of the day getting to know each other. They all walked uptown and bought sodas from the grocery store and then Gail and Maggie left and went to visit one of Gail's friends across town. Molly and Doris went back to the Riker's to play games and jump rope. The girls had a great day.

That evening Molly and Maggie were very tired. They had one of Grandma's great suppers, and later they sat in the backyard with Grandma and Grandpa and talked.

"I think we're going to have fun here," said Molly.

"I'm so glad Gail and Doris live right next door," added Maggie.

Soon it was getting dark, and it was time to get ready for bed. Grandma came to tuck in the girls and make sure the curtains were far apart to let in the night breeze. As she tucked the girls in, she told them that their bed was the same bed their mother and her two sisters slept in all those years ago. The bed felt cool and cozy, and soon both girls were fast asleep.

All the windows in the house were open with screens, because Grandma and Grandpa never used their window air conditioner.

In the middle of the night Molly was abruptly awakened by a strange noise. She sat up in bed and listened intently while a slight breeze rustled the curtains, and a strange odor permeated the room. She heard someone walking on the sidewalk. She heard swoosh, swoosh, swoosh. The sound was terrifying. She whispered to Maggie, but all Maggie did was turn over and continue to sleep. She sat up in bed, frozen, staring at the window. The swooshing noise got louder as it neared the window and then stopped. Molly could hear someone's wheezy breathing. The moonlight shone through the window to the opposite wall, so she

Molly O'Neal   27

could see a dark shadow on the wall of someone standing right outside the window. She couldn't move or breathe. She tried to scream, but no sound came out. After what seemed like an eternity, the swooshing steps started up again and began to move away from the window and onto the front porch. Molly heard the person jiggle the front doorknob to see if it was unlocked. Molly started breathing again when she realized the door was locked. She heard the harsh clanging of Grandma's wind chimes that hung on the front porch. The person had to hit the chimes hard to make them clang. Then she heard swoosh, swoosh, swoosh, as the person walked down the sidewalk toward the road.

Molly sat frozen in terror. She couldn't run to Grandma's room, because she'd have to pass the open window. All she could do was pull the covers up over her head and listen. She was afraid the person would return to the window. She fought sleep, afraid of what might happen, but eventually dozed off.

Chapter Four

Grandma was up early making breakfast, and Grandpa was having a cup of coffee at the kitchen table. When Grandma finished preparing the breakfast surprise, she went and opened the girls' bedroom door and said, "Breakfast is ready, girls, rise and shine. It's Sunday, and we'll be leaving for church in one hour."

Molly sat up in bed, surprised to be alive. She turned to Maggie and whispered, "Did you hear the footsteps and breathing at the window last night?"

Maggie looked at her like she was crazy and said, "You must have had one of your fever dreams again. I'm starving. Let's go eat."

Molly started to wonder if it was all just a dream. She got up, got dressed, and went into breakfast. Grandma made the girls homemade fried donuts. The donuts were hot and coated with sugar. They were heavenly. Grandma was a wonderful cook.

Soon Grandma, Grandpa, and the girls were walking to church. It was a beautiful Sunday morning: sunny and warm. The church was about four blocks away. The walk gave Molly time to think about her scary night.

"You look like you've seen a zombie. Stop talking to yourself," Maggie said.

Molly gave her a dirty look. She was deep in thought - *did it really happen or was it just a dream?* Soon they were entering the intricately carved wooden doors of the little church. The steeple bell was ringing. Everything seemed so safe.

After church, Grandma served a great fried chicken dinner. The girls helped Grandma wash the dishes after lunch and then they changed their clothes and went outside. Molly and Maggie sat on the large wooden swing near the flower garden, and Molly told Maggie what she heard in the middle of the night. Maggie listened to the awful details of the night, and she couldn't believe Molly didn't wake her up. Molly explained that she didn't wake her up, because she was frozen with fear. Maggie wanted to investigate.

"Let's go to the front of the house by the window and see if we can find any evidence," Maggie said.

"That's a good idea. Let's go," said Molly as she jumped off the swing.

The girls walked around to the front, and began to investigate around the large pine tree near the window and the ivy covering the ground. Maggie thought the ivy did look a bit matted near the window. The window was only about three feet off the ground, so it was easy for the girls to look in the bedroom. The girls were looking closer at the ivy, when Maggie jumped back and screamed, as a bunny jumped up and ran across the yard.

Maggie got mad and yelled, "There's your swooshing noise! I'm not going to waste any more time investigating your dream! You and your dreams," Maggie muttered as she ran off to see if Gail was home.

Molly was left standing alone by the big pine tree, when the chimes rang gently. She began to feel like she wasn't alone. She could feel her heart pounding. She ran around to the back of the house and ran in the back door. She ran from room to room searching for Grandma, but she wasn't in the house anywhere. Molly was frantic. She ran out to the shed, where Grandma made rugs, and there she was threading her loom. Molly was very relieved to find a familiar face and soon calmed down.

"Why are you so out of breath?" asked Grandma.

Molly wasn't ready to tell Grandma about the night, so she said, "I was just running around outside. Can I watch you make rugs?"

"Of course you can, anytime."

Grandma asked Molly if she wanted to wind some of the blue colored strips of fabric into balls. She was very anxious to get her mind off of the scary night, so she was very happy to help her grandma. As they both worked in the shed, the conversation was lively and interesting. Grandma asked her questions about school and the family. They had been working in the shed for about an hour, when Molly asked Grandma if anything weird ever happened around the neighborhood.

Grandma said, "Yes, come to think of it. One evening last month, I was sitting on the swing with your grandfather, talking about your visit, when I saw a real mangy looking black cat crouched in my flowerbed. The cat was staring at us with big green eyes. It reminded me of some bad memories, so I got my broom and shooed it away. It screeched and hissed at me before it ran away. It was probably just a stray." Grandma got a strange look on her face and continued, "It reminded me of when she was, oh, never mind, nothing bad ever happens in Coaltown anymore."

"What do you mean, anymore?"

"Well, there was a time, long ago. Oh well, no need to go into that. Nothing strange has happened here for years. Do people ever ask you about your beautiful eyes?"

Molly O'Neal   31

"My friends say they look yellow when we play out in the sun, but my family says they look exactly like Mom's," Molly said as she finished winding the fabric strips into a ball. "Doris is busy today, so I'm going to take a little walk, okay, Grandma?"

"Sure, just check in, in a couple of hours," Grandma answered.

❖

Mrs. Skora was Grandma's cousin. She was a widow, and lived across the street, over one house, from Grandma. She was born in Pennsylvania, but both of her parents were born in Austria-Hungary, and they came to the United States in 1895. Her one-story house was quaint looking and covered in red asphalt shingles. It had a nice front porch with a wood floor that was painted dark green. A picket fence lined the yard with beautiful pink, yellow, and lavender flowers. Molly decided to pay a visit to Mrs. Skora and see if she could get her to talk about the past. She was a wise woman and loved to talk. If anyone knew anything about the past, she would.

Molly walked across the street. As she walked down the sidewalk, she ran a stick along the picket fence. Soon she got to the opening in the fence and stood there for a while getting up her nerve to knock on the door. She was trying to think of a reason for her visit. Before she could think of anything, Mrs. Skora appeared at the door. She was a jolly looking older lady, with gray hair she wore in a bun, and like Grandma, she always wore dresses.

"Hi there! Aren't you Joanna's granddaughter? I see you at your Grandma's house from time to time. Are you spending the summer with her?"

"Yes, a couple of months," Molly answered. Molly stammered a little trying to think of something to say. "I love your flowers. What are they called?"

Molly and Mrs. Skora walked to the garden, and Mrs. Skora began to tell her about all the types of flowers she grew. Molly kept trying to think of a way to get her to talk about the mysteries of the past. She finally asked her if she had any grandchildren.

"Yes, seven grandchildren, all living in the city, and two of them are boys close to your age. They're going to stay with me for two weeks. They're coming a week before the Homecoming."

Molly decided to just blurt it out, "I think someone was walking around the neighborhood last night"

Mrs. Skora looked at Molly curiously, "What do you mean?"

"Well, late last night I heard footsteps outside my bedroom window."

Mrs. Skora looked startled and sat down on her porch swing. She mumbled to herself, "It can't be happening again, no, and here I am living alone. I've got to close my windows at night."

She turned to Molly and said, "Did you hear any noises or laughing, or the name Reza?"

"All I heard was swooshing footsteps and wheezy breathing. I'm not sure if it was a dream or not, but it really scared me. Oh, and there was a weird, awful smell."

Mrs. Skora looked worried and said, "Let's hope you were dreaming and it isn't happening again."

"What do you mean, again?"

Mrs. Skora began to tell Molly a story. "Many years ago, when your mother was about your age, strange things were happening in this town. Until that time, not many people around here even locked their doors and windows, but since then almost everyone does. It all started when the two Krenshaw sisters were walking home from choir practice one night near the end of October."

Mrs. Skora sat on the porch swing and stared out into space as she told the story.

"I remember it like it was yesterday. My husband, may he rest in peace, was the chief of the volunteer fire department in this town. We had no police in those days, so people would send for him when they needed help. That night, Bobby Tucker, the Krenshaw's neighbor, rode his bicycle over to our house. He started banging on our door. He told my husband to get to the Krenshaw sisters fast. He said the sisters were at his house, and they were afraid to go home. My husband put Bobby's bike in the trunk of his car, and they drove to Bobby's house. When they got there, Thelma was practically in shock, so Tillie did all of the talking.

"Tillie said they were walking home from choir practice and turned down Oak Street, when suddenly, the wind picked up. They thought a storm might be brewing, so they started walking faster. Leaves were falling off the trees and swirling all around. They heard a horrible cackling sound, but they couldn't tell where it was coming from. They stopped to see who it was. Dust was blowing in their eyes, so it was hard to see. They were holding on to each other's arms, when Thelma screamed for Tillie to look at the Albrech's house. A black shadow was floating around the side of the house, coming toward them. When it got closer, it looked like a woman dressed in black. She was shaking her head and cackling. She was riding a broom and had one of their cats under her arm. They started screaming and running home, but they were stopped in their tracks when the Albrech's huge dog ran toward them growling and barking ferociously. They froze, terrified, thinking he was going to attack them. Instead, he ran past them and lunged at the figure floating in the air. The dog must have knocked her off balance, because she shrieked and dropped the cat. The sisters ran home, and when they got there, the front door was wide open and so were all the windows. Their curtains were blowing in the wind, and leaves were blowing inside the house. They were too scared, so they ran out of their house and went over to the Tucker's."

Mrs. Skora sighed and continued. "My husband and Bobby went over to the Krenshaw sisters' house. They walked inside the open door to a dark house. They turned on the lights and saw that the house was a wreck. Cat fur was everywhere, and the four cats were nowhere to be found. A lamp was broken, and chairs were knocked over. The backdoor was open, so my husband went to the backyard to have a look around. He heard crying sounds coming from under the back porch. He looked under the porch with a flashlight and could vaguely make out the figures of four cats, so he knew they were safe. Back inside, Bobby and my husband went upstairs to check out the bedrooms. Bobby was closing the windows, when he thought he saw a black figure hovering outside. He yelled for my husband to look out the window, and the figure flew away. He thought, maybe, he was imagining things with all of the wind and the story he had just heard.

"Anyway, the Krenshaw sisters spent the night with Bobby's family. The cats wouldn't come out from under the porch until the next day. After that, lots of people complained of missing pets. People in the village started locking their doors and getting suspicious of their neighbors. We never could prove who it was. Some people thought it was a Halloween prank, but I figured it had to be Mrs. Vedick: the witch. Your grandmother knew her family from the old country. She married Mr. Vedick, but her family's name is Bunyak, and they're supposed to be witches."

Mrs. Skora suddenly turned to Molly and said, "Oh my, I bet I'm scaring you, and everything happened so long ago. Anyway, I bet your grandma is wondering where you are."

"She probably is. I better go. May I come back tomorrow?"

"Sure, we'll have some cake, and I'll tell you about Mrs. Vedick," said Mrs. Skora. "Tell your Grandma I said hello."

"Okay, I'll see you tomorrow."

Molly was going over the story in her mind as she walked back to Grandma's house. She walked past her bedroom window, and the hair on the back of her neck stood up. She felt a chill and ran to the backyard. She found Maggie and Gail making a chewing gum wrapper necklace. Maggie handed Molly some wrappers to fold.

"Hey, Molly, your sister was telling me about your nightmare," Gail said.

Molly gave Maggie a dirty look.

"I have lots of nightmares. Mine are usually about cemeteries and dead people," Gail said. "I've only heard stories about an old witch who lived outside the village years ago until she got sent away. Everyone who knew of her said she was a nightmare walking. She was real scary looking. She always wore a black scarf on her head that she tied under her chin. Kids said she had beady green eyes and pointy teeth. She always wore a dark moth-eaten sweater and a long black skirt. She had real thick ankles and droopy stockings. She wore men's, house slippers, the black leather ones with no backs, so when she walked, they made a creepy swooshing sound. She's a legend around Coaltown."

Molly and Maggie were listening intently.

"People say she carried a scythe when she walked down the streets," Gail added.

"What's a scythe?" asked Molly.

"Have you ever seen pictures of the grim reaper? He's usually carrying a scythe. It's a tool with a long wooden handle and a curved blade on one end. Here, this is how it looks," Gail said as she used chalk to draw a scythe on the sidewalk.

Maggie stared at the picture and looked back at Gail and asked, "Is she a witch?"

"Some people say she is. Your grandmother thinks Mrs. Vedick is a witch, ask her."

"This town is creepy. Do you have any other odd people?" asked Maggie.

"Oh yeah!" replied Gail. "There's old Billy May. He wears funny tight clothes, usually green plaid, and his shoes always turn up at the toes. I'm sure you'll see him if you go to Livingood's store. He walks all the way from his family farm, almost every day, just to put five pennies in the gumball machine. He's trying to get one of the tiger eye gumballs, so he can win a silver dollar. He wins every once in a while. He's been doing it for years. My dad says he keeps the silver dollars in a pot under his bed, and he thinks he's a leprechaun with a pot of gold."

"He sounds scary," Molly said.

"Oh! And then there's Alice. My aunt told me about Alice. She's been weird ever since she was a kid. In one night, her hair turned white. Now she hides from strangers. If she's outside and anyone walks by her house, she hides behind a tree or runs inside. We have some pretty peculiar people in this town," Gail said.

"You sure do," Molly said. "What happened to her?"

"No one knows. Alice won't talk about it," Gail answered.

Grandma opened the back-porch screen door and called the girls for supper. The girls were so involved in Gail's stories, that Grandma startled them, and they screamed.

"You silly girls, come in and eat."

"Bye, Gail, see you tomorrow," said Maggie.

Grandma made chicken soup with homemade noodles and sweet bread. Being the month of June, it was pretty hot for soup, but the heat didn't matter, because the soup was heavenly.

Soon it was getting dark outside, and as always, Grandma had all the windows open for the night. Molly was sitting on the couch watching television. Maggie was in bed reading a book, and Grandma and Grandpa were playing cards at the kitchen table. Molly was trying to watch television, but she felt like someone was watching her through the window. Looking at the window, all Molly could see was the black night. She started to imagine a person looking in at her. She tried to ignore her feelings, but the thoughts of someone or something watching her became stronger and stronger. She sat on the couch, frozen, clutching a pillow, when suddenly a horrible commercial came on showing the shadow of a man stabbing a woman. The music was creepy. That was all Molly could take. She flew off the couch, ran into bed, and pulled the covers over her head.

Maggie yelled, "You scaredy cat!"

"If something happens tonight, I'm waking you up."

"Yeah, you do that," said Maggie sarcastically as she turned off the reading lamp.

It seemed like Molly had just closed her eyes and Grandma was calling, "Breakfast."

Molly made it through the night safely. She didn't even have a nightmare.

Chapter Five

The next day was bright and sunny. Molly and Maggie walked to the post office with Grandma. As they walked, Molly played step on a crack, break your mother's back. Maggie stepped on all the cracks on purpose, because she didn't like the game and wouldn't play. They stopped off at Livingood's grocery store on the way home, and Grandma bought some things. She gave the girls three pennies each to put in the gumball machine. They didn't have any luck finding a tiger eye gumball. They helped Grandma carry the groceries home and then went out to play. Molly told Maggie she was going to go visit Mrs. Skora, and she would find her and Doris and Gail later.

Molly ran across the street to Mrs. Skora's house. She was very excited to see she was home and waiting for her with a piece of chocolate cake and a glass of milk.

"I can't wait to hear the story of Mrs. Vedick," Molly told Mrs. Skora.

"I don't think your grandma will mind me telling you this story. Well, where should I start? As you know, your grandma knew Mrs. Vedick from the old country. Her family lived in the next farming village. Children in these villages, at that time, were born at home. A midwife named Ezabet was to help with the delivery of babies. Ezabet was very busy with her own family and traveling between several villages when needed. Your grandma was pregnant the same time Mrs. Vedick was. Your grandpa went to fetch Ezabet when your grandma went into labor. Nobody knew, but in the next village Mrs. Vedick went into labor too early and was having a very hard time. A couple of village women came to help her, but most of the women were afraid of Mrs. Vedick, because of her green eyes and the mystical ways of her family. The baby came too soon, and the little girl did not make it. In the other village, your grandmother gave birth to a beautiful baby girl she named Anna, your mother. She and Stefan already had a little girl named Veronica."

"That would be Aunt Veronica," Molly said.

"Yes, you're right," said Mrs. Skora as she continued her story. "As the months went by, your grandma noticed Anna's eyes changed from gray to a bright green. Your grandmother was worried, because everyone believed the legend about witches and green eyes. It doesn't mean every person with green eyes is a witch, but the legend does say all witches have green eyes. The word got around that your grandma had a green-eyed girl. Mrs. Vedick was still mourning her baby when she walked over to your grandma's village to look for the green-eyed baby girl. She went door to door asking about the girl. She told everyone she thought there had been a mistake and a lady from this village had her baby girl. She told each person she met that they could tell she was the real mother by her green eyes. The people of the village were very protective of each other. They lied and told Mrs. Vedick that there was no baby in their village with green eyes. A while later, Mrs. Vedick saw Veronica and Joanna working in the garden, and little Anna was on a blanket near them. She walked in the garden gate and

Molly O'Neal 41

picked up the baby. Your grandmother turned around and saw her walking out of the garden gate with Anna."

"She ran over and grabbed the baby out of Mrs. Vedick's arms and yelled, 'What are you doing? What is wrong with you?'

"Mrs. Vedick began to cry. She reached for the baby and screamed, 'She is my Reza! You have her by mistake!' She wanted your grandmother to give Anna to her."

"Oh my gosh!" Molly said.

"By then your grandfather came out of the cottage, and a few of the villagers gathered around. Your grandpa took your grandma, Anna, and Veronica in the house, and the villagers made Mrs. Vedick go home.

"After that, your grandmother and Anna were followed by Mrs. Vedick. She started coming by their cottage at night, and she would always try to open the door. One night she sang a lullaby outside one of their windows. There weren't any police in the villages in those days, so your grandma and grandpa had to deal with her by themselves.

"At that time, it was very hard for your grandpa to get work, so they decided to move to America. Some of your grandma's uncles had already moved to Pennsylvania to work in the coal mines. That's where my father lived, and some moved to Oklahoma and other states to work in coal mines. I'd like to tell you about my father sometime, but I'll stick to the subject. So, where was I?"

"Grandpa couldn't find work."

"Right, okay. Stefan, your grandfather, packed up the family, and they came to America on a huge ship. Unfortunately, the Vedicks found out about the move and followed the next year. They moved right outside of town, and Mr. Vedick worked in the mine right alongside of your grandfather. Soon Mrs. Vedick had a baby boy, and she seemed to accept the fact that Anna wasn't hers. Then a few years later, when her husband and son died in a car crash, she lost her mind. She went back to her old-world ways and started conjuring and doing spells. She would walk through town at night and steal cats and puppies and call for Reza.

"One horrible night when Anna was a little girl, she and her two sisters were sleeping in the front bedroom. They were all in the same big bed, when the witch quietly ripped the screen on the window and climbed into the bedroom. She picked up Anna and was trying to leave with her. The girls started to scream, and woke your grandma and grandpa. Your grandpa stopped her while your grandmother called the police in the next town. That's the night Mrs. Vedick was taken to an insane asylum."

"My mother never told us," said Molly.

"Well, Anna was so shaken by what happened, she never spoke of it after that. She was worried that she might be a witch, because of her green eyes, but your grandmother assured her the legend of the green-eyed witches was just that: a legend. And now you have the same color eyes as your mother," Mrs. Skora said.

"Well, I'm not a witch," said Molly, obviously shaken by the story. "I better check in with Grandma. She may be worried about me."

"Of course you're not, sweetie. It's just a legend. Bye now. The next time you come for a visit bring your sister."

"I will, bye," said Molly as she got up to leave.

Molly was beginning to get a little homesick. She wondered if she should tell Maggie the story Mrs. Skora told her. She really never had time to tell Maggie, because Maggie was either playing with Gail or reading a book and didn't want to be disturbed.

❖

THE NEXT DAY MRS. RIKER ASKED GRANDMA IF MOLLY AND Maggie could go swimming with her girls at the Stanton Country Club. Molly and Maggie had brought their swimming suits and caps just in case, so Grandma was glad to let them go. Mrs. Riker assured Grandma that she would keep an eye on the girls. She was going to be in and out of the pool area all day, and she would have them home around three o'clock. Grandma sent them with a dollar a piece to buy some lunch.

"Isn't this great, Molly? We get to go swimming, and we don't have to babysit."

"Great for me, you never babysat."

Maggie laughed and rolled her eyes.

❖

ON THE WAY TO THE COUNTRY CLUB, THEY DROVE BY A cemetery.

"Look at those two boys running around the cemetery, and there's a guy waving at us," Molly said as she waved back.

"I don't see anyone," Doris said.

"Oh," Molly said. She tried to change the subject. "I've never been to a country club."

"Stanton Country Club is fairly small. We only have one clubhouse, a pool, and a golf course. Stanton is a small town, but a lot bigger than Coaltown," said Mrs. Riker.

"We love to swim at the club, and we can bring a guest anytime," Gail said.

"I was born in Stanton," Molly told Mrs. Riker.

"Were you born in Stanton, Maggie?" Mrs. Riker asked.

"No, I was born in California, and so was my brother Nathan."

"All of my children were born in Stanton Hospital," Mrs. Riker said as they pulled up next to the pool and parked.

The girls went in the pool house and changed into their suits and went out to the pool. Gail and Doris headed straight for the diving boards, and Maggie and Molly slowly got used to the cold water in the shallow side of the pool.

Around twelve o'clock, Mrs. Riker told the girls to wrap up in a towel and go with her to the restaurant to get hamburgers and a soda. Since they were wet, they brought their food outside and sat at a picnic table to eat. After lunch they played shuffle board and then Doris and Gail gave them a tour of the club. After their food was digested, they went back in the pool.

About an hour later, Mrs. Riker called the girls to get out of the pool and get dressed.

On the way back to town, Molly couldn't help but look at the cemetery as they drove by. She was very relieved that she didn't see anyone.

"I thought we could go to the library for a few minutes. I have some books of the girls to return. Maggie, Gail tells me you read books all the time, so I thought we could check a couple of books out for you, and you can give them to Gail when you're finished with them," Mrs. Riker said.

"That would be great!" Maggie said.

"You can check out a book or two also, Molly," Doris said.

"Good, something happy to read before bed," Molly said. "I'll look for a couple of books."

Molly O'Neal

Mrs. Riker parked in front of the library and said, "You girls go on into the library. I'll be in after a few minutes. I'm going over to the produce stand and buy some fruit."

"Okay, Mom," said Doris and Gail together.

Mrs. Riker bought some fruit and put it in the car. When she met up with the girls in the library, they had a stack of books ready for her to check out. When they got home, Molly and Maggie thanked Mrs. Riker for the great day and the library books.

❖

Tired from swimming, Molly and Maggie spent the evening reading.

That night Molly fell asleep reading, and she soon began to dream. She was walking in deep woods, and she came across a small waterfall. She saw twinkling lights floating around. One of the lights got close to her, and she could see it was a fairy.

The fairy said, "Hello, Molly. You can stay, but she can't." The fairy pointed over by a large tree, and Molly saw a woman in a black cloak. As Molly looked at the woman, she took off the cloak and started walking toward Molly. She had on a shimmery gold dress. She had long red hair, and as she got close, Molly could see her green eyes.

"Don't be fooled, Molly," warned the fairy. "That's Sarah. She may be beautiful on the outside, but she's ugly on the inside."

Sarah pulled an iron rod from the air and swatted at the fairy.

"I want to take care of all these fairies, and I don't need anyone like you to interfere," Sarah said as she smiled at Molly and raised the rod up over her head. The fairies started screaming, and Sarah brought the iron rod down hard trying to smash it into the top of Molly's head. Molly woke up screaming.

"Molly, wake up. Are you all right?" said Grandma as she turned on the light.

"No, I had the dream about the fairies again, but this time a witch named Sarah was in it, and she tried to kill me!" cried Molly.

"Let's go to the kitchen and get a drink of water," Grandma said.

Maggie got up too. She was afraid to stay in the room alone in the middle of the night.

"Is everything under control?" Grandpa asked.

"Yes, Stefan, go back to sleep."

After they had a drink of water, they went back to the bedroom, and Grandma sat on the edge of the bed.

"Grandma, is Mrs. Vedick's first name Sarah?" asked Molly.

"No, her name is Berta. Do you think she's the witch in your dream?"

"It's that stupid dream," Maggie said sarcastically.

"Shut up, Maggie. Grandma, I have dreams about fairies in some woods usually by a waterfall, and they talk about a witch named Sarah."

"Hmm, that's interesting. I'd be wary of any strange woman named Sarah until we find out who she is," Grandma said.

"Do you think she's real, Grandma?" asked Maggie.

"She could be. Since Molly had the dream more than once, the fairies could be trying to tell her something."

"Are fairies friendly?" Molly asked.

"Some are, and some aren't. Do they seem friendly in your dreams?"

"Yes, and they seem like they need my help."

"I don't think your dream is about Coaltown. We don't

have any waterfalls here, so this may be about the future. Tell me right away if you come across any fairies or a woman named Sarah. Don't go with her or do anything she says. Tell your mother about your dream, so she can look out for a Sarah too."

Grandma went out onto the back porch and made a big bouquet of lavender and sage to hang on the bed. She sat down on the side of the bed and reached into her pocket and pulled out a beautiful rosary and said, "Hold this in your hand or put it around your neck as you sleep."

"Okay, Grandma." There was a slight pause. "I will," Molly said as she fell asleep.

"Just like her. She wakes me up with one of her dreams and then she falls back to sleep first," Maggie said.

"You'll sleep soon. Just smell the beautiful herbs," Grandma said soothingly.

Grandma said a prayer in Slovak over Molly, Maggie, and the whole house. Molly slept quietly the rest of the night.

♣

The next couple of days went by without anything strange happening. Molly was having a good time, and she and Doris became good friends. They had a lot to do in the neighborhood. One great place to meet friends was the school playground.

The town's elementary school was right next door to the Riker's house. The two school buildings were very old. They were two stories high and made of red brick. In the back of one building, coming from the second story, were two fire escapes. The fire escapes were long metal tubes the students were to slide down in case of a fire. The playground had two sliding boards, a merry-go-round, two big swing sets, and two teeter-totters. The girls enjoyed going to the playground.

Doris and Gail had an older sister named Sherry. She was tall and slim with dark brown hair. Sherry was very pretty and always had a boyfriend. She had just turned sixteen years old, and started a new job at Schuete's ice cream parlor on Lincoln Street. The ice cream parlor was about three blocks from Grandma's house.

One evening, after supper, Grandma allowed Molly and Maggie to walk to Schuete's for dessert. The girls usually went to get ice cream after lunch, but Grandma thought it would be all right for them to go since the ice cream parlor was on a corner surrounded by houses. It was a steamy evening and everything looked hazy. The sun was setting, and the lightning bugs were coming out.

"We better walk a little faster. It's beginning to get dark," said Molly.

"Don't be a chicken," sneered Maggie. "It's not far."

They made it to Schuete's in record time. Molly felt safe in the ice cream parlor, because everything was so bright and cheery. Molly ordered a double chocolate cone, and Maggie ordered a double strawberry cone. Sherry made the ice cream cones and added sprinkles for free.

"You girls will be my last customers today. I have to clean up the place, and then I'll be heading home," Sherry said as she followed the girls to the door. "Bye now."

The girls heard the lock click behind them, and saw Sherry turn the open sign around to say closed.

It was difficult to walk and eat the melting ice cream. Molly and Maggie were about two streets from Grandma's house when Maggie stopped dead in her tracks. She was

Molly O'Neal

staring down an alley next to a vacant lot with high weeds. Molly looked into the alley and saw – HER.

It had to be Mrs. Vedick. The person was exactly as Gail had described. They both stood petrified, as she walked toward them with her scythe. In the haziness of the alley, she looked just like a witch. She began to point the scythe at the girls and cackled. Her cackling laugh was bone chilling. Maggie dropped her ice cream cone and ran away, leaving Molly alone. Molly screamed and squeezed her cone so hard it mashed apart in her hand. She began to run, trying to catch up to Maggie, but Maggie was older and faster. Soon Maggie was out of sight. Molly ran down the street without watching where she was going. She was terrified. She turned a corner, and none of the houses looked familiar, so she began to panic. She yelled for Maggie, but she was nowhere to be found. She ran back a block and looked to see if she recognized any houses. She ran around a corner and almost ran into the witch. She was waving her arms and yelling something Molly couldn't understand. Molly screamed and turned around. She started running so fast everything became a blur. She turned another corner and looked up the street and saw the school buildings over the houses. Finally, something she recognized. Her heart was pounding, and she couldn't catch her breath, but she had to get back to Grandma's house. She finally ran through Grandma's front yard and all the way to the back door. Molly kept trying to open the kitchen door, but it was locked.

"Open up!" Molly screamed as she banged on the door.

Grandma came to the door, and she could tell Molly was upset. Molly finally caught her breath and cried, "Why did you lock the door?"

"I didn't lock it," said Grandma.

Maggie peeked out of the bedroom and said, "I locked the door. I didn't want the witch to get in."

Molly eventually calmed down enough to tell Grandma what happened. Grandma tried to stay calm. She tried to comfort Molly by telling her everything was all right, and she was safe with her and Grandpa.

"How about we close all the windows and turn on the air conditioner tonight? You and Maggie have some cookies, and get ready for bed."

Molly felt safer with the windows and the curtains closed. She also insisted that the bedroom door was always open. The girls sat up in bed and talked for a long time. During the conversation, Molly asked Maggie why she left her behind.

Maggie said, "I thought you were right behind me. I can't help it if you can't keep up."

Molly didn't believe her sister, because she'd left her behind before.

When Grandpa came home from his card game, Grandma met him at the door.

"Why is the air conditioner on?" he asked.

"Shh," Grandma whispered. "I think the witch is up to her old tricks again."

"What do you mean?" he said.

"The witch they described has to be Mrs. Vedick, and she scared the daylights out of the girls tonight when they were walking home from Schuete's. She has to be back."

"Do you think she knows they're Anna's girls?" asked Grandpa.

"She must have heard that Anna had two girls who were visiting for the summer. She probably looked in her crystal

Molly O'Neal   51

ball," Grandma said sarcastically. "She's a witch I tell you. All this makes me so mad. I can't believe she's back. She tried to kidnap Anna, and now she's after our Molly. She's been gone for more than twenty-five years. What in the world is she doing out of the asylum?" Grandma whispered.

"Oh, Joanna, we're going to have to protect the girls, especially at night. Tomorrow we'll tell them just enough about the witch so they'll watch out for her, and we'll have to watch them very carefully. We won't tell them about their mother's connection to her or the legend about women with green eyes. Old Vedick always thought Anna was supposed to be her daughter, because of those green eyes. Molly has green eyes and Maggie's are blue. She only wants Molly. Nothing will happen to Molly as long as we're alive."

Suddenly, something started flopping against the bedroom window. The girls started to scream. Grandpa ran outside with a broom, and as he was shutting the front door, three bats tried to get in the house, but they hit an invisible barrier. They turned back to the bedroom window and continued to thrash against it. The girls looked outside through the living room window in horror. The bats saw them and started ramming that window. Molly thought she heard them screeching something.

"What are they saying?" cried Molly.

"Nothing, get away from the window!" cried Grandma as she pulled the girls away.

Grandpa started hitting the bats with the broom. He killed one of them, and the other two flew away.

"Come in, Stefan," Grandma said calmly. "Okay girls, the bats are gone now. We have to calm down. Nothing can get in this house, I assure you."

Pamela Gillette

"Joanna, check the windows again, and I'll check all the doors. Everyone, go to bed now," said Grandpa in a very worried tone.

"Well Maggie, I guess when I heard someone at the window, I wasn't having a fever dream after all."

Grandma went to the closet and pulled out a cot. She set it up in the girls' room. Molly slept on the cot and Grandma slept in the bed with Maggie. Grandpa stayed up most of the night playing solitaire at the dining room table: keeping watch.

Chapter Six

On a Saturday morning in mid-June, Molly noticed a strange car at Mrs. Skora's house. She remembered that two of her grandchildren were coming for a visit. She watched out the window for quite a while trying to get a look at the boys, but she never saw them.

Later that afternoon, Molly and Doris walked up to Livingood's to buy popsicles. They walked in the door, the bell rang, and the door banged behind them. Molly turned the corner and looked down the aisle by the gumball machine and saw two boys buying gum.

"I got the tiger eye!" the smaller boy said as he showed the gumball to Mr. Livingood.

"Then you win a silver dollar. Here you go," said Mr. Livingood. "Hey, Doris, Molly, come here. I'd like for you to meet Mrs. Skora's grandsons. This is Tyler and his older brother Alan. They're visiting their grandmother for a couple of weeks. Maybe you two can show the boys around town."

The girls were kind of shy, but they managed to get out a "sure" and a nod.

Tyler was nine, and Alan was twelve years old. Molly felt embarrassed talking to Tyler. He had blond hair, brown eyes, and a dark tan. Both he and Alan were cute. Alan had red hair and brown eyes.

As the group was trying to think of something to say, the bell above the door rang, and old Billy May walked in. Molly's eyes got huge as he came closer. He was mumbling to himself as he headed to the gumball machine. Molly, Alan, and Tyler stared at Billy as he put five pennies in the gumball machine. Doris didn't pay any attention to him. She saw him around town all the time.

"May we have two popsicles, Mr. Livingood?" asked Doris. She paid Mr. Livingood and pulled Molly outside. The boys followed.

"Do you know who that guy is?" asked Molly

"Yes, that's Billy May," answered Doris.

"Oh, he's the guy Gail told us about the first week we were here. She said he thinks he's a leprechaun. This is the first time I've seen him."

"Who are you talking about?" asked Alan.

"It's a long story. All we really know, is that the guy in the store who was talking to himself, is a very strange person," said Doris.

Billy walked out of the store, and he was still mumbling to himself. He was a thin man, and he was wearing green plaid pants and a tight orange shirt. His shoes were a couple sizes too big and turned up at the toes. He had a long beard that came to a point at the end. They watched Billy walk down the street until he was out of sight.

"How long are you guys staying with your grandmother?" Doris asked.

"We're only going to stay here for two weeks," Alan said.

"Where do you guys live?" asked Doris

"Springfield," Tyler answered.

"Are you going to the Homecoming?" asked Doris.

"Yeah, maybe we could go together," Alan suggested.

"I have an older sister and so does Molly. They can go too," said Doris

"Sounds like fun," said Molly.

Molly looked over at Tyler. He was smiling at her. She could feel her face burning. She knew she was turning red with embarrassment, so she turned away.

"Do you guys want to ride bikes around town?" asked Alan.

"Molly doesn't have a bike, but I do and so does my sister. We'll go home and get the bikes and meet you back here," answered Doris.

Doris and Molly walked home, and Doris asked her mother if she and Molly could use the bikes. Her mother was fine with it, so they got the bikes and left. Molly and Doris found Tyler and Alan waiting at the road in front of their grandma's house. They rode around town most of the afternoon. They stopped off at the grocery store uptown and got sodas. Later they went to the schoolyard and found Gail and Maggie.

"Where have you two been? We've been looking for you, and what are you doing on my bike?" asked Gail.

"Mom said we could take the bikes. We've been riding around town with Mrs. Skora's grandsons. This is Tyler and his brother Alan. They're going to be staying with her for two weeks," answered Doris.

For Gail, it was love at first sight. For once she was speechless as she looked at Alan.

Maggie broke the silence and said, "We're staying right across the street from your grandmother."

"Have you guys ever seen fire escapes like these?" said Gail, finding her voice and pointing to the long metal tubes.

The group went over to the fire escapes. Alan climbed

up one of the tubes and tried to open the door at the top, but it was locked, so he slid back down.

After hanging around the playground, the group went over to Mrs. Skora's house to watch television and have some lemonade. About four-thirty, the girls went home to help with supper.

Molly was on cloud nine. She forgot all about how scary it was around there at night. For the rest of the evening, she couldn't get Tyler off her mind. That night, everything was quiet. Nothing unusual happened.

※

THE BOYS SPENT A LOT OF THEIR TIME FISHING AND HANGing around with other boys in the neighborhood. Molly and Doris always managed to bump into the boys at the store or the playground. One day Molly, Doris, Maggie, and Gail were riding their bikes on Main Street. Maggie and Gail were doing the peddling, and Doris and Molly were on the back-fender seats. They saw Alan and Tyler coming out of the post office with their grandma's mail. Alan saw the girls and asked them if they wanted to go to the ice cream parlor.

"Our sister works there. Maybe we can get some ice cream for free," Gail said. They all rode to the ice cream parlor.

"Hi, you guys. What are you doing in this part of town, and who are your friends?" Sherry asked with a big grin on her face.

"This is, Alan and Tyler, Mrs. Skora's grandsons," said Gail.

"That's nice," Sherry said. She smiled, because she could tell the boys were kind of shy.

"So, what do you guys want?" asked Sherry.

As they ordered their ice cream cones, Gail tried to

Molly O'Neal

get hers for free, but Sherry refused, although she did give everyone free sprinkles. The kids went outside and sat on the ground under a shade tree. They ate their ice cream and talked about school and other friends. Maggie didn't say much, because she was a bit shy, and Molly blushed a lot, because she had a crush on Tyler. Doris wouldn't admit it, but she had a crush on him too. Everyone could tell Gail had a crush on Alan. She was very outgoing, so she could easily talk to him, but it was pretty obvious he liked Sherry. She was too old for him and had a boyfriend her own age.

"We're going swimming with some guys, so we'll see you all later," said Alan. He and Tyler got on their bikes and started down the street.

"Bye, see you later," yelled the girls.

After the boys left, the girls felt a little bored.

"I know what we can do," said Gail. "Let's go to old Alice's house."

"Mom told us to never bother her," said Doris.

"We won't be bothering her. We'll see if she's afraid of us. Let's go," said Gail.

"I don't know. Is she scary?" asked Molly.

"No, she looks like a nice lady," said Doris.

The girls rode to Alice's house. Her house was a little run down with paint peeling off the clapboards, and a cracked window in the front door. The front porch went around both sides of the house, and big trees shaded the front yard. The garage out back was leaning to one side and needed a coat of paint. As the girls approached, they saw a woman run up the porch stairs and around to the side of the house. The girls parked the bikes outside the front gate.

"Come on in the gate. We'll knock on the door," said Gail.

Reluctantly, Molly followed the rest of the girls. She felt

very leery of Alice. They went to the front door and knocked. They knew Alice was at the side of the house, hiding, so they kept knocking.

"What do you want?" said a weak voice from around the corner.

"We're just checking up on you, Alice. We haven't seen you around town or at church for a long time. It's Gail Riker. Remember me?"

"Oh yes, I've known your family for years," Alice said as she poked her head around the corner of the porch.

Molly jumped back. She didn't trust Alice.

"Don't be afraid of me little girl. I don't get many visitors. You look just like someone I knew a long time ago," Alice said as she sat on the porch swing.

"This is Molly and Maggie O'Neal. They're staying with their grandma and grandpa. You know them, Mr. and Mrs. Giba," Gail said.

"Oh, so you're Anna's girls. That's who you look like, Molly. What can I do for you girls today?"

Gail was so bold, she came right out and asked, "Is it true your hair turned white, over night, when you were a young girl?"

"Well, people say it did and they stare at me and point, but I don't think it's true. I always had light blonde hair."

"What happened to you that night?" asked Gail.

Alice looked fearful and said, "You kids better be careful in this town. No one listens to me. For years I couldn't remember what happened. The doctor said I had amnesia."

"Tell us what happened. We'll believe you," Gail said.

"On my thirteenth birthday my mother brought home a yellow Labrador retriever. The new puppy looked exactly like Roscoe. He was the puppy I was given for my tenth birthday. I loved Roscoe. He was the first pet I ever had. Anyway, at my thirteenth birthday dinner with Mom and Dad, Mom told me to close my eyes, because she had a birthday surprise for me. She put the new puppy on my lap, and they all began to sing *Happy Birthday*. When I opened my eyes, the horror of that winter evening, three years before, came flooding back."

"What did happen?" asked Doris.

Alice's eyes welled up with tears as she began to tell the story.

"It was a winter evening about six o'clock. I was walking home from a babysitting job with my puppy, Roscoe. The snow had been falling all day. By evening it was about four inches deep and still coming down. I carried Roscoe some of the way home, because when I put him down, his belly would drag in the snow. He was only three months old. A couple blocks from home, I put him down. As I walked on, he ran circles around me and jumped on my snow boots. It was dark, but the snow helped light my way. Everyone in town was tucked in for the evening, so the streets were deserted. Little Roscoe and I were enjoying the walk home, when Roscoe began to bark at something behind me. I spun around and stared into the snow. I could vaguely make out a dark shadow coming toward me. I yelled, asking it who it was, and Roscoe continued to bark.

"I heard a creaky, hoarse voice mocking me, 'Who is it? Who is it?' I tried to grab Roscoe and run, but the person lunged at me and pushed me down in the snow. The dark figure was wearing a ragged black hooded cape. When it pushed me, the wind caught the hood and it blew off exposing her head. I could see it was the witch, Mrs. Vedick. Her gray hair was all matted to her head. I saw her big nose and pointy chin. She pulled the hood back over her head and ran for Roscoe. I yelled, "Run, run Roscoe!" She kicked him right off his feet. He yelped and cried as she leaned over to grab him. I screamed and ran at her, pushing and pulling on her cape and screaming for help. She shoved me down and told me to shut up, in an evil whisper. She grabbed Roscoe and started running down the street. I could hear Roscoe crying. I got up and ran after her. She abruptly stopped and spun around. She hissed and stared at me. I kept running at her and yelling for Roscoe. I grabbed her cape, and suddenly I felt myself lifting off of the ground. Vedick had transformed into a huge black vulture. She cackled as we flew higher. The cape I grabbed was now part of the vulture's tail. I hung on screaming for help. She didn't want me hanging on. She began to hit me with her wings, but I wouldn't let go. She tried to kill me! We flew over houses and trees. She finally landed in the deserted school playground. She was still carrying Roscoe in the claws of her feet. I was half-dazed from the landing, so I let go of the tail. I could hear Roscoe's sad cries as she flew away with him, leaving me in the snow all alone and crying.

"I didn't remember anything. I don't even know how I got home. I woke up in my own bed with a terrible headache. My mom and dad were hovering over me, calling my name. Mom was crying. I asked them what happened. Mom said I was late coming home, so my father went out looking for me. He found me in the schoolyard crying and muttering something about Roscoe. Dad said that when he tried to help me, I screamed and fainted. Mom told me I had an awful lump on by forehead.

"I didn't remember any of this until three years later on my birthday. Mom told me not to tell anyone, because they wouldn't believe my story. My father said I fell in the snow and hit my head, and Roscoe wandered off. They never believed my story. Sometimes I wonder if it was all a bad dream."

"We believe it," said Molly and Doris.

"I believe you too," said Gail.

"I don't know. You did bump your head," said Maggie.

"All of this is too scary," said Molly.

"My mom and dad think Mrs. Vedick is a witch, and so does your grandmother, Molly," said Doris.

"I do know she was sent to an insane asylum long ago, but I swear I heard her cackling near my house one-night last week," Alice said. "Both my parents moved into Stanton years ago. I live here alone. I hope she isn't back."

"She is back," said Molly. "Maggie and I saw her one evening. She chased us."

"I guess she is real, but why chase us?" asked Maggie.

"Ask your grandmother about it, girls. I have to go in now. All of you better be careful," Alice said as she pointed at Molly. "You look just like your mother. Everyone around town knows the story. I'm surprised your mother never told you anything."

"I know a little," said Molly.

"Bye girls."

The girls got on the bikes and left.

Chapter Seven

The Homecoming was scheduled for the following Friday and Saturday nights, at Coaltown Park. Everyone from neighboring communities and family and friends were invited to enjoy the festivities. The park was only a block from Grandma's house. The anticipation was running high. On Wednesday the big trucks started rolling into town carrying the carnival rides. The carnival workers began to assemble the rides and booths as soon as they arrived on Wednesday and all-day Thursday. "May we go watch them put up the rides?" Maggie asked Grandma.

"No, that's not a good idea. You'll get in the way, and I could use some help today baking cookies for the bake sale for our church. I also have to make a double chocolate cake for the cake walk."

"I guess we can help with the baking as long as we can sample the cookies," Molly said smiling.

❖

The Homecoming opened on Friday night, but that night was mostly for the adults, so Molly and Maggie stayed home with Grandma. Two different bands were going to play in the evenings. On Friday night, a polka band played.

Grandma and Grandpa and Maggie and Molly sat in the backyard and listened to the polka band. They could hear the music just fine from the park. The band started around five o'clock and continued until ten o'clock. Grandma and Grandpa stayed outside, but Molly and Maggie had to go to bed around nine-thirty. Grandma's street only had one big light, and it was outside of Livingood's store in the next block, so the neighborhood was very dark.

At nine-thirty, Grandma said, "You girls go to bed. I'll come in after the music stops and tuck you in and close the windows."

The girls were tired and ready to go to sleep, so they went in without a fuss.

"The window is open," Molly said.

"Grandma said she'll come in and close the windows soon," said Maggie. "Some awful smell is coming in the window. It smells like a skunk or something dead."

"Is the smell getting stronger?" Molly asked. "Shh, I hear something outside. Turn off the light."

Maggie turned off the light in the bedroom, and the girls stood looking out the window into the darkness.

"Do you hear someone breathing?" Maggie said.

"Shut the window!" Molly cried as she reached up and started pushing the window down. "Help, it's stuck!"

Molly and Maggie were panicking while they tried to close the window. The stench was strong as Mrs. Vedick jumped in front of the window and started laughing and scratching on the screen. The girls screamed and ran to the kitchen. Grandma and Grandpa had gone to the front of the house to see what was going on, but no one was there. The girls were standing in the kitchen waiting for Grandma to come inside, when Mrs. Vedick knocked on the window behind them. They turned around and saw her ugly face in the window. She was smiling at them. The girls started screaming again. Grandma and Grandpa heard them and ran in the kitchen door. Grandpa found his flashlight and went back outside. He shined the flashlight all around the house and down the sidewalk on both sides of the street. He never found anyone, so they closed up the house for the night and turned on the air conditioner.

※

Bright and early on Saturday, Grandma and Grandpa walked with Molly, Maggie, Doris, and Gail to the Homecoming. Each girl carried a plate of cookies for the bake sale, and Grandpa carried the cake. They delivered the goodies to the church booth and the cakewalk area and then Grandma went to work at the booth selling raffle tickets for a quilt the ladies from her church made. She was always nearby if the girls needed her. Grandpa was helping out in the refreshment area, and Mrs. Skora was working with the cakewalk.

Booths were set up all over selling hotdogs, fried chicken, cotton candy, snow cones, and soda. Many of the booths were games of chance, for example, shooting metal ducks, ring tosses, and darts. The town even had a dunking booth. Only the best cooks in town donated cakes to be won at the cakewalk. Over in one corner of the park was a tent with a gypsy fortuneteller. Molly and Maggie were mostly looking forward to the carnival rides. Each ride cost one ten-cent ticket. A kid could be entertained all day for only a couple of dollars. Molly and Doris, and Maggie and Gail planned to pair up for the rides. The girls were hoping to see Tyler and Alan there too.

Maggie and Doris took off for the ticket booth. Everyone had to buy tickets to get on the rides or play the games. They knew there would be a long line.

Grandpa had made the ticket booth out of scrap lumber. A large window was cut out of the front, and the back of the booth was open. A row of flashing lights lined the top, and under the lights was a sign that read *Tickets 10 Cents*. As Maggie and Doris were nearing the line, Alan and Tyler came out of nowhere and cut them off. The boys reached the end of the line first.

"You cut!" yelled Doris.

"No, we didn't. You're just too slow," laughed Alan. "Hey, Molly, why don't you and Tyler go in the fun house together?"

"Shut up, Alan," Tyler said as he pushed him.

Alan laughed and pushed him back. Doris shoved Molly in front of her, so she could be next to Tyler.

"Stop it," whispered Molly as she went back to the end of the line.

The kids all bought long strings of tickets. Alan took off toward the Ferris wheel, and Molly and Doris went the opposite way.

"See you later, Molly," yelled Tyler as he followed after Alan.

"He is cute, isn't he?" asked Molly.

"Of course he is," replied Doris.

Molly and Doris made their way around the park a few times during the day. They found Grandpa about mid-day and got a couple more dollars from him. Then they begged a couple more dollars off of Mr. Riker. They rode the swings and the merry-go-round several times. They each bought a hot dog for lunch and washed it down with grape soda. For dessert they had cotton candy. They played lots of games and rode more rides during the afternoon. They had a pretty extravagant day with the extra money they finagled out of Grandpa and Mr. Riker.

Soon the day was just about over, and they didn't have many tickets left. They decided to take one last ride on the Ferris wheel. As they rode around and around, Molly noticed a strange looking woman standing at the entrance platform. She seemed to be staring at them.

Molly nudged Doris and said, "Do you know that weird looking lady down there?"

"Who?" Doris questioned.

"The woman down there in the long dress, with the veil on her head," said Molly as she pointed at the woman.

As they swooped down, Doris could look her straight in the face.

"No. She's a stranger."

As the girls rose backwards into the air, the Ferris wheel slowed down and stopped with the girls half way up. They moved up each time the carnival worker let passengers off and new ones on. Soon the girls were stopped at the top.

"I want off this thing. I want to find Grandma!" Molly said.

Doris looked down to see the woman. When she did, she caused the seat to lean forward and begin to rock.

"Don't move, Doris, we'll fall out!"

"Okay, hang on," Doris said as she tried to steady the seat.

The Ferris wheel moved again. Then it stopped so fast it caused the girls seat to rock even more. The girls screamed.

"I'm getting dizzy!" cried Molly.

"Don't look down!" said Doris.

"My eyes are closed," Molly said as she clutched the safety bar.

"Why doesn't he move this thing?" cried Doris.

Stopped half way down the front of the Ferris wheel, the girls could see the strange woman watching them. They finally reached the bottom; it was their turn to get off. The worker removed the bar from their laps, and the strange woman moved right up to the platform and was practically touching Molly. She just stared. The girls left the platform, and the woman followed them.

She reached out for Molly's arm and mumbled, "I see graves, Reza, darkness."

"Run! She's crazy!" yelled Doris.

"I am!" Molly yelled as they made their way through the crowd.

It was easy for the little girls to lose her in the crowd.

"Molly, you look like you've seen a ghost," said Tyler, tapping Molly on her shoulder.

Molly jumped and screamed. She thought it was the strange woman.

"Oh! It's you," said Molly, relieved to see it was Tyler.

"Gee thanks," Tyler said as he began to walk away.

"I thought you were someone else," said Molly. "Don't go."

"Well, in that case I'll stay. Did you guys ride everything?" asked Tyler.

"Two or three times," answered Molly.

"Are you hungry? We're going to get some food. Want to go with us?" asked Alan.

"Sure!" said Molly and Doris simultaneously.

The food booths and picnic tables were on the other side of the park, so the foursome walked through the crowds.

"Hey wait! I want to shoot the ducks again. I'm feeling lucky," said Tyler.

Tyler gave the man in the booth a ticket and grabbed

one of the guns. The metal ducks were going by in a nice straight row. Tyler had three chances to shoot. Ping, he knocked one down. Ping, ping, he knocked two more down. He won and got to pick a stuffed animal. He chose a fluffy white bear and handed it to Molly. Of course, she blushed and thanked him for the bear.

"Let's go eat," said Alan as he walked off.

They all followed Alan to a food vender. The kids ordered their food and sat down at a picnic table. The girls sat on one side, and the boys sat on the other. Molly was careful not to get food on her bear. As they ate, they talked about all the rides they had been on and the games they played all day. Molly started thinking that Tyler might like her. She hoped it wasn't just wishful thinking.

When they finished eating, Tyler said, "There is only one thing left to do here and that's to see the gypsy and have our fortunes read."

Alan noticed Maggie and Gail and waved them over and said, "Come on, let's get in line for the fortune teller."

The line for the fortuneteller was pretty long, but the group passed the time talking and laughing. As they got close to the tent, they could read the sign above the door. The sign said *Madam Seezall Fortuneteller to the Stars*. The tent looked mysterious and dark. One person at a time entered the tent, paid one ticket, and sat down across the table from Madam Seezall. She wore lots of bracelets and rings, and her dress was a bright purple and orange print. She wore a long black shawl with fringe on the ends, and she had a shiny veil on her head trimmed with what looked like gold coins. She wore thick black eyeliner and blue eyeshadow. Her lipstick was bright red and went over her lip line to make her lips look bigger. She looked old and scary.

Molly was the last customer to go in the tent to see the gypsy. She sat down at the table across from Madam Seezall and gave her a ticket. Molly looked up at the gypsy, who was glaring at her, and she realized Madame Seezall was the crazy woman at the Ferris wheel. Molly started to leave.

Madam Seezall said, "No, Molly, wait. I have some very important things to say to you. I felt a strange presence today. I walked outside my tent and something led me to you. Let's look in my crystal ball."

"How did you know my name?"

"Madam Seezall, sees all, Molly. You are here visiting your grandmother. You are with your sister, aren't you? Hmm, I am getting a picture of a bedroom window at the front of a house."

Molly started to panic.

"Something evil is lurking at your bedroom window. All I see is a dark shadow. You must protect yourself from this evil. It is trying to take your very soul. I see graves and headstones, and I see people crying."

"Is it the witch?" Molly cried.

"THAT'S ALL!" Madam Seezall shouted.

Molly jumped out of her chair, knocking it over.

"Just beware of these things. Times up! GO!"

Molly's eyes were huge, and she was trembling as she ran out of the tent. She found Alan, Tyler, and the girls near the tent waiting for her.

Tyler said, "She's crazy. She told me I would do great in school and grow up to be a lawyer. She told Alan he was going to work in a circus. She's a fake. What did she tell you, Molly?"

"Nothing, nothing, I have to find my grandma," answered Molly.

"Let's check out the sing-a-long. We'll see if we can find your grandmother there," Tyler said.

They walked over to the sing-a-long and found Mr. and Mrs. Riker. Everyone was singing and swaying side to side. Molly couldn't concentrate on the songs. She was worried about what Madame Seezall said about the evil outside the bedroom window. A song with a good beat started, and everyone was clapping, and Doris was singing along. She nudged Molly to at least clap. Finally, they sang the last slow song, and everyone started to disperse. Tyler and Alan left to look for Mrs. Skora. Molly saw Grandma and Grandpa sitting at a picnic table holding hands. The Rikers, and Molly and her family, slowly walked home while they heard the beautiful song being repeated again to serenade people as they left the park. On the walk home, everyone shared stories of their day. Molly was very quiet. She was worrying about the night. She wondered if Mrs. Vedick would be back.

 After they got home, Grandpa took the flashlight outside and made sure no one was in the yard. Molly told Grandma and Maggie what the gypsy said. Grandma pulled out the cot again and this time Maggie slept on it, and Molly and Grandma slept in the bed. Grandpa peeked in and told them good night and not to worry.

Molly O'Neal

Chapter Eight

Molly thought Mrs. Skora might be interested in what the fortuneteller told her. She knew the boys were going fishing that morning at Coal Mine Lake, so she watched the house and saw them leave before she even had breakfast. She ate some cereal and told Grandma she was going out to play.

"It's too early to bother the Rikers. Come with me to the post office and grocery store. I like your company."

Molly had to put off her conversation with Mrs. Skora until later that morning. Molly and Grandma walked to the post office, and the mail clerk, who was also the postmaster, had a lot of local gossip for Grandma. Then they shopped at Livingood's store, and Grandma met one of the neighbors there, and they talked for a long time. By the time they got home, it had been almost three hours since the boys had left to go fishing.

Molly told Grandma she was going out to play. She ran straight for Mrs. Skora's house and knocked on the door. Mrs. Skora came to the door and told Molly the boys had gone fishing. Molly said she came to talk to her and not the boys. Molly followed her into the kitchen. She told Molly to sit down while she ironed some clothes.

"What's on your mind?" she asked Molly.

"Saturday, I went into the fortuneteller's tent at the Homecoming. She looked in her crystal ball and saw an evil shadow lurking outside my bedroom window. She knew the window was at the front of Grandma's house, next to a pine tree, and she knew my name."

"Oh my, that's scary. Did you tell Joanna about it?" asked Mrs. Skora.

"Yes, she keeps the bedroom window closed every night now, and she turns on the air conditioner."

"Good idea. Your family had a lot of trouble at the house when Anna was about your age."

"What kind of trouble?" she asked.

"It was so long ago. One night, I remember it was cold, and there was a pack of dogs growling and barking outside your mother's bedroom window. There were so many dogs, all the neighbors, including me, were looking out their windows trying to see what was going on. Everyone was afraid to go outside and chase them away. After a few minutes, your grandpa got his shotgun, loaded it, and went outside. The dogs ran off, and when they got to the corner by Livingood's store, they disappeared. Everyone thought Mrs. Vedick sent them.

"In the old country, witches could take the form of animals and attack someone. They could also send evil spirits into animals and send them out to attack people. Vedick is her married name. I told you about Mrs. Vedick's family, didn't I?"

"Yes, you said they were witches in the old country," Molly said.

"Yes, they were. No one could ever prove that she sent the dogs. I hope she's still in the insane asylum. All the trouble stopped when she was sent away. If she is back, I won't know what to do. I'm so glad your grandparents live across the street. We are family, and we take care of each other," Mrs. Skora said. She stood up and looked out the kitchen window.

"I better go help Grandma, bye," said Molly as she walked toward the door.

"I'm going to start lunch. The boys should be back from fishing soon," said Mrs. Skora.

Molly was stunned by the story Mrs. Skora told her. She was standing on the sidewalk in front of Grandma's house, deep in thought, when she saw Alan and Tyler coming down the road. They waved at her and seemed anxious to tell her something.

"After lunch we'll meet you and your sister at the playground. Bring the Rikers too and the bikes. We have something to show you," Alan said.

"Okay, see you later," Molly said.

After lunch Molly, Maggie, Doris, and Gail met the boys at the playground. Gail asked them why they needed their bikes.

Alan quietly explained. "Gather around. Tyler and I went fishing this morning at Coal Mine Lake. On the way home we did some exploring. We saw an old weedy road on the other side of the tracks. We figured no one lived back there, so we rode our bikes down the road. It wound around like a snake for a long stretch. Every so often there was a faded sign on an old fence post. I could barely make out the words *Keep Out* on one of the signs. Of course, that made us want to see what was at the end of the road even more. We finally came to a real creepy house. It was old and dark, and it looked like a log cabin. Junk was everywhere. We thought you guys would like to go with us and explore. Nobody's lived in the house for years."

Maggie and Gail were anxious to go.

"I think we should ask Grandma," Molly said nervously.

"Don't be such a scaredy cat. You'll be with all of us," said Maggie in her usual know-it-all tone.

"There's nothing back there but a bunch of old junk," said Tyler.

"All right, I'll go. Who do I ride with?" asked Molly.

"You ride on my handle bars," said Alan. "Tyler can ride his bike, and Doris can let Maggie ride her bike."

"My sister can ride on my back fender," said Gail. "Let's go."

As they crossed the railroad tracks, Molly mentioned that it was getting cloudy, but everyone ignored her. Soon they came to the old weedy road. Weedy was an understatement. The weeds on both sides of the road were about five feet tall, and the road was very narrow, more like a path. They began to peddle slower and listened for any strange noises. They rounded one of the bends and stopped at the rickety, old cabin.

"Let's explore," Alan said as he and Molly got off his bike.

"Be careful, and wait for us," said Doris

They left their bikes on the dirt road. The kids opened the gate of the old picket fence and went in the yard. The grass was high and weeds were everywhere.

"I wonder who used to live here. I hope no one lives here now," Molly said.

"Oh, Molly, no one could live in a dump like this," Alan said.

Gail and Maggie walked to the side of the house on a stone path. They saw a wrought iron fence with a broken gate.

"Oh, look! Inside the fence there aren't any weeds. Are those gravestones?" Maggie said in a high-pitched voice.

Gail was very curious and brave. She walked through the open gate and tried to read the stones. They were old and weathered, so most of the carving was illegible. The only words she could read on the stones were husband and son.

Tyler ran over to the graveyard and said, "Get out of there. Graveyards are even too creepy for me. Let's hurry up. It looks like a storm is brewing."

Molly wished they would all leave and go home. She didn't want anything to do with the awful place. Alan and Tyler walked up the three rotting steps onto the porch, and the girls followed.

"Why don't we go home now? It's going to storm any minute!" cried Molly.

"We've come too far to turn back now," said Alan, determined to go in the cabin.

Most of the windows were cracked. An old rocker on the porch started to creak, and Doris jumped.

"It's just rocking with the wind. It does look like a storm is coming. If it starts to rain, we'll wait it out in the cabin. Let's go in," Gail said.

Alan tried the door. It wasn't locked, so he slowly opened it and walked in. "It smells like something died in here," said Alan.

The floor of the cabin creaked as they walked around inside. All they could see was one big room with a large fireplace.

"I don't know guys, there's furniture in here," said Molly with a tremor in her voice.

"Nobody lives here, but it sure does stink," said Maggie."

Gail walked over to a cupboard and peeked inside.

"Look at this stuff. All these jars are labeled, but it's in a different language. Eww, there are creepy things in these jars!" Gail said.

"Don't touch them!" Doris said.

"I bet this stuff was used by a witch to make potions. I bet a witch lives here now," said Maggie.

"Mrs. Vedick could live here. Let's go back to Grandma's. I hear thunder!" cried Molly.

"I bet they used the big iron pot in the fireplace to make potions," said Tyler. He looked out the door and said, "It's getting dark outside. We'll have to wait out the storm in here."

"It's better to be in here than riding back in the rain, but I do hope Grandma won't be worried. While we're here, keep exploring," said Maggie.

Molly and Doris walked over to a corner of the room and noticed a door handle on the wall. They pulled on the handle, and a door hidden in the wall opened up. They looked in and thought it was a bedroom. The room was dark. Doris saw a window on the far wall with closed shutters. She went over and opened the shutters. With more light in the room, Molly noticed an old dresser with a dirty gray doily on top. Next to the dresser were two rocking chairs. One chair was normal size, and the other chair was for a doll or small child. Molly looked at Doris who had turned away from the window. Molly's heart started pounding as she looked at her terror-stricken face.

"What's wrong, Doris?"

"Molly, LOOK!" Doris screamed as she pointed behind her.

Terrified, Molly slowly turned around. She felt like her legs had turned to mush. She could see a bed in the corner, and SOMEONE WAS IN IT. Molly thought the person was dead. All she could see was a lot of stringy gray hair. Then it started to move, and Molly screamed.

The person in the bed sat up and cried in a low, muffled voice, "Reza, Reza, come to Momma, Reza!"

Molly screamed again. By that time Gail, Maggie, Alan, and Tyler were running into the room blocking Doris and Molly's exit.

"What's wrong? What happened?" they were yelling.

Molly and Doris took no time to explain. They ran out of the room, pushing through the others. They flew through the cabin and ran straight to their bikes. They could hear screams and soon the others had caught up to them.

Alan said, "Get on the bike, Molly! Let's get out of here!"

The sky was dark purple, gray, and green. Lighting was flashing and the thunder was getting louder. They were peddling as fast as they could. No one slowed down for any reason. Soon they crossed the tracks and stopped in front of the post office to catch their breath.

"She almost touched me! I want to go home and I mean to Mom and Dad! Do you think she's following us?" cried Molly.

"That was Mrs. Vedick, the witch!" exclaimed Gail.

"What was that? Who's Mrs. Vedick?" Alan asked nervously.

"I bet it was her," said Maggie. She was so afraid, she was trembling.

"Oh no, I bet she's going to be after us again tonight!" cried Molly.

"I'm afraid to tell Grandma. She told us to stay around where she could keep an eye on us," said Maggie.

"I'm not telling my mom!" cried Doris.

"Me either. She'll be so mad at us if she found out we rode our bikes over the tracks. If she finds out about this, we'll be grounded forever!" cried Gail.

"We're not going out there anymore, not even to go fishing," said Tyler, still looking down the road to see if they were being followed.

"I agree, Tyler. I can't wait to get out of this town. Who's this Mrs. Vedick anyway?" Alan asked again.

"She's a witch," said Gail.

"I believe it," Alan said.

Big drops of rain began to fall as they started toward Grandma's. They rode as fast as they could, trying to beat the storm. The kids had about two blocks to go, when the clouds opened up, drenching them. It was raining so hard they could barely see. Rain was pounding them. They all rode into Grandma's backyard. Molly jumped off Alan's bike and ran inside. Gail and Doris ran next door. Maggie left the bike in Riker's backyard and ran in Grandma's house. Alan and Tyler rode across the street to their grandma's, and just as they got to the porch, the wind started blowing hard.

Grandma and Grandpa met the girls at the kitchen door. They had called all over town looking for them. They were worried, because the radio had reported a tornado in the area.

"Where were you girls? Mrs. Skora and Mrs. Riker were frantically looking for you kids," said Grandpa as he went to get some towels for the girls.

Maggie spoke up, "We were riding our bikes and lost track of time."

Suddenly, the wind started slamming rain against the windows. The wind sounded like a train roaring by the house.

"Get in the cellar! It's a tornado!" Grandpa yelled.

They all ran downstairs as the storm raged outside. Grandma and the girls huddled in the corner. Everyone was quiet, listening to the storm and then the lights went out, and both the girls screamed. Grandma held them tighter, and Grandpa tried to reassure everyone that everything was going to be all right. The wind finally died down, but the thunder, lightning, and rain continued. Grandpa went upstairs to check on the house. He got two flashlights and came back downstairs to get Grandma and the girls.

The house withstood the storm, but Grandma didn't have time to close all the windows, so rain blew in the kitchen and bathroom. Grandpa began to mop up the floor as he told the girls to listen to the weather report on the radio and keep him posted.

"Oh, I forgot, we can't listen to the radio without electricity," said Grandpa. "How are we going to know what's going on?"

Grandma lit candles and placed one in every room.

The rain finally stopped, and Grandma, Grandpa, and the girls went outside to look around. It was still scary outside. The sky was dark, with gray and green clouds swirling overhead, and thunder could still be heard in the distance. Limbs were all over the ground, and Grandma's old apple tree split in half and one half fell on her shed. People were out all over the neighborhood checking the damage. Mr. Riker came home from work, and told Grandpa that trees were down all over town, and Livingood's garage blew over. As he spoke, rain started falling again, so everyone ran inside.

Grandma made sandwiches for supper. Everyone was very tired after the terrifying day, so Grandma suggested an early bedtime. Molly and Maggie were tired, but too afraid to sleep. The girl's got ready for bed and spent what seemed like hours whispering about what happened at the cabin and how scary the tornado was.

"I can't believe you guys talked me into going there," said Molly.

"We had no idea it was Vedick's house. The place is creepy and the graveyard, wow. Didn't Grandma say Vedick thought Mom was her baby, way back in the old country?" asked Maggie.

"Yes and Mrs. Skora told me all about a legend and about how Mrs. Vedick tried to steal Mom when she was a baby. Should we tell Grandma what happened today?"

"No, we can't. We weren't supposed to be there. They'll ground us until it's time to go home," whispered Maggie.

"Okay, but I'm scared," said Molly in a shrill whisper.

Grandma and Grandpa peeked in the door and said, "The electricity's back on, so blow out the candle. Good night you two. No more talking now."

The girls finally dozed off. Molly was awakened in the night by a loud crash of lightning. Another storm had blown in. The lightning flashes were lighting up the bedroom through the curtains. Molly sat up and became transfixed on the window. She swore she saw a silhouette of a person at the window whenever the lightning flashed. She pushed Maggie's shoulder until she woke up. Molly was so afraid, she could only whisper.

"Maggie, there's someone at the window!"

Both the girls were staring at the window while the rain poured down outside. They sat up in bed, staring at the window, frozen in terror. The lightning flashed, and both girls saw the figure at the window. Both gasped and began to scream.

Hearing the screams, the figure began pounding on the window yelling, "Reza, Reza, come home, Reza!"

Grandma and Grandpa came in the room and saw the figure at the window. Grandpa ran in the kitchen and got the rolling pin and ran outside in the rain. By the time he got to the window, no one was there.

"I'm calling the police!" he yelled.

It took a state policeman about twenty minutes to show up, and by then the rain had stopped. Grandpa went outside and talked to the officer for a long time.

Grandpa came in fuming. "He's just a kid, Joanna. He doesn't know anything about Vedick. He assured me he would look into the matter. What a waste of time."

"At least we reported it, Stefan. That's all we can do."

Grandma draped a heavy blanket over the window of the girl's bedroom. She got the cot out for Maggie to sleep on, and she slept in the bed with Molly.

Chapter Nine

The next day all anyone could talk about was the storm, and the whole town was out cleaning up all of the damage. Alan and Tyler were helping neighbors clean up branches, and they helped Grandpa clean up the part of the tree that had fallen on the shed. The girls were picking up small branches all over the yard. The kids were kept busy working all day.

❖

Alan and Tyler's parents surprised the boys the next day when they showed up two days early. They were worried about them because of the storm.

Molly saw a strange car parked in front of Mrs. Skora's house, so she went outside and sat on the front porch step. She was afraid it might be Tyler's parents' car. She saw Tyler come out of his grandma's house and start walking her way. She got up and met him at the street.

"My mom wants to meet you, Molly."

Tyler's mother came out on the porch to meet Molly. She took one look at Molly and called back to Tyler's dad, "Honey, come look at Molly. Who do you think she looks like?" She turned to Molly, "You look exactly like your mother, except she had dark hair. Oh my, it brings back so many memories of all the good times we had together. Your mother was like a sister to me. I wish I could see her again. We all grew up and moved away. When is she coming to pick you up?"

"I don't know when they're coming."

"Too bad I won't be able to see her. Maybe I'll see her at the next class reunion."

"Sorry to interrupt, but we have everything packed and should be on our way," said Tyler's dad.

"Bye," Molly said sadly as she turned to walk away.

Tyler followed Molly across the street and tapped her on the shoulder.

"I'm going to be here for the Homecoming next summer," he said shyly. "Will you be back?"

"I think my whole family will be going next year," Molly said as she gave him a quick hug.

Tyler blushed and ran back across the street. Soon Molly was standing on the sidewalk waving goodbye to Tyler as they drove off.

"It's going to be kind of boring around here now and really boring after you leave," Doris said as she sat on her front porch steps. "Tyler was so cute. I'm sure he'll be back next summer."

"We'll be back for the Homecoming. I think my whole family will want to go next year. We'll have to see," said Molly.

※

THAT EVENING WAS HOT AND HAZY. GRANDMA LET Molly and Maggie have sleep overs. Maggie was at the Riker's, and Doris came to spend the night with Molly.

Doris and Molly were sitting at the dining room table playing Monopoly, and Grandma and Grandpa were watching a television show where everyone was dancing the polka.

"Let's go next door and tap on Gail's bedroom window and scare them," whispered Doris.

"Grandma and Grandpa won't let us go outside," whispered Molly.

"It isn't dark yet. We can sneak out while they're watching TV and only be gone for a minute. Come on, Molly."

"Well, just for a minute," whispered Molly.

The girls crept outside through the back door. Gail's window was just out of reach, so Doris looked around and found a small tree branch on the ground. She picked it up and scratched it across the window.

"This should get their attention," Doris said. Molly and Doris started laughing as quietly as they could.

"I bet they're staring at each other right now and afraid to look at the window," whispered Molly.

Doris scratched at the window again. This time they heard muffled talking inside the house.

"One more time," Doris whispered.

"Okay," replied Molly, having a hard time controlling her laughter.

Both girls had one arm pressed against their stomachs and one hand over their mouths trying to stifle their laughter and not be heard. As Doris scratched at the window again, a sudden cold breeze flew around the corner of the house. Molly and Doris turned to each other with wide eyes. They slowly walked to the front of the house and looked down the road. They were holding on to each other's arms and straining their eyes to see through the now hazy darkness. Both of their chins dropped when they saw a figure of a person slowly walking up the street toward their houses. The figure stopped in the street even with them, turned, and looked their way.

"It's the witch!" screamed Doris as she tried to pull Molly between the houses. "We have to get inside! Why can't we move faster? My legs won't move!"

"I can't run!" cried Molly as they trudged to the backyard.

As Mrs. Vedick walked up Grandma's sidewalk and around to the backyard, she was quietly chanting a spell to freeze the girls in place, but all it did was slow them down.

She came up behind them and grabbed at Molly and caught the back of her shirt.

"Come with me. Come with me, Reza," Vedick said in a horrifying whisper.

Molly grabbed Doris around the waist. Doris grabbed the wooden support of the yard swing and screamed for Molly to hang on and not to let go. Molly hung on for dear life, and both girls screamed loudly. The back-porch lights flashed on, and Grandpa ran outside. As Grandpa ran out, Vedick let go of Molly's shirt, and both girls fell to the ground. Vedick transformed into a huge ugly vulture. The vulture perched on the roof of Grandma's house and stared down at Molly. Everyone was completely stunned. Grandpa grabbed a broom by the back door and began swinging it at the bird.

"Get away, Vedick! Get away!" he yelled as the bird flew away.

Grandma ran out of the house yelling, "What happened? Why are you girls outside?"

"The girls were being attacked by a huge vulture!" Grandpa said as he tried to calm down.

Molly and Doris were too terrified to speak.

Mr. Riker ran out of his back door and said, "What's going on out here! You girls shouldn't be outside after dark!"

Maggie and Gail peeked out the Riker's back door, and Gail yelled, "I knew it was you guys scratching at my window. You didn't scare us."

"Well, they sure had a scare," said Grandpa.

Doris finally found her voice, "It was Vedick, the witch! She grabbed Molly. I was trying to save her life, right Molly?"

"Yes! She was walking down the street and then she came at us! She told me to come with her, and she kept calling me Reza! When Grandpa came outside, she turned into a vulture! I swear!"

"Everyone inside," said Mr. Riker sternly. "I want to talk to Stefan."

Grandma and the girls went inside, and Mrs. Riker, Gail, and Maggie went into the Riker's house. Everyone was badly shaken, especially Molly and Doris. Grandpa and Mr. Riker had a muffled conversation in the garden.

"Stefan, do you believe that Mrs. Vedick is out of the insane asylum and came into your backyard? Do you believe she turned into a vulture? The whole story sounds like two girls with wild imaginations to me. I'm confused," said Mr. Riker.

"Well, that crazy woman has been around here before when Anna was young, harassing us and doing insane things. I think she's back, and she thinks Molly is Reza, her daughter who died at birth. I have a policeman who assured me he would look into the situation," explained Grandpa. "As for the vulture, it could be sick or something."

Grandpa couldn't go into a lot of detail about the legend of the green-eyed witches in the old country, and that he thought Mrs. Vedick was a witch, and she turned into a vulture. No one believed in witches anymore. After a few minutes, Grandpa came in the house. He told Grandma they have to let the police handle this, and he thought Anna

Molly O'Neal 87

should be informed. He called Anna and asked her to pick up the girls as soon as she could.

Grandma went into the girls' room and told Molly that her mom and dad were coming to pick them up the next day. Molly was happy to be going home.

"I sure will miss you, Doris, but I'm too afraid to stay here any longer."

"I understand," Doris said sadly.

The girls talked for about an hour and then dozed off. Everything had remained quiet the rest of the night.

❖

Early in the morning, Maggie and Gail came running into Molly's bedroom and woke her and Doris up.

"Do you believe we get to go home today?" Maggie said excitedly.

"What time is it? When is Mom coming? We better pack," said Molly as she yawned.

"Grandpa said they're coming after lunch," said Maggie.

The girls packed up all their things and went outside and talked with Doris and Gail. The girls were glad to be going home but sad to leave their new friends.

"I want to give you my address and you give me yours. We can be pen pals," said Molly.

"I've never had a pen pal," said Doris

"We can be pen pals too," Gail said to Maggie.

"Okay and we can always be friends. We visit Grandma all the time. We'll see you guys when we visit on Sundays," said Maggie.

Just then, the doorbell rang. Molly looked out the window and saw a police car. Grandpa opened the door and asked the officer to come in. Molly and Doris stood behind the bedroom door and listened as they talked. Maggie and Gail went out through the kitchen and ran to the front yard and listened through the window.

"Well, Mr. Giba, I did some investigation on your claim that a Mrs. Vedick was harassing your grandchildren. In the records I found complaints about her dating back to the 1920s. She apparently had lived in a cabin on the outskirts of town. The complaints went on for years. In 1933, Mr. Vedick and their son died car accident. That seemed to be the cause of Mrs. Vedick losing her mind, and she was placed in an insane asylum. I called down there and talked to a secretary named Sara. She had to find Mrs. Vedick's records and call me back. Now, Mr. Giba, you and Mrs. Giba will have to sit down for this news. Sara called me back and told me that the mental institution released Mrs. Vedick in 1959. They thought she was getting old and wouldn't be a bother to anyone anymore. She went back to her cabin, and no formal complaints were made, but several people accused her of stealing their cats, but there was no proof. They also accused her of being a witch, but we don't hang witches anymore," the officer said with a chuckle.

"Then last fall, a man and his wife were awakened by some noise on their back porch. They had a brand-new litter of puppies on the porch, so they went to check on them. The man said he turned on the light and saw a black figure putting the puppies in a gunny sack. It took him by such surprise, his wife reports, that he actually screamed. His wife came running, and she screamed. The screams scared the person, but not enough to keep her from gathering up the gunny sack of puppies before she left. The couple called the police, and they found Mrs. Vedick walking home with the gunny sack containing the

Molly O'Neal 89

puppies. The puppies were returned, and the couple pressed charges. Mrs. Vedick was taken to the hospital. She was examined by a psychiatrist and sent back to the asylum. This is the shocking part of the story, Mr. and Mrs. Giba, are you ready?"

"Yes, we're very anxious to end this story," said Grandpa, as Grandma nodded her head in agreement.

"Well," continued the officer. "Sara said, according to the records, Mrs. Vedick died of a heart attack in the asylum last December 14th. I asked her to double-check her records. She checked the records again and assured me Mrs. Vedick had died. Her grave is in the cemetery on the asylum grounds. She had no next of kin in this country. She is going to send me a copy of the death certificate as soon as she can. I will bring it out and show you in a few days."

"I don't know what to say," said Grandpa.

"Vedick is up to her old tricks, even in death," Grandma whispered.

"We'll have to discuss this, Joanna," said Grandpa quietly.

Molly and Doris were still listening behind the bedroom door. They were dumbfounded. They couldn't even speak.

The officer continued. "I went out to the old cabin yesterday, and you could tell it hadn't been lived in for quite a while. It sure is a spooky place. It gave me the creeps. Anyway, I wanted to let you folks know Mrs. Vedick is dead. I don't know what was here last night. Maybe a vulture did attack the girls, but that would be very odd. Something I've never heard of." The officer walked toward the door saying, "If you folks have any more trouble, give me a call."

"Thank you, officer. We appreciate the information," said Grandpa.

As the officer drove off, Grandpa turned to Grandma and said, "She is haunting us. Will it ever be over?"

"We'll take care of this problem," Grandma whispered. "We must go to the cabin and finish this," said Grandpa. Molly and Maggie were to spend the rest of the morning with Mrs. Riker, while Mr. Riker drove Grandma and Grandpa out to the cabin. Mr. Riker walked around the yard, and Grandma and Grandpa went inside the cabin. They noticed all the odd ingredients in the jars in the cupboard. Grandma recognized the ingredients and could read the Slovak labels. She knew that some of those things were used for dark magic. They went in the bedroom and noticed the awful smell and saw the bed in the corner. A rag doll lay on the bed missing an eye and an arm, and next to the rag doll, was a porcelain doll with brown hair and green eyes. The face was cracked and the once fancy clothes were all stained.

Grandma looked at the doll and said, "Stefan, this doll looks like Anna and Molly. She was obsessed with Anna, and now she's obsessed with Molly, even in death."

Mr. Riker yelled from outside, "Stefan, Joanna, come out here! You'll want to see this!"

Mr. Riker was in the little graveyard at the side of the house. He pointed out the two primitive grave stones.

"I'm going in the cabin to look around," said Mr. Riker. He left Grandma and Grandpa in the little graveyard.

"She's probably watching us right now," said Grandma calmly.

Grandpa held Grandma closely and said, "You know what to do. You can take care of the problem once and for all."

Grandma raised her arms up and calmly began to speak to Mrs. Vedick in Slovak, "You can't have her. She's ours. We'll never let you get to her. It is OVER!" She lowered her arms and said, "It is done. No need to be afraid any more.

Molly O'Neal

She knows she has to go. She will pass over now."

Immediately after Grandma said those words, Mr. Riker ran out of the cabin as it burst into flames. With all the tall weeds around the cabin, they were in danger.

"Run for the car!" shouted Mr. Riker. "I didn't do it, I swear!"

"We know you didn't," Grandpa said. They looked back one last time and saw the cabin totally engulfed in flames.

"As soon as we get home, I'll call the fire department in the next town," said Mr. Riker.

Back at the Riker's house, Molly was sitting on the Riker's front porch with Doris. Suddenly, she felt a cold, icy wind, blow right through her and then was gone. She shuddered and looked around and noticed how beautiful the day was.

"Will you ever be around on Sundays when we visit my Grandma?" Molly asked Doris.

"We take turns on Sundays visiting my Mom and Dad's parents, so we'll just have to write letters," answered Doris as she shrugged her shoulders.

"We can even send pictures, okay?" said Molly.

"That's a great idea," Doris said looking rather sad, realizing Molly was leaving soon.

Molly looked down the street and saw her parents' station wagon coming. They parked in the front of the house, and the whole family got out of the car. Molly ran to greet them, and Doris went in her house.

"Were you worried about us, Mom?" asked Molly.

"I knew you two would be fine with Grandma watching over you, but it's time to come home," Mom said as she gave Molly and Maggie hugs.

The family visited for a while, and soon it was time to go home. Dad and Nathan loaded up the station wagon, and everyone went out the front door to the car.

Molly went to give Grandma a goodbye hug. Grandma bent down and looked into Molly's sweet face and said, "Don't worry anymore. It's all over, and you're safe."

"Grandma, you have such pretty eyes."

"They're just like your eyes, and your momma's," Grandma said as she winked and smiled at Molly.

As the station wagon loaded with O'Neals pulled away, Molly waved out of the back window until Grandma and Grandpa were out of sight.

Chapter Ten

Molly and Maggie had been home from Grandma's a couple of days. It was a Tuesday night, just after dark, and Molly and Mary had fallen asleep. Maggie was reading by lamplight, when she heard footsteps on the stairs to the small landing right outside their bedroom. She turned off her lamp and stared at the window in the door.

"Molly, wake up," Maggie whispered.

BANG, BANG, BANG. A man was at the side door.

"O'Neal, I know your home!" BANG, BANG, BANG.

Molly and Mary were awakened by the banging and yelling. All three girls started screaming and running into the living room where Mom and Dad were. Mom went to the bedroom, turned on the light, and told the man to come around to the front door.

"It's the man who used to live here," she said with a worried look on her face. "He came to see your dad. Go back in your room and try to get to sleep."

Molly's dad met the man on the front porch. All Molly could hear were muffled voices, so she couldn't understand what they were talking about.

Adam, Molly's oldest brother, came home as the man was leaving. He and Dad talked on the porch for a few minutes. They came inside, and Mom and Molly's other brother,

Nathan, joined them at the kitchen table to talk about it. Mary fell back to sleep, but Molly and Maggie snuck out of the bedroom and listened by the kitchen door.

"I'm in financial trouble, and the man banging on the door was the landlord. He wanted the back-rent money today, and since I don't have it, he said we have to be out by the end of the month, or he'll have us evicted. Tomorrow I'll find another place for us to live. I have a friend who might know of a place."

Molly and Maggie snuck back to bed and talked for a long time.

"I'm scared. I like it here, and our school is just around the corner," said Molly.

"I'm scared too. The man was yelling, and Mom seems so worried."

"Turn off the lamp and go to sleep. You girls don't need to worry about anything," Mom said as she looked in on the girls.

Everything looked very bleak for the O'Neals, with only two weeks to find another place to live.

❖

ADAM CAME HOME FROM SCHOOL THE NEXT DAY AND talked to Mom. He said, "My friend Sam Campbell told me a farmhouse on County Road, close to where he lives, has been empty since the old farmer died around ten years ago. His son, Mr. Paul Doyle, inherited the farmhouse and land, but he doesn't farm it himself. He leases the land out to the Campbells. Mr. Doyle lives across the road in his own home, so the farmhouse is empty. We can look his number up in the telephone book, and Dad can call him."

Molly O'Neal

"What did he die from?" asked Mom.

"He got caught in a combine."

"Oh," said Mom, looking worried. "Is it a nice place?"

"It's an old farmhouse. I haven't actually seen it."

"We'll tell your dad when he gets home."

When Dad got home, he told Mom he didn't have any luck finding the family a place to live. She told him about the old farmhouse and asked him what he thought.

"Let's call Mr. Doyle, and hopefully, I can go out tomorrow and look at the place," said Dad.

Dad called Mr. Doyle that evening. Mr. Doyle said he would like a family to live in the house and look after the place. He said the land was leased by a neighboring farmer, so the out buildings, land, and field roads would be pretty busy for most of the growing season. He said there will be soy beans in the big shed, and the barn is full of hay, and the family could use the garage and the chicken coop. He told Dad the house had three bedrooms, one bathroom, and a good well.

The house sounded good to Dad, because the rent was only thirty-five dollars a month. He was going to check out the house the next day.

❖

THE NEXT DAY AT BREAKFAST, MOM SAID, "We're probably going to be moving soon, so I want you girls to go to the swim club as much as you can until we leave. We joined the club for the entire summer. If your father likes this house, we're going to move far out in the country, so you won't be able to walk to the store or swim club anymore."

"Okay, Mom," said Molly. "Will I be able to go to the same school?"

"I'm pretty sure you'll be able to. We should know for sure after supper if we're moving out to the country and then we'll find out about school," Mom said in a sad tone.

Mom thought to herself, *Way out on a farm, no grocery store, and I don't drive. We'll be so isolated.*

After lunch, Adam actually offered to take Nathan and the girls to the swim club in his old car. The girls jumped at the chance to get a ride.

"I'm only going to stay until about four o'clock and then I'll find everybody and bring you back home. Get your stuff and let's go," Adam said.

It was such a strange day with Adam being nice to the girls and moving to a new house on their minds.

Adam brought the girls home in time to help with supper. Nathan stayed at the pool with friends and assured Adam he would be home for supper. The house was pretty quiet except for the clanging of pots and pans. Molly and Maggie were helping Mom in the kitchen, and Mary was watching television in the living room.

Dad came home, and he was in a pretty somber mood. They ate supper and while everyone was around the table, Dad said, "Well, I went to see the farmhouse today. It's really far out, and there's no close neighbor. The nearest neighbor is about a half mile away, because the driveway or lane as everyone out there calls it, is a half mile long. Mr. Doyle lives on County Road directly across from our lane. We are going to move in this weekend, and everyone is going to help. I called your Uncle David and Aunt Julie, and they're going to pick up Grandma and Grandpa to help pack and set up everything in the new house. Aunt Veronica and Uncle Tim can't get away from the store at such short notice."

Molly O'Neal   97

"My friends Sam and Chuck can bring their fathers' pickup trucks and help with the heavy lifting," Adam added.

"That's what we need," said Dad.

"Will I get to go to St. Patrick's?" Molly asked.

"Mr. Doyle said the school bus will come by and pick up all the kids at the end of the lane, early every school day and bring them home in the afternoon. I asked him if the public-school bus would take you guys to the Catholic school, and he didn't know, so Mom will call the school office soon and ask about it. Right now, I think we should drive to the back of the grocery store and get as many boxes as we can fit in the station wagon and start packing. Not your tooth brushes, just things you won't need for a couple of days, like books and games, pictures, and winter clothes. Saturday will be the big moving day."

※

Saturday morning came quickly. Sam and Chuck showed up at about six o'clock and began working. Aunt Julie, Uncle David, Cousin Chris, and Grandma and Grandpa showed up about seven o'clock to start working. The whole O'Neal family had finished breakfast and was packing boxes. Molly worked with Grandma bringing her all the quilts and bed linens to pack. Maggie was with Aunt Julie packing everything from the bathrooms and kitchen. Mom was packing up all of the closets in the house and secured all the dressers. She made sure that Molly's white bear and any other stuffed animals were in their own separate box and packed in the station wagon. Soon the two trucks were full, and the station wagon was packed to the brim, so Dad and the men left with the first load.

When Grandpa came back with the others to start loading the trucks again, he asked Anna and Grandma to come in the back room with him, so he could talk to them in private. They went into the back bedroom and closed the door.

"I feel the house has a dark presence or something. Joanna, I think you should go with us on the next load and tell me what you feel, if anything," said Grandpa with a worried expression.

"When Charles called, he told me a little about the house, so I brought some things just in case. I'll go with you on the next trip, and we'll see if I can sense anything." In her native Slovak language, Grandma said, "We'll do a cleansing of the house and a protection blessing."

"Good, you should have access to all the corners and dark places since the house is half empty," said Anna feeling a bit more secure. "We have to let Molly be as carefree as possible. Have you noticed that when she sings, Mary and even Maggie go right to sleep?"

"We've known now for quite some time that Molly inherited special gifts," answered Grandma.

"Mom, will you take Molly and Maggie with you on the second load and stay there and start unpacking the boxes?"

"Sure, I love their company," said Grandma.

The second load was packed and everyone who was going, squeezed into a vehicle and off they went.

Molly was surprised at how far out in the country they were going. The road was hilly and wound around sharp corners. As they were driving down the road, Molly looked to her left, and far back off the road, she saw a fantastic white house with a small room at the very top with lots of windows. She thought the farm and house looked magical, and she wished that was the house they were moving into, but the car drove on.

Finally, they turned into their new lane. Corn was growing on one side of the lane and soybeans on the other. The fields were lush and green. The land was flat at the beginning and dipped down to a very small creek and then up a fairly steep grade to the house. The lane was mostly dirt with big rocks dumped into the creek, so cars could get through it when the water was high. The two trucks rocked back and forth going through all the pot holes and the creek, so it was a pretty rough ride. The lane split off to the left into two field roads with one going along a tree line, and the other road continuing around to the back fields. To the right of the lane was the house, and on the left was a large grain storage shed. Straight ahead were the chicken coop and the garage, and in back of the garage was an outhouse. Next to the garage was another large building that housed farm equipment. Next to that building were two corn cribs. In back of the house to the right was a large red barn. The lane wound around between the back of the house and the outbuildings, and then continued to the back fields. A large pigpen, fenced with barbed wire, was connected to the barn and ran alongside the front yard of the house.

Mr. Doyle had mowed the grass with a tractor, so the house looked a bit neat, but the tractor couldn't get into the tight places between the buildings, and he didn't mow the pigpen, so there were a lot of high weeds.

The two-story house was covered in brown asphalt shingles. The covered front porch had a stone foundation and wooden floor and steps. A sidewalk started at the bottom of the steps and led to a concrete slab that covered a well with a working hand pump. The front door didn't really have a purpose. Everyone entered the house from the back screened in porch. The lane wound around to the back of the house, like it forgot the front door.

"This is going to be so different than living in town," said Molly as they drove up to the house.

"I bet there won't be a bookmobile out here," said Maggie, looking distressed.

They all got out of the car and started unloading the trucks.

The boys and Dad took the kids' beds upstairs. The second floor was really the attic, so it didn't have anything but wallboard between the ceiling and the roof. The walls weren't finished either. The seams of the wallboard showed, and it wasn't even painted. The attic was in the shape of a triangle, so both bedrooms were the same size. The roof was slanted, with the tallest part of the ceiling at the wall between the rooms. Each room had a normal size window on the far wall. Because of the slant of the ceiling, the window was only about four inches above the floor. The boys called for the bedroom on the left and moved their beds in and set them up.

Molly and Mary got the other bedroom. As the boys set up the beds, especially in the girls' room, they kept bumping their heads on the low ceilings. Mary's twin bed was to the right, and Molly's was in the far corner. On the opposite wall, the boys placed the girls' two small dressers. A plasterboard covered chimney was between the dressers. Molly's headboard was only a foot or so from the big window. The only thing separating the foot of Molly's bed and Mary's bed, was a small rectangular window next to the floor. It overlooked the back-porch roof. An electric wire hung from the ceiling with one socket for a lightbulb. A chain hung from the light to turn it off or on. The chain was too high for Mary to reach, so Mom had to eventually tie a ribbon to the end of the chain to lengthen it. A vent was cut in the floor near the window. It was in the ceiling of Mom and Dad's bedroom downstairs, and it was the only way to get heat into the upstairs.

At the top of the stairs was a little nook big enough for one twin bed to tuck under the eave. Maggie called for that area. Another small window was next to her bed. On the opposite wall from Maggie's bed was a very creepy, dark closet. The closet was too low to hang clothes in. The door to the closet was short and wide with metal hinges and latch. There was no light in the closet, so all they could see was some old junk on the floor.

The upstairs was not ideal for the O'Neals: with no real closet, no bathroom, and more importantly, no real heat and absolutely no air conditioning.

When Grandma heard about the house, she went out to her garden and cut lots of different herbs to use to cleanse the house. She also transplanted some herbs into big pots for Molly. Grandma braided some garlic into a wreath and put a bow on it. The wreath of garlic was to hang on the front door.

Grandma and Grandpa Giba still practiced old world ways, and Grandma planned to perform a cleansing of the house to rid it of any evil or bad energy. Molly had never seen this done before, so she was intrigued by it. First, they opened all the windows and doors. Grandma had prepared a tightly bound bundle of sage. She lit the bundle and then blew out the fire and allowed the embers to smoke. She started upstairs in the girls' room. She was speaking in Slovak and waving the bundle so the smoke would drift into all the cracks and crevices of the windows. She waved the bundle, so the smoke drifted to all the roof lines, the floor vent, under all of the girls' beds, and in all the corners of the room. She moved to the boys' room and did the same thing in there. She went to the odd little door of the closet and opened it. She spent extra time with the scary closet making sure the smoke penetrated every inch of it since she really couldn't see in the darkness. Then she went to Maggie's area. She cleansed under the bed, all the corners, the roof line, and the little window. She waved the sage as she went down the stairs and continued to speak in Slovak. She left the sage in a large bowl on the kitchen counter and lit another bundle. She went to Mom and Dad's room and waved the smoke into all the corners, under the bed, and in the closet. She did the same in the living room, bathroom, and kitchen, concentrating on the windows and doors. She ended in the pantry and then out to the back screened in porch. She went back into the kitchen and put the smoking sage in the bowl with the other bundle. She took a bundle of rosemary mixed with several other herbs and burned it in another bowl. She continued to speak almost in a chant and then turned to Molly and said, "Everything's fine now. Let's unpack some boxes."

Molly smiled and said, "Okay."

After a few minutes, Dad said, "This is the last trip back to the old house to get anything that's left and pick up your Mom and Mary. Do you want to come with us for one last look, or stay here with Grandma?"

"I'll stay here," said Molly.

"I'll go with you for one last look," said Maggie.

Molly and Grandma and Grandpa went outside to walk around and check the place out. They looked in the garage and went to the barn. While they walked, Grandma and Grandpa were speaking in Slovak so Molly wouldn't understand them. The barn was full of hay bales stacked from the floor to the ceiling with a few scattered bales on the dirt floor near the door. Two beautiful cats were sitting on the bales. Both cats jumped off the bales and came over to Molly. One cat was light gray with darker gray swirls and beautiful green eyes, and the other cat was coal black with one white foot and big blue eyes.

"These cats are beautiful, Grandma. Can I name them?"

"I'm sure you can. They live here, so now they're your pets. They're both girls, so think of pretty names."

"I'm going to name this one Sock and this one Swirl," Molly said as she was petting the cats.

"Perfect names," said Grandma. "They're working cats, so let's let them get back to work hunting critters."

They walked out of the barn and looked at the house, and Grandpa shook his head. Molly looked at the house and noticed the tall metal rods on the roof and a long wire attached to one that dangled on the side of the house and was buried in the ground. She asked what the pointy things were doing on the roof. Grandpa told her they were lightning rods, and they were supposed to direct the lightning into the ground if the house was hit.

"What about the shadow on the roof?" Molly asked.

"I don't see a shadow on the roof, but the sun is shining through the trees and can cast lots of shadows," Grandma said as she looked at Grandpa and said something in Slovak. "What does the shadow look like, Molly?"

"I really can't tell. It's kind of like someone is dancing around and spinning," Molly said as she stared at the roof.

"Can you sing a song for us, Molly? Your favorite one?" asked Grandma.

Molly began to sing a lovely tune Grandma had never heard. She sang in a language no one could understand. The song seemed to be a lullaby with a very haunting melody.

"Your song is beautiful. Where did you learn it?" asked Grandma.

"I learned it from my dreams: the good dreams, not the bad ones."

"Sing that song any time you get scared, okay, Molly?"

"Okay, Grandma, I love to sing it."

Grandma, Grandpa, and Molly turned around and marveled at the magnificent view from behind the barn of rolling fields and woods. The house and the outbuildings were on the crest of a hill, so the view went on for miles.

"Grandma, I can see so far."

"It's a beautiful view, Molly."

"Grandpa, what are those things over there and that machine?"

"Those are corn cribs, where the farmer will store his corn after he harvests it, and the big old machine is called a combine. No one uses it anymore, so Mr. Doyle parked it there to get it out of the way. Stay away from it, because it's all rusty, and you don't want to get lock jaw," said Grandpa, trying to keep Molly away from the combine.

Grandma and Grandpa started talking in Slovak again. Grandma took Molly's hand, and they all walked over to a large outbuilding full of farm equipment.

"This is another building you children should stay out of. Let's go check out the chicken coop," said Grandpa.

They noticed the old wooden outhouse as they walked past the garage. Grandpa opened the door and noticed it was a two-seater.

"The farmhands must use this outhouse, because there's toilet paper in there."

They walked over to the chicken coop. It was a fenced in area and even had chicken wire across the top of the pen to protect the chickens at night. They opened the gate and went in the pen. They went in the chicken coop, and Molly said, "It stinks in here."

"Your momma can raise good chickens in here, and you'll have eggs for breakfast every morning. Your dad can clean it out and put down fresh straw, and it won't smell bad at all," said Grandpa.

Mom and the girls came with the last load. They walked in the back door, right into the kitchen. Immediately to the right of the back door was the only bathroom. To the left was the kitchen cooking and dining area. Straight ahead, on the right, was the door to Mom and Dad's bedroom, and straight on from there was the living room.

The kitchen was set up quickly with Mom, Aunt Julie, Grandma, and Maggie unpacking all the food, plates, cups, and pots and pans. The cooking area was small with only two cabinets, but the small walk-in pantry under the stairs was a life saver. The table and seven chairs fit just fine in the kitchen. Mom's sewing machine was also set up on a desk in the kitchen. There was still room for people to walk from the back door, to the living room, or upstairs.

"Where's my bed?" said Mary.

"It's upstairs by mine. Let's go up, and I'll show you," said Molly.

"It's dark up here, and it's hot too," said Maggie as she came up the stairs.

Even though all the windows had been opened all day, the house was still hot and stuffy. The place had been closed up for years. The upstairs seemed even hotter.

"There's no light on the stairs or by my bed, so I have this lamp plugged in with an extension cord, because there's no outlet out here," Maggie said as she turned on her lamp. "The cord fits under the door, so there's no problem."

"We have to pull the chain to turn on our bedroom light. Can you reach it, Mary?" said Molly.

"No, not even if I jump."

The one lightbulb was fairly dim and made the room look rather drab. Grandma, Aunt Julie, and Mom came up with the bedding and made up all five beds. Grandma's quilts brightened up the girls' room and Maggie's corner, but the boys' beds were made with dark green blankets, because they thought Grandma's quilts were too girly.

Soon it was time for Uncle David, Aunt Julie, and Chris to take Grandma and Grandpa home. "Call us if you need anything, Anna," said Aunt Julie.

Before Grandma left, she found Molly and said, "Don't forget to sing your song anytime you get scared even if it's in the middle of the night, and if your mom or your sisters get scared, sing to them too. You promise?"

"Yes, I promise. I love you, Grandma," said Molly as she hugged her goodbye and kissed her cheek. "I love you too, Grandpa."

Grandma and Grandpa kissed Anna goodbye and spoke in Slovak for a few seconds. They got in Uncle David's car and left. Molly watched as the car kicked up dust as it drove down the lane, through the shallow creek, onto County Road, and out of sight.

Adam and his friends took off in the trucks, and the rest of the family went inside. Everyone was hungry, so Mom made sandwiches, and the family sat around the kitchen table and talked until bedtime. The girls had to take turns using the bathroom before they went upstairs for bed.

While they were waiting their turn Maggie asked Dad, "When are we going to get a phone?"

"The phone guy should be here on Monday. It's getting late. You kids need to get up to bed."

"We have to wait in line for the bathroom. Mary's in there now," said Molly.

Adam came home and he, Nathan, and Dad went in the living room to see if they could get the television to work.

The girls finally had their turns in the bathroom, so they went up to change into their pajamas. Maggie ran ahead and shut the girls' bedroom door and locked it. Molly and Mary were standing by the door in the dark. Molly could barely find Maggie's lamp to turn it on.

"You should have turned on your lamp, Maggie. We could fall down these stairs in the dark," cried Mary.

"Hurry up, it's spooky out here," said Molly.

It was a very hot July and no air was moving in the bedrooms. Finally, Maggie opened the door, but by then Mom was coming up the stairs, because the girls made such a ruckus.

"Wow! It's too hot up here. We're going to have to get some kind of a fan, so until we do, don't sleep with any covers. Hopefully the night air will cool down the bedrooms," said Mom.

Mom folded the quilts down to the end of the beds and let the girls decide for themselves whether they wanted to use the top sheets or not. She kissed each girl on the forehead and turned off the light.

"I'll leave the light on above the kitchen sink, so if anyone has to go to the bathroom in the middle of the night, the light should glow at the bottom of the stairs. Just be sure to hold on tight to the rope whenever you come downstairs. Mary, you wake up Molly if you have to go to the bathroom, so she can go with you, okay? Good night girls, sweet dreams," Mom said as she started down the stairs.

Maggie was able to read as long as she wanted, and Molly was glad the lamplight was glowing into her room. Adam and Nathan finally came upstairs to go to bed. They shut their door to change, but after they changed, they decided it was too hot to have the door shut, so they told Maggie she had to turn off her lamp, so they could get to sleep.

Chapter Eleven

Molly woke up bright and early with the sun coming through the bedroom window. She woke up Mary, and they went downstairs. Mom was already up fixing breakfast. Someone was already in the bathroom, so the girls had to wait their turn.

"It's cereal for everyone this morning. We have to leave for church in about an hour," Mom said.

"Hurry up in the bathroom. We gotta go." said Mary.

The bathroom door opened and Adam came out. Nathan was next in line, so he went on in. He was in the bathroom for at least fifteen minutes, and he was hurrying. Next turn was Maggie's, and then Mary, and finally Molly had her turn. Molly barely had time to eat a bowl of cereal and get ready for church. Every morning was unorganized until they made a schedule for the bathroom. If one person missed their scheduled time, by sleeping late, they had to go to the end of the line. It was grueling.

Dad drove everyone to church, except Adam. He went with friends, if he went at all. Dad dropped the family off and said he would be back in an hour to pick them up. He was ten minutes late, and almost everyone else who attended the Mass was gone. As the family was getting in the car, Father Roberts was leaving to walk across the parking lot to the rectory.

He stopped at the O'Neal's car and said, "Charles, I miss you at Mass. You have a lovely family who attends church every Sunday, but I haven't seen you for quite a while."

"I know, Father, but at least I drive them." Father Roberts shook his head and walked off.

Molly missed being able to walk to church, like they did at the old house.

❖

WHEN MOLLY AND THE FAMILY GOT HOME FROM CHURCH, Mr. Doyle was waiting for them.

"Hey folks, I'd like to tell you a few things about the place. First off, this is a working farm, so farm machinery is going to be coming and going all the time, especially at planting and harvest time. You're on well water here. This place has two working wells. The one in the front yard has a hand pump, and the one there on the porch is for drinking and washing. The hand pump is so you can fill those two wash tubs and the wringer washer on the porch. Those are for you to use. Back in the day, it was pretty modern to have the well right there on the porch. I realize that using a wringer washer is hard work and impossible in bad weather, so I would recommend the laundromat in town. To get the water into the house, we installed an electric pump in the cellar years ago. It has always worked fine. You'll hear it kick on when you use the water. The old cistern is around the side of the house. It hasn't been used for decades. My father covered it over with concrete the same time he had the well in the front yard covered, so no one will fall in."

They walked around to the cellar and Mr. Doyle said, "Mr. O'Neal, do you want to go down in the cellar, and I can show you some tricks to keep the pump running?"

"Sure, let's go on down," Dad said.

The cellar door was right next to the screened in porch in the back of the house. One thin wooden door, with a metal handle and hinges, covered the stair opening. Mr. Doyle pulled the door up and put it to the side. The rest of the family stayed outside the cellar, but couldn't help but notice the large snake skin hanging at the opening of the cellar door.

"I hate snakes. This is not a good sign. Snakes in the cellar, great," said Maggie. Molly agreed.

Mr. Doyle showed Dad the pump, water heater, and propane furnace. As they came out of the cellar, Mr. Doyle took the snake skin and asked Nathan if he wanted it. Nathan thought it was cool, so he took it. They went in the house so Mr. Doyle could show Dad the fuse box in the pantry under the stairs.

"My grandfather owned all this land and everything on it. My father inherited it, and to make a long story short, he lived here until he died about ten years ago, and I inherited everything."

"Mr. Doyle, does the creek in the lane ever flood?" asked Nathan.

"It's actually a spring, so it's always wet, and it does flood if we have heavy rains."

"Can we have the cats in the barn?" asked Molly.

"Sure, I didn't know there were any cats in the barn. Cats are always welcome on a farm."

Mr. Doyle, Dad, Nathan, and Molly went back outside, and he continued to tell them about the farm.

"We don't get trash pickup out here, so you're welcome to use the burning barrels over behind the shed. Behind the garage and chicken coop is a great place for a garden. I have some pumpkins planted there now. You're welcome to them, but I see the weeds got away from me. I guess that's it for now. If you need any help with anything, you have my number."

"Thanks for coming by," said Dad, as Mr. Doyle got in his truck and started down the lane.

Molly started talking to herself, "One bathroom, steaming hot bedrooms, no friends, no swimming, no stores, and snakes in the cellar. What else could be wrong with this place?"

❖

ON MONDAY THE TELEPHONE MAN SHOWED UP. HE RAN the telephone line to the wall in the kitchen, and he hooked up a black dial phone. He worked on the lines for a few minutes and then told Mom everything was ready to use. He told her they were on a party line with four other families and their ring would be two short ones. Everybody on the party line had a different ring. He wrote the number down for her to give to friends and family and then he left. Mom was anxious to try the phone, so she called her sister Veronica. She lived in town, so the call wasn't long distance. She was excited to hear her sister's voice, and now she didn't feel so isolated.

Molly and her family were trying to get accustomed to the place. There was no plaza nearby to wash clothes or buy groceries. Molly couldn't walk to the swimming pool anymore. There wasn't much to do around the place, and the reception on the television didn't work very well. The only antenna they had was a set of rabbit ears with a bunch of foil wrapped around them.

Molly O'Neal

❖

Molly went out to the barn and was talking to Sock and Swirl when she heard a big motor start up. A famer had driven up and parked his truck near the big equipment building. He had started up a combine and was going to harvest the wheat fields. The machine was big and loud, and it scared Molly. She watched him as he drove by the old abandoned combine and went out to the fields. Mary came in the barn and snuck up behind Molly and touched her shoulder and yelled, "Boo!" Molly screamed and started running out the back of the barn.

Molly realized it was Mary who scared her, and she yelled, "How would you like it if I did that to you?"

"I wouldn't," Mary said as she continued to laugh.

Both girls watched the farmer for most of the day. The wheat field was huge and rolling. Down at one end, Molly could see a patch of trees that bordered the field and part of the roof of a house. She wondered if anyone lived there and if they had any children. The house was awfully far away though. She was watching the wheat flow in the breeze, when she thought she saw a person waving. The person was standing on the side of the field next to the house. Molly waved back, and Mary asked her who she was waving at.

"There's a person way over there by a house."

"I'm too short. I can't see anything," said Mary.

"Let's go in the barn and climb up on some hay so we can see better," said Molly.

The back of the barn had a large section open to the field. The girls climbed up on some bales of hay, and looked over by the house. It looked like a young girl was waving to them.

"After the wheat is gone, we can walk over to her house," said Molly in a hopeful tone.

"I hope she can play with us," said Mary.

Sock and Swirl jumped up and sat by the girls on the hay. The girls looked down at the cats, and when they looked back up, the girl was gone. A big truck roared by and went out to join the combine in the field. They could faintly hear Mom calling them to help with the laundry.

"Coming," yelled Molly as she and Mary jumped down from the hay.

The girls were helping Mom hang clothes on the lines. Mom looked pretty disgusted and said, "Those farmers are kicking up too much dust. All this dust is ruining my wash. You girls keep hanging the clothes. Hopefully, we won't have to rewash them. I'm going in the house to close the windows. This is terrible!"

Mom had stormed off just as Maggie screamed, "Snake!"

Molly stopped hanging clothes and looked over where Maggie had been and saw a huge black snake slithering off toward the pigpen. Mom grabbed a broom from the back porch and came running around the side of the house.

"Where is it?" she shouted.

"It slithered into the pigpen," Molly answered.

Mom grabbed Maggie's basket of clothes and told Molly and the girls to go in the house. As they walked in the house, Mom mumbled to herself.

"I have work to do, and it must be ninety-five degrees outside and one hundred in here." She turned on an oscillating fan Dad had brought home. "Lay the rest of the clothes over the kitchen chairs," Mom said as she tried to calm down.

Dad brought home a huge metal fan to put in the window above the stairs. The fan was heavy, so Adam helped him put it in the window. The fan blades were exposed to the outside. The blades had a grate in front of them, on the inside, to protect peoples' heads as they came up the stairs, but there was nothing to stop the bugs from coming in. Sometimes a big bug would hit the blades and make a ping noise. The fan was supposed to suck the hot air out of the house and pull cool air in through all of the other open windows. It was loud, awkward, and never successful at pulling in a breeze. The bedrooms remained unbearably hot and humid.

That evening at dusk, Molly went upstairs to get her pen pal's address. She got to the top of the stairs, and she noticed the creepy closet door was open. She felt very scared looking into the dark closet. She imagined a monster peeking out of the door. She stood at the top of the stairs for a few seconds and then ran and slammed the door shut. She locked the door by twisting a piece of wood that was nailed near the top of the door. When she slammed the door, she apparently disturbed a couple of wasps, and they started flying around her head. She screamed and ran down the stairs almost falling. She didn't get the address or write to Doris that evening. Later, Mom went upstairs with a broom and killed the wasps.

The ceiling was low where Molly's bed was, and her headboard barely fit in the corner. Later at bedtime, Mom came up to tuck the girls in. Molly started getting in bed and yelled, "Mom, look, daddy-longlegs in the corner by my bed!"

"I have to go down and get my broom," Mom said.

"Just leave it up here, Mom!" cried Molly.

Mom came back up with her broom and killed the daddy-longlegs. "How am I supposed to sleep in here with all these bugs? I'm going to have nightmares," Molly said.

"I killed them all, now hush, you're going to scare your sisters." Mom said as she turned out the light.

"Like we can't hear what's going on. I killed a roach in the kitchen the other day," said Maggie. "And don't think I didn't notice the mouse traps under the sink."

"It was a water bug, and the mouse traps are a precaution. Now go to sleep," Mom said as she walked down the stairs.

Molly and Mary were upset by all the insects and so was Maggie, so Molly decided she was going to sing. Soon all the girls were asleep.

Molly woke up in the middle of the night and felt disoriented. She didn't have a pillow under her head, and she saw the moonlight coming through the window. She soon realized she had been sleeping with her head at the foot of the bed. She quickly moved around, grabbed her bear, and pulled the sheet over her head.

※

IN THREE DAYS, THE FARMERS WERE FINISHED HARVESTing the wheat, and the day after they were finished, it rained. The rain helped to settle the dust, but by then, everything in the house was already coated with dust.

Molly went to the back of the barn and looked across the empty field where she had seen the girl. She walked over by the old combine singing her favorite song. She looked over the field again and saw the girl waving at her. She waved back and started walking across the field toward the girl, and the girl started walking to Molly.

"Molly, where are you going?" called Mary as she ran to catch up to her.

Hearing Mary calling, Molly stopped and turned around to wait for her. When she turned back around, the girl was only a few feet away from her. Molly thought, w*ow, she sure must run fast.*

The little girl looked about Molly's age. She had long blonde hair with waves and curls, and big blue eyes. She had on a light blue dress with yellow flowers. She was very thin and very pale, and she had bare feet.

"I heard you singing," said the little girl. "My name is Lucy. I know who you are. You're Molly."

"How did you know my name?"

"I don't know. I just heard it in the wind I guess," Lucy said.

"This is my little sister, Mary."

"Hi, Mary, do you want to take a walk?"

"Just a little one, because Mom doesn't know we're out here," said Molly.

As the three girls walked along, they got to know each other a little.

"Where do you go to school, Lucy?" asked Molly.

"I go to school down County Road on School House Hill. It's a far walk, but sometimes I get a ride in my father's wagon."

"We have a station wagon too," said Molly.

Lucy giggled and said, "Will you go to school on the hill?"

"No, we go to the Saint Patrick's School in town. I think we'll have to catch a bus. We just moved here, so we aren't sure yet. We walked to school at our old house."

"I'm starting first grade, and my birthday is next week," said Mary proudly.

"That's nice. I'm nine years old," said Lucy.

"I'm nine, and my birthday is in February," said Molly.

"Maybe you can come over to our house sometime."

"I can, but I will have to stay outside though. My mom doesn't let me go in peoples' houses."

"We have two gorgeous cats in our barn, and we can jump rope and play hopscotch," said Molly excitedly. She was happy at the thought of having a friend who didn't live too far away.

They were so far out in the fields that Molly's house and barn looked very small. "We better go back now," said Mary. "Mom is going to worry about us."

"You're right. Let's go back. Do you want to come over tomorrow, Lucy?" asked Molly.

"When you want to play, go out in the field and sing your gorgeous song, and I'll hear it," said Lucy.

"How can you hear my singing so far away?"

"I'll hear it, and I'll be watching for you."

The girls continued to chat as they walked back. About half way between the houses, Lucy turned left to go home, and Molly and Mary veered to the right.

The girls were very happy to tell Mom about the friend they met. Mom asked all about Lucy. Molly told her Lucy went to a school on the big hill down the road. Mary asked if she could go to Lucy's school. Mom told Mary, that even though the school on the hill was close, she still had to go to Saint Patrick's.

※

THAT NIGHT, THE MOON WAS BRIGHT WHEN THE GIRLS went up to bed. The big, loud fan was humming in the window above the stairs. It had been on all day, but it was still very hot upstairs. Maggie wanted to read for a while, so she turned on her lamp. Molly walked in the bedroom and pulled the chain to turn on the light. After Mary got in bed, Molly turned off the light and found her way to bed by the dim light coming in their room from Maggie's lamp. As Molly lay there, trying to go to sleep, she heard some scratching noise on the porch roof next to her bed. She got out of bed and looked out the little window under the eve. It was pretty light out, and the garage light was on, so Molly could tell the window was fogged up. She ran her finger down the window to see if she could make a mark. She tried again, and she realized the fog was on the outside of the window. She went over to the big window to see if it was foggy, but it was clear. She went back to the little window and saw a small yellow circle that looked like it was on fire. At one point it got brighter and then faded away. Molly climbed back into bed thinking it was just a big lightning bug.

⁂

AT BREAKFAST, MARY TOLD EVERYONE ABOUT HER IMAGinary friend who lived in the garage. He was real to her, so everyone humored her. It got a little creepy when she told them he was a big boy, and he was watching them eat breakfast through the window in the back door.
"Why doesn't he come in and say hello?" asked Nathan.
"He told me he can't come in, and he doesn't want to anyway," said Mary defensively.
"Who knows, maybe the weird voodoo that Grandma did before we moved in, helped," said Nathan mockingly.
"I love Grandma. Shut up, Nathan," Molly said.
"Okay, everyone, settle down," Mom said as she turned

to Nathan. "Your grandma knows what she's doing. Be quiet and leave your sisters alone."

"Molly, don't forget to water your plants today. They need a lot of water in this heat."

"Okay, Mom."

Molly went outside and got her watering can, and she used the pump on the back porch to fill it up. Grandma had given her a few herbs in big pots that were too heavy for Molly to move, so her dad placed them right outside the back porch, so they would get plenty of sun. Molly refilled the watering can two more times and gave all the pots a good watering. She went back in and told Mom she was going to see if Lucy was outside. She walked to the crest of the hill behind the barn and looked down by Lucy's house. She couldn't see anyone. She looked back toward her house and saw Mary walking and talking to her imaginary friend. She watched her walk around the outbuilding and corn cribs.

"Where are you going?" Molly yelled.

"To play on the combine with John," Mary yelled back.

"Oh, no you're not. Mom said to stay away from the combine. You and your friend have to stay in the yard," Molly shouted.

"Okay," Mary said as she turned around and walked to the backyard.

Molly was still standing in the field. She looked down toward Lucy's and still no one was there. She remembered that Lucy told her to sing and she would hear her. Molly thought it was odd, but she decided to try. She closed her eyes and began to sing words she didn't even understand, but she loved the melody. She opened her eyes and looked toward Lucy's house and still saw no one.

"Hello!" called Lucy from inside the barn. Lucy waved at Molly as she held Swirl.

Molly waved and ran to the barn. "I see you've met Swirl. She was here with Sock the first day we moved in. Mr. Doyle said we could have them."

"I've known Swirl for a long time. She used to hang around our barn until my brother chased her away. I called her Agatha back then, but I like the name Swirl too. I never saw Sock before. She's beautiful," said Lucy dreamily.

"Do you want to take Swirl home, since she's your cat?" asked Molly.

"Oh no, my brother is still around. I don't know if he would be nice to her, or if he's sorry for what he did," Lucy replied as her eyes welled up with tears. "Let's go for a hike," Lucy said, trying to change the subject. "I know where there's a little waterfall. We might see some fairies there."

"I have to ask my Mom. Do you want to come in with me?"

"No, I can't, so I'll wait out here with Swirl and Sock."

Molly ran inside and asked Mom if she could go on a hike with Lucy. Mom asked Nathan if he wanted to go on a hike with the girls, so they wouldn't get lost. He actually wanted to go. He ran upstairs and got his canteen and filled it with water at the kitchen sink. He grabbed a package of saltines for a snack and said, "Let's go."

Mom told Molly to wear a straw hat and Nathan to wear his baseball cap to protect them from the sun. Molly asked if she could bring Maggie's hat for Lucy, and Mom said she could. Nathan and Molly went out to the barn, and Molly introduced Nathan to Lucy. He noticed she was barefoot and asked her if she wanted to go by her house and get some shoes.

"Heavens no, I never wear shoes in the summer."

"I brought you this hat to wear to protect you from the sun," Molly said as she handed Lucy the straw hat. Lucy put the hat on and twirled around a few times.

They walked along the field road for a long time until it ended at a cornfield. Lucy led them through the cornfield to the edge of the woods. She knew right where the path was that wound through the woods. The woods were very dense and dark. Finally, they came to an opening in the trees and saw the waterfall. The water trickled over it making a soothing sound. The sun shining through the trees and the water glistening on the rocks, made everything look magical.

Lucy began lifting fern leaves and looking around fallen logs. "I'm looking for fairies," Lucy said. "My mom told me there are fairies in these woods, and I could always find fairies around waterfalls."

"She's kind of weird," Nathan whispered to Molly.

Nathan and Molly got a drink from the canteen and then Molly went over by Lucy.

"Lucy, I've dreamed about this place. They weren't good dreams. They were awful. I talked to fairies, and a witch named Sarah showed up. The fairies tried to warn me about her."

"I know of Sarah. I've seen her here. She has no power over me or Agatha," Lucy said looking very confident. "She has moved far away, and I don't think she'll be back for a long time. She lived over there," Lucy said as she pointed east. "She hung around the Campbell graveyard at night many times. I've even heard her running through these woods screaming for no reason. She is evil and trouble."

"In my dreams the fairies ask me to make her go away. I wouldn't know how to do that," Molly said.

"Remember the love you share with your grandmother and your sister Mary. You three are strong. Your grandmother can help you if you need it, but remember Sarah has moved away. I don't know what she would want with the fairies unless she thinks she could control them and use their powers. I don't know what she could be up to. Hopefully, she will never show up here again."

"What are you two talking about over there?" Nathan asked. "Do you want some crackers or a drink?"

"Molly needs some more water. She looks a little pale. I don't need anything," Lucy said as she danced around the creek.

"She's a little freaky, and why aren't those stones hurting her feet?" Nathan whispered to Molly.

"She's just happy," said Molly.

"Look over here in this patch of clover. It's a fairy circle!" Lucy said. "This is where fairies danced and flattened the clover. We can't step in it or mess it up in any way, because that would make the fairies angry."

Molly went over by the circle, and she was careful not to step in it. The whirling clover was sparkling as if it were covered with dew. "It's beautiful," she said.

"My mother gave me this necklace. She said she got it from her mother, and the beryl stone will help me find fairies. It really works. Here, Molly, you should have it."

"Thank you, Lucy, I love it," Molly said as she put the necklace on.

"What next, trolls?" Nathan whispered to Molly, who was ignoring him.

"Do you have any brothers or sisters?" Nathan asked Lucy.

"I have an older brother, and he did a bad thing, so I don't ever talk about him."

"Look, its Agatha. Sorry, I mean Swirl. What are you doing here, naughty kitty?" Lucy asked as she picked up Swirl. "You want Molly to go home now? Okay, let's walk back." Lucy put Swirl down, and Swirl started trotting down the path. She stopped and looked back at them and meowed loudly.

"I guess we better go," said Molly, not thinking that was odd at all.

"Wow, this is weird. Let's go," Nathan said as he shuddered.

Swirl led the group down the path. They went single file, because the path was so narrow. At one point they stopped at a path crossing, and Swirl looked back at Lucy and meowed loudly. "Okay I will," said Lucy. She picked up two sticks and started knocking them together and yelling, "Shoo, get away, shoo!"

"What are you doing, Lucy?" Nathan asked, looking stunned.

"Making sure nothing evil follows us home."

"The only person following you is me," Nathan said.

"I can see you silly, and I know you aren't evil."

"I don't know about that," Molly said.

"Oh brother," Nathan mumbled.

Molly was smiling and having a good time. They finally exited the woods and walked through the cornfield to get to the field road, where it was much easier to walk. They still had a pretty long hike home, and the sun was beating down on them. Molly took another drink of water from the canteen and offered it to Lucy, but she refused again.

"I'm going to cut through the field to get home. Swirl, you go home with Molly," Lucy said as she veered to the left.

"Bye, remember if you want to hike again or play games, just go out by the barn and sing, and I'll hear you."

"Okay, I had fun. Bye, Lucy," said Molly.

"What did she mean for you to sing? Is she crazy? If she lives in the house way over there, how could she hear you sing?" Nathan asked as he rolled his eyes.

"Don't be a party pooper, Nathan. She's really a nice girl," Molly said as she looked up at Nathan.

"Nice and weird, but so are you. I guess you guys are just alike, and don't look at me with your weird yellow eyes. They're freaky too."

"They're only yellow in the sun, and you're the weird one!" shouted Molly.

They didn't say anything else the rest of the way home.

"Mom, I tell you, Lucy is one weird girl," Nathan said as he walked in the kitchen.

"She's not weird, Mom. I like her."

"It would be nice if sometime we could meet her parents," said Mom.

When Mom and Molly were alone, Molly told her about the waterfall in the woods. It was the same place she had dreamed about. Mom told her to never go back to the waterfall.

❖

Later that night, Dad took Mom and the girls into town to get some groceries, because they were going to have a picnic in the backyard on Sunday. It was a house warming party and Mary's birthday party. Mom's two sisters and their families and Grandma and Grandpa were coming. Mom bought extra treats for the whole family to eat after they got home from the store. She bought six packaged chocolate cupcakes and a yellow cupcake for herself.

As they were driving down the long lane home, something black crossed their path. Its eyes glowed in the headlights.

"What is it, Charles?" asked Mom.

"It's probably Sock out hunting," answered Dad.

They pulled around to the back of the house. They left for the store before dark, so no one had turned on any lights. Everything was very dark. The only light was from the car's headlights. Dad turned off the car and the headlights and everyone got out to go into the house. Mom went first to turn on some lights so no one would trip on anything. As Molly was walking into the house, she looked over by the barn and saw a yellow circle. This time the circle was moving from the barn to the outbuildings.

"Look, can you see it?" Molly asked Maggie. "Over there by the barn."

"No, I don't see anything."

"It's gone now. It was a little yellow circle. It looked like it was on fire, and it moved from the barn to that other building," Molly said as she pointed to an outbuilding.

"I'm going in to eat my cupcake," said Maggie.

❧

Mom had made a big bowl of potato salad on Saturday and fried up a few chickens, and made Mary a big chocolate cake, so she would have more time to enjoy the picnic on Sunday. Everyone loved Mom's cold fried chicken and potato salad.

❧

Sunday morning came quickly, and it was time to go to church. Dad dropped the family off and came back about an hour later to pick them up. By the time they got home, Anna's side of the family had arrived. Her sister, Molly's Aunt Veronica, brought Waldorf salad, soda and chips, which were treats the O'Neals rarely had anymore. Aunt Julie brought paper plates and cups, and plastic forks and spoons, baked beans, and Grandma and Grandpa. Grandma brought nut bread and fresh tomatoes, peas, and green beans from her garden. She also brought large cuttings of fresh herbs.

❖

Aunt Julie was Molly's mom's younger sister. She was married to Uncle David. They lived in a big house in Laton. Uncle David had a good job, but he had to travel a lot. Aunt Julie volunteered for charities and was a member of the Ladies Society of Laton. She was very glamourous. She wore beautiful expensive clothes, and jewelry. She had a red Christmas dress with white mink around the neck and sleeves, and of course she had a mink coat or two.

Aunt Julie and Uncle David had one son. His name was Chris, and he was ten years old. He was what Molly's family would call, "spoiled." He had just about every toy ever made. He also flaunted his bag of silver dollars he had collected. He got a lot of them from Mr. Livingood's store, near Grandma's house. Chris and Uncle David would bring a hundred pennies or more to Livingood's to put in the gumball machine. They were determined to get all of the tiger eye gumballs and win all the silver dollars they could. Fortunately for Mr. Livingood, they usually visited Grandma on Sundays and holidays, so most of the time the store was closed.

❖

AUNT VERONICA WAS MOLLY'S MOM'S OLDER SISTER. SHE was born in Czechoslovakia. She married Uncle Tim. He worked at his family-owned hardware store in Laton, and they lived in a house a couple of blocks from the store. Aunt Veronica looked and dressed Bohemian style. She had inherited some of Grandma's *gifts*. She was sensitive to the spirit world as a child, but as she grew older, she denied having the gifts. She always said she wanted to blend in and have a normal life. She claimed to be able to see ghosts on very rare occasions, but she would never talk about it. Aunt Veronica was nice looking and kind, but Uncle Tim was a character and made Molly uncomfortable most of the time. He had a glass eye, and he would take it out and scare the children with it. Mary thought he was really a pirate.

Aunt Veronica and Uncle Tim only had one four-year-old boy named, Jimmy. Cousin Jimmy was mild mannered and sweet. He was a good boy and never caused any trouble.

❖

"MARY, DID YOU INVITE YOUR FRIEND, WHAT'S HIS NAME, to the picnic, and Molly, did you ask weird Lucy to come over?" sneered Nathan.

"Shut up, Nathan, you're stupid," Maggie said disgustedly. She turned to Molly and said, "Next week we can invite

Lucy over to play hopscotch or something in the front yard."

"I hope we can. I'm sure you'll like her, Maggie."

Uncle David opened the trunk of his car and got out a badminton set, two card tables, and six lawn chairs. He handed Chris the badminton set and told him to ask Adam and Nathan to help put it up. Uncle David set up the card tables and the lawn chairs.

The ladies laid out all the food on the kitchen table. Everyone lined up in the kitchen, filled their plates, and went outside to eat. The adults sat at the two card tables, and the children sat on lawn chairs or Grandma's rugs.

After everyone's stomachs were full, Grandma and Mom went in the kitchen to put the leftovers away and talk. Grandma asked how everything was going at their new home, and Mom assured her everything inside the house seemed safe and secure. She told Grandma about Mary's new imaginary friend who seemed a little strange, because he couldn't come inside.

"He only hangs around outside, and she says he watches us through the window in the back door," Mom said.

"I think that's pretty odd. You should keep an eye on Mary," Grandma said.

Mom also told Grandma about Lucy. As the ladies went back outside, Grandma assured Mom she would talk to each of the girls sometime during the day.

"Speaking of Molly, here she is," Grandma said as she walked out the back door and saw Molly standing by her plants. "How are your plants doing, Molly? By the way, I brought a bunch of sage to hang on the window of your back door. I need someone to hammer in a nail above the window, and I'm sure your mother has some pretty yarn or ribbon to make a bow."

After the sage was hung in the window, Grandma asked Molly to show her the cats in the barn. She really wanted to talk to Molly about Lucy and the house.

"Grandma, I'm so glad I have a friend who lives kind of close. She lives in the house over there. We went for a hike, and she showed me and Nathan a waterfall. She's very nice."

"Do you like your house?"

"No, our bedroom is too hot, and the closet upstairs is scary. This house is too far away from my school and stores and my best friend, Paula."

"Have you been getting scared at night?"

"One time we got a little scared because of the wasps and daddy longlegs in our bedroom, but I sang my song, and everything was okay."

"I'm glad you remembered to sing. Whenever you have bad feelings and even when you're happy, sing your lovely song. Promise me you will."

"I will, Grandma. I promise."

"I've got a packet of special salt here. Come with me, and we'll put some on the window sills of your bedroom and on Maggie's window sills. This house is protected with love, but I'm going to add a little more protection. I still haven't figured out if Mary's friend is a good thing or not. Would you and Maggie include her in a lot of your games, so she won't spend so much time imagining? Have her walk with you every day to get the mail, and when Lucy comes over, let Mary play with you sometimes."

"Okay, Grandma."

Molly and Grandma went upstairs and sprinkled a tiny line of salt on each window ledge.

"Why salt, Grandma?"

Molly O'Neal

"It's not only salt. I mixed it with crushed lavender and cloves. It smells good and protects you girls from bad thoughts and nightmares."

Grandma was really protecting the girls from any evil or unwanted spirits who might try to enter the house. She was very leery of the house because of its history.

Back downstairs, Grandma set up a line of string on the back porch, so when Mom cut Molly's herbs, she could hang them on the line.

"Let's cut some of your basil for your mom to use in her cooking. We'll gather it in a bunch, tie it off, and hang it here on the porch. Let's also gather a bunch of the chamomile, so your mom will have plenty for tea."

When Molly was finished helping Grandma, she and Maggie played a game of badminton.

Everyone who didn't live at the farmhouse, except for Grandma and Grandpa, thought it was a fantastic place with the fields, farm equipment, and fresh air.

A little later, Grandma pulled Mary aside and asked her if she could meet her friend. Mary told Grandma her friend said he would wait for her by the corn cribs when she wanted to play.

"What's his name, Mary?"

"His name is John, and he told me that he's fourteen years old. He's kind of old, but he wants to be my friend."

"Let's walk over to the corn cribs, and you can introduce me to him, okay?"

"Okay, Grandma, let's go."

Grandma and Mary walked around behind the outbuilding and over to the corn cribs. Mary looked for John and called his name, but he didn't respond. Grandma called out for John, but still no response.

"Grandma, look Swirl came out to see us," Mary said as she picked the cat up. "Listen to her purr."

"Hello, Swirl. Well, we should go back and join the others. I guess John's not here right now."

Chris, Nathan, Maggie, and Molly were playing badminton. Uncles Tim and David, and Dad and Adam were playing horseshoes at the side of the house. Grandpa was waiting for his turn to play. The men were working up quite a thirst.

"Can I get a drink from this well?" Uncle Tim asked.

"That's what the cup's dangling on the chain for," Dad answered.

Molly heard the conversation and commented to Chris. "I wouldn't drink out of the well. I pumped water out of it the other day, and a frog came out with the first gush from the spout."

"Should we tell them?" Chris asked while he laughed and had no intention of telling them.

"Nah," Molly said, chuckling, as Uncle Tim took a long drink from the well.

The Aunts and Mom were icing the birthday cake and cutting up Grandma's nut bread, and Jimmy was sitting at the kitchen table, when Grandma came in the house to talk with her girls.

"Anna, do you think it would be a good idea if Mary spent a week or so with me or one of your sisters, to give her a break from her imaginary friend? I don't have a good feeling about him," Grandma said.

"You don't think she made him up because of the stress of moving?" asked Anna.

"Mary told me he was fourteen. I don't know why she would come up with that age, and why can't he come in the house to watch television with her or play inside?" Grandma asked sounding very concerned.

"My Christopher always had imaginary friends. One of them was a cowboy. I thought it was because he was an only child," said Julie.

"Anna, she can stay with us and play with Jimmy. He has lots of toys. Let me spoil her for a week or two and then we'll bring her home. By then, she may have forgotten all about her friend," suggested Veronica.

"I guess it'll be all right. I'm sure she'll have a good time. It'll be good for her to get away from her "friend" for a while. Thanks, Veronica."

The ladies brought out the sliced nut bread and the birthday cake. They lit the candles, and Mary blew them out while everyone sang *Happy Birthday*. Mary opened some presents and then everyone went back to playing games. Mom and Aunt Veronica told Mary she was going over to Aunt Veronica's house for a week or two. Mary was happy to go as long as Uncle Tim didn't take his eye out. Aunt Veronica assured her he wouldn't take out his eye, so Mom and Mary went upstairs and packed plenty of clothes in Molly's suitcase. They brought the suitcase down and put it on the back porch.

Mary saw Molly and asked, "Is it okay if I borrowed your suitcase, Molly?"

"I don't mind. I'll miss you while you're gone."

All the games continued until dusk and then everyone started packing up to go home.

"We'll leave the badminton game here since it's all set up," said Uncle David as he loaded his lawn chairs and card tables into the trunk of his car. Aunt Julie, Chris, Grandma, and Grandpa said their goodbyes and hugged everyone.

They got in Uncle David's car and took off down the lane. Uncle Tim put Mary's little suitcase in the trunk. Aunt Veronica got in the front seat, and Jimmy and Mary got in the back seat. Mary brought her pillow with her and her stuffed dog. Mom gave Mary one last hug and kiss. She told Mary to be a good girl and off they went.

Everything seemed so quiet after they all left. The rest of the family finished cleaning up, and Molly sat at the table to write Doris, a letter. Mom was milling around the kitchen making Dad, Adam, and Nathan a snack, and Maggie turned the television on to see if she could get any reception. All in all, it was a great day.

Before the girls went up to bed, Molly pulled Maggie over by the kitchen sink. Dad was watching television and not paying attention to what the girls were doing.

"Before we go up, let's poke holes in Dad's cigarettes with one of Mom's sewing needles," Molly whispered to Maggie. "If he asks us who did it, we'll tell him we think Mary did it. She's gone for a week or two, and he won't remember it by the time she gets back. He smokes too much."

"Okay. I'm tired of him stinking up the house. Look at him in there, puffing away. Hurry before Mom notices what we're doing," Maggie whispered.

The girls poked holes in several cigarettes and neatly placed them back in the pack. They giggled when Mom told them it was time to go to bed.

Mom walked the girls upstairs and asked Maggie if she wanted to sleep in Mary's bed while she was away. Maggie agreed to try it for the night and see if she liked it. She thought she might miss her reading lamp, so she asked Mom if she would pull the nightstand into the bedroom and put it next to Mary's bed. Mom agreed since the lamp was plugged into the girls' room with an extension cord anyway. All was quiet that night. The only sound was the hum of the fan in the window above the stairs.

Chapter Twelve

Bright and early Monday morning, Dad went off to work, and it was wash day for Mom. She had a huge pile of dirty clothes to wash. Adam helped her fill the two rinse water tubs and the wringer washer with water pumped from the well on the porch and then Nathan and Adam took turns pushing the lawn mower around the yard. They had to especially mow in the front yard under the clotheslines to make sure there weren't any snakes in the grass.

Maggie and Molly helped Mom wash the clothes. Washing and hanging the clothes on the clotheslines took most of the morning. Soon it was bologna sandwiches for lunch.

"Do you want to play in the front yard with Lucy, if she can come over?" Molly asked Maggie.

"Sure, and later Nathan can join us for badminton or horseshoes," said Maggie.

Molly finished eating and went outside by the barn. She yelled for Lucy but got no response. She went in the barn and called Swirl and Sock, but she couldn't find them either. She began to sing her favorite song. She walked out of the back of the barn and there was Sock, Swirl, and Lucy peeking around the far side of the barn.

"Hello! Do you want to play with us today?"

"Yes, I would love to play," said Lucy in a melodic voice as she stroked Swirl.

Lucy was wearing a simple pink dress with fancy pearl buttons down the front but still no shoes. They walked to the front of the house where Maggie had already drawn a fresh hopscotch with chalk. Molly introduced Maggie to Lucy, and they each chose from the rocks Maggie had arranged on the porch and began to play hopscotch. It was Lucy's turn when Maggie noticed some black soot on the bottom of Lucy's dress. Lucy tried to dust it off, but it wouldn't budge.

"I must have sat on something," said Lucy as she continued to play.

"Where's, Mary?" Lucy asked.

"She went to stay with my aunt for a week or two," answered Maggie.

"Is it because of her imaginary friend? Do you know what they talk about? Molly, have you seen her friend?"

"No, he's her imaginary friend, so he isn't real like my sweet Chester was."

"Does Mary call him by his name?"

"I don't know. I never asked her. I think she calls him, the boy," answered Molly.

Lucy seemed very happy with Molly's answer. She began twirling around and humming. She stopped suddenly and looked at the house and said in a melodic voice, "You have a spell on your house. It's a good one, not a bad one. I'm glad your house is protected."

"Whoa, that's weird. How would you know about Grandma's voodoo?" said Maggie.

"I can see it. Can't you, Maggie? Can you see it, Molly? It's strong, and it's not voodoo. It's a blessing put on with love. Nothing harmful can enter your house."

Mom was making Maggie's dress for her upcoming birthday. She was sitting by her sewing machine facing the window of the front porch, so she could hear everything the girls were saying and see everything they were doing. Lucy amazed her with her intuition, and she was impressed by Grandma's protective blessing on the house, because Mom didn't seem to have any of the gifts that Grandma possessed.

Mom tapped on the screen and told the girls to check and see if any of the clothes were dry.

Lucy stood by Molly while she checked some of the towels. "I helped my mom hang her clothes on the line," said Lucy.

"Does she go to the laundromat now?" asked Molly.

"What do you mean?" asked Lucy as she began to twirl and hum.

"Oh nothing."

The girls told Mom the clothes were still damp.

Nathan walked around the side of the house and asked the girls if they wanted to play horseshoes, and of course, they did. He gave Molly and Lucy a two-step advantage. Lucy did a little dance before she threw each of the horseshoes.

"This is fun!" she said.

Maggie and Nathan won all the games. Lucy acted like she had never played horseshoes before.

"I should go now," Lucy said. She walked toward the field behind the barn. Molly could hear her tell Swirl, "Stay with Molly and watch."

"Bye, Lucy," Molly and Maggie shouted as they turned to go in the house.

Molly forgot to ask Lucy if she and Maggie could go over to her house the next day. Molly and Maggie ran to

Molly O'Neal 139

the back of the barn, and Lucy was already almost home. Lucy was too far away to hear them.

"Lucy must really be able to run fast and barefoot too," said Maggie.

"She really has pretty dresses, doesn't she?" Molly asked Maggie.

"Yes, she does. I wonder if she'll get in trouble for getting soot on that one."

The girls walked back to the house and went in to get a drink.

"Good news girls, Adam has offered to take you and Nathan to the swim club tomorrow. I told him I'm sure you would love to go."

"I thought we'd never get to go again," said Molly.

"Yippee, and we don't have to take Mary!" cried Maggie. "I can't wait."

Molly and Maggie were excited to get to go swimming. They hoped they would see some friends from school, so they could tell them they moved, but they'll be at school in September.

"I'm glad I didn't catch up with Lucy to make plans for tomorrow. Next time I see her, I'm going to ask her for her phone number. She may even be on our party line," said Molly. "I'm going to walk up and see if we got any mail. Anyone want to go?"

"I will," said Maggie.

"Wear your hats," said Mom.

"I hope I get a letter from Doris. I had to write her last week to make sure she had our new address. I told her to be sure to tell Gail for you," Molly said as they walked down the lane.

Both girls got a letter. They were very excited to hear from Doris and Gail, but neither opened their letter until they got home, so they could savor every word.

Molly wanted to go to bed a little early. She was extra tired from all of the walking she did that day. She went upstairs and turned on Maggie's lamp in the bedroom next to Mary's bed. No one else was upstairs, so she left the light on and went to bed and closed her eyes.

Molly heard someone whisper, "Secrets, bad secrets." She sat up in bed. She was so glad she had left the lamp on. She heard a long creaking sound coming from the hallway by Maggie's bed. She called for Maggie, but she didn't answer. She got out of bed to go downstairs, and when she got to the bedroom door, she looked over at the closet in the hallway, and the door was open. It looked like a black hole. She heard someone whisper, "Secrets and lies." She ran down the stairs and yelled for Mom, but no one was in the kitchen or living room. She ran to the back door and turned on the porch light. Something was drawing her outside. She stepped out of the screen door and looked to her right. All she could see in the porch light and moonlight were rows of fresh graves in the backyard. She ran out and read the tombstones. She read the names: Mom, Dad, Adam, Nathan, Maggie, and Mary. Next to Mary's grave was a deep hole dug waiting for her. Molly screamed and woke up Maggie.

"What's wrong?" cried Maggie. "Please not again. Did you have another one of your dreams? Go back to sleep."

"I have to go to the bathroom, but I'm too afraid to go downstairs by myself," Molly said.

"Okay, I'll go with you," Maggie moaned.

Mom had given Molly and Maggie flashlights to help them get to the bathroom at night. The girls kept them in their beds. The house was dark except for the light above the kitchen sink and the girls' flashlights. Molly and Maggie had to walk past the back door, with the big window, to get to the bathroom. The curtains were open, and Molly swore she saw the small round light again.

"Let's get in there and close the door," Molly said as she shuddered. When they were finished in the bathroom, Molly said, "When I open this door, run for the stairs, okay?"

"This place gives me the creeps," Maggie said.

Molly opened the bathroom door, and both girls were surprised to see that the back door was open all the way. It was blocking their way out of the bathroom. They could hear the wind outside and coyotes howling in the distance.

"Close the back door," Molly whispered.

"How did it get open?" Maggie whispered. "I bet Nathan is playing a joke on us. I bet he's in the pantry watching and laughing to himself."

The girls heard something fall on the porch and then a cat screamed.

The girls screamed, and Mom came out of her bedroom and said, "What's wrong!" She closed the back door and turned on the kitchen light.

Dad was close behind her. The girls hysterically told them what happened. Dad went over to the pantry, but Nathan wasn't there. He took Maggie's flashlight and went out the back door. Mom and the girls stood at the door while he shined the flashlight around the back porch.

"The wind must have blown this washtub off its hook and blew the back door open," Dad said.

"How could the wind blow the washtub off a hook?" Mom asked. "Look over there."

Dad shined his flashlight over by the barn, and they saw Swirl standing in the yard.

"Do you see the little yellow circle over by the garage?" Molly asked.

"I see it," Maggie said.

Dad shined the flashlight by the garage and said, "It must be a lightning bug. Get back in the house and lock the door. If Nathan is out here, he can sleep out here."

"Did someone say my name," Nathan said as he stood in the kitchen.

"What are you doing down here?" Mom asked.

"He was trying to scare us," Maggie said. "He was probably hiding in the living room."

"I was upstairs and heard all the commotion down here. Adam woke up too. He told me to come down here and see what's going on."

"We heard the noise outside and the cat scream. I guess he couldn't have been outside. This door is the only way in here, and we didn't see him come in," Maggie said.

"I'm scared, Mom. If Nathan didn't open the back door, who did?" Molly asked.

"I don't know, Molly. Come on girls. I'll walk you up to bed."

Mom walked the girls back upstairs, and she told them she was going to keep the kitchen light on for the rest of the night. The big loud fan was humming in the window above the stairs. Even though it was hot upstairs, Molly pulled her quilt up over her head, and after a while she fell back to sleep.

❖

LATER THAT NIGHT MOLLY WOKE UP, AND THE BEDROOM light was on. She realized she had kicked her quilt onto the floor. She could tell it was still dark outside, so she got up and put her quilt back on her bed and pulled the chain to turn the light off. She figured Maggie turned the light on, because she was scared. About an hour later she woke up again, and the light was on.

She got up to turn it off, and Maggie woke up and asked, "Why did you turn the light on?"

"I didn't turn it on. I thought you did," Molly said.

"Well, turn it off and try to get some sleep. I hate this place."

Molly pulled the chain and turned the light off again. She had no idea what was going on. She went back to bed and put her pillow over her head determined not to wake up if the light came on again.

※

DURING BREAKFAST, THE FAMILY WAS DISCUSSING WHAT happened that night. Molly added to the suspense by telling them about the light coming on, two times, in the middle of the night.

"OOO, I bet old man Doyle's back!" said Nathan. "Could you also hear the old combine start up?"

"He is not!" Molly cried.

"Be quiet, Nathan," Mom said as she glared at him. "It's probably bad electrical wiring in this old house."

"What about the creaking on the stairs I hear all the time? It sounds like someone is walking up the stairs." said Maggie, obviously upset by it all.

"I don't know what caused the washtub to fall off the hook on the wall. I think we should leave the lights on in the garage for a few days to light up the backyard. As for the light upstairs, it's probably just the house settling at night," said Dad.

"I think a house this old has settled already," Mom said looking worried. "Before you kids go swimming today, I want you to clean your rooms and make your beds."

Molly was pretty tired, but she perked up at the swim club and had a wonderful time. She got to hang around with friends from school and tell them the reason she wasn't able to go swimming anymore.

❖

BY NOW IT WAS MID-AUGUST. MARY WAS BACK FROM Aunt Veronica's house. Maggie turned twelve, and it was time to start preparing to go back to school. Mom had called the school office and found out that the public-school bus came down County Road. The bus driver picked up all grades from first through twelfth. The driver would only take Mary and Molly as far as North Junior High School. Maggie and Nathan would get off there too. Nathan was going in the ninth grade, and Maggie was starting seventh grade at North. Adam would stay on the bus and it would continue on to the high school. Molly and Mary would have to wait in the gymnasium, at North, until the teacher on duty called their bus number. The Catholic school bus would pick them up and take them to St. Patrick's. In the afternoon the process would be reversed.

Since Mary was starting first grade, she needed a new uniform. She would normally have a hand-me-down uniform from Molly, but all of her old uniforms had been hand-me-downs, and they had no life left in them. Adam took Mom and the girls to the store to buy one. After they bought a uniform for Mary and a blouse for Molly, they drove downtown to the fabric store.

The fabric store was Mom's favorite place to go. Two older men ran the shop and waited on customers. Maggie picked out a couple of new patterns and a few yards of material for some new dresses. Maggie didn't have to wear a uniform to school anymore, so she needed some new clothes. Mom was also able to buy some material to make Molly a new dress for church.

Molly had to wear Maggie's hand-me-down uniforms. They were old and ill-fitting, but that's all they could afford.

After they got home Mary wanted to talk to John, her imaginary friend. Mom put up two lawn chairs in the garage so Mary and John had a place to sit.

Molly went in the barn to pet Swirl and Sock. She sat on a bale of hay and began to sing and pet Swirl. Sock ran out of the barn opening, and as soon as she did, Lucy snatched her up and said, "Hello, Sock. Is Molly in the barn?" She came around the corner and said, "I heard you singing. Is everything all right?"

"Yes, I'm happy school is going to start soon, but I miss our old house in town."

"Why don't you go to my school on the hill?" asked Lucy.

"I can't. My mom said I have to go to St. Patrick's."

The girls sat for a while looking out across the fields. "Have you found any old books or newspapers in the house?" Lucy asked.

"No, but I haven't looked for any."

"You would think the old farmer would have left something in the house," Lucy said.

"Well, the upstairs closet has a box tucked way under the eaves, way back in the dark and a bunch of old junk on the floor," Molly said.

"Why don't you pull the box out, and see what's in it?" Lucy asked as she began to dance around.

"Should I ask my father to ask Mr. Doyle if we can look in the box?"

"No, he probably doesn't even know the box is up there," Lucy said as she stopped dancing and began to look worried. "You see my brother did a terrible, horrible thing." Lucy began to cry and said, "I need your help. It's been so long now."

"I'll help you, but what can I do?"

"You can look in the box, and see if he saved anything."

"Will you come with me, Lucy? It's scary in the closet."

"I can't go in your house, remember?"

"I'll try to sneak up there tonight and look in the box," Molly said.

"Maybe I can finally have some peace," Lucy said as she sighed.

Dad drove up and honked his horn. "I gotta go and see what's going on," said Molly. "I won't forget to look. I'll see you tomorrow."

Dad brought home a box of baby chicks. He put them in the chicken coop and set up the feeder and the water, and he hooked up a heat light for the cool night air.

"The chicks are a few weeks old, so all we need is a lamp on at night for a couple of weeks. We'll put straw in the box, and with food and water, they'll be fine. We only have fifteen chicks, so they'll be easy to care for, and Nathan will be in charge of them," Dad said.

"Now let's go in and have supper," Dad said.

Molly didn't remember about the closet until it was time to go to bed. As they all went upstairs, she stopped and stared at the closet. Maggie had moved back into her own bed in the hallway after Mary got home from Aunt Veronica's house. She noticed Molly staring at the closet and thought it was odd.

"Why are you looking at the closet?" Maggie asked.

"Do you know there's a box in there? It's pushed way over to the side, and there's a bunch of old stuff on the floor? I saw some of the junk when Grandma was cleansing the house," Molly said.

"No, I never looked in there."

"Do you want to look in there with me tomorrow, in the daytime?" Molly asked.

"I'm sure the closet is full spiders."

"I might try to look in the box tomorrow morning with my flashlight," said Molly. She went in her bedroom and reached to turn off the light.

As Molly got comfortable in bed, she heard four loud thuds on the little window at the foot of her bed. They sounded like something was trying to get in. Maggie heard it too. Mary didn't wake up.

"What was that?" said Maggie as she came in Molly's room.

"Something banged on this window four times," Molly whispered. The big window fan wasn't on, so every noise could be heard. "Let's look outside and see if we can see anything."

Molly and Maggie walked to the big window and looked out. They were looking down at the side of the house, driveway, and grain storage building. The light was on inside the garage, and the big garage door was always open, so with light coming from the garage and the moonlight, they could see some shadows. Molly saw a yellow circle again. This time it was right outside the big window.

"What is it, a lightning bug?" whispered Maggie.

"I don't know. It's moving down the side of the house."

The girls heard a loud hiss and what sounded like a cat fight. The yellow light went around to the back of the house. The girls moved to the small window and looked out. They could see a large cat sitting under the light of the garage.

"I bet that's Swirl," whispered Molly.

"She scared away whatever it was," whispered Maggie. "Whatever it was is gone. Let's go back to bed."

"You're right. See you in the morning."

※

THE NEXT MORNING DAD LEFT FOR WORK, ADAM LEFT to work on a local farm, and Nathan was tending the chicks. All three girls were sitting at the table having cereal, when Mary said, "Do you hear John calling me? He said I have to get to the garage, now!"

"Finish your cereal and get some shoes on first," Mom said.

Mary finished eating her cereal while she stared at the back door. She finally finished, ran and got her shoes, and trotted out the back door.

Molly looked out the door and said, "Maggie look, Swirl is still by the garage. Finish eating, and let's go outside."

"Yeah, good idea, Molly."

The girls finished eating and went in the garage. Mary walked up to them very quickly with her fists clenched. "You made John mad, Molly!" she shouted.

Molly O'Neal

"What are you talking about?" asked Molly.

"He's mad at you! He said Lucy is awful, and you can't talk to her anymore, and you have to stay out of the closet."

"What? How do you know about the closet?"

"It's not me, Molly. John is mad at you for wanting to look in the box."

"She must have heard us talking about the closet last night, or else how would she know you're planning to look in the box?" asked Maggie. She was worried about how angry Mary was.

Swirl came in the garage and meowed loudly at Mary. She picked up the cat and seemed to calm down.

"Okay bye, John," said Mary. "John said he doesn't want to be around the watcher, so he's going to sit in the old combine."

"Oh, that's weird. What does she mean, *watcher*? Let's get out of here," said Maggie. She headed for the door with the other girls following. Mary put down Swirl and started walking around the outbuilding toward the combine. Swirl meowed loudly at Mary.

"Where do you think you're going, Mary?" asked Maggie.

"I'm going to the old combine to talk to my friend," Mary said defiantly.

"No you're not! I'm telling Mom if you don't get in the house!" shouted Maggie.

"I hate you, and I hate you too, Molly!"

"She's probably just jealous, because Lucy is your friend, and she doesn't have a real friend," Maggie said as they walked inside the house.

Maggie went in the living room and started watching television with Mary, and Molly went upstairs. Molly made her bed and got her flashlight. She was planning to look in the box. She stood in front of the closet door and stared at it for a couple of minutes while she was getting up the courage to unlock the door and look inside. She turned the piece of wood nailed to the door frame to unlock it, and she slowly opened the door. She noticed Mom had put a box of old clothes right inside the door. She pulled Mom's box out and put it to the side, and she ducked into the closet. She shined her flashlight to the right and could see the old box and a bunch of junk scattered on the floor. She had to duck low to try to reach it. The rafters were so low she couldn't see inside the box, so she tried to pull it toward her, dragging it through the junk. She pulled as hard as she could and inched the box out of the corner and into the light of the door. Now she had enough head space to look inside the box. Everything in it was covered with a heavy layer of dust. She could see a large picture frame on top of some clothes. She pulled the box out into the hallway to get a better look at everything. She took the picture out and laid it on the floor. With it gone, she could see a large brown envelope, and under the envelope was a parcel tied with string. She put the envelope next to the picture frame on the floor and pulled out the parcel. It was wrapped in old brown paper. She pulled off the string and brown paper and saw a small stack of newspapers. She looked back in the box and found a journal. The cover of the journal had a handwritten message that read, *Open this book and Die!*

    It was already hot upstairs, so she gathered up the newspapers and went outside and sat on the back-porch step to examine them. The newspaper on the top was from the year 1903. The sun was too bright, so she went around to the front of the house and sat on the shaded front porch stairs and began to read the papers.

The first newspaper had a headline, *Bad Seed Burns Down House and Kills Parents and Self*. Molly looked through the whole paper and couldn't find anything more interesting than the front-page article about a fire, so she began to read it. She read about a fourteen-year-old boy named John Doyle. He was interviewed after he survived a fire in his house. John said his parents were dead and it was entirely Lucy's fault. He said she was always leaving candles lit in her bedroom at night, and she played with matches. He said she always started fires outside in the weeds, and she hated her parents because they were so strict and mean. "My sister was a bad seed from the start."

John told the reporter that the fire started in Lucy's bedroom and spread to his parents' bedroom and then to his room. He said he was awakened choking on smoke and barely got out of the house with his life. He said he tried to save his family, but it was too late. John said, "I knew Lucy would do something horrible someday, but I didn't think she would kill our parents."

During the fire it began to rain, so part of the house wasn't burned completely. Since John was only fourteen, he went up the hill to stay with his uncle. He would inherit all the land, his uncle's house, and his parent's homestead when he turned eighteen. Until then, his uncle was in charge of him and the property.

Molly wondered what her friend Lucy's last name was and if she could be any relation to the John Doyle in the article.

She found an article in the next paper with an ink drawing of two horse-drawn wagons. The first wagon had one coffin on it and the other had two coffins: one adult size and the other child size. The article told about the sad procession to the Campbell Cemetery and how John Doyle, the son of the deceased, was emotionally distraught during the funeral.

The article also said, "Mr. and Mrs. Doyle and daughter Lucy, were laid to rest in the Campbell Cemetery off County Road. Mrs. Doyle's unborn baby was placed in the coffin with her. They leave behind their son John Doyle and Mr. Doyle's brother, Joseph Doyle. Mr. and Mrs. Doyle were members in good standing at the First Baptist Church. Mr. Doyle was born locally, and Mrs. Doyle was an immigrant from Ireland. Her maiden name was Dunagan. They will be sadly missed."

❖

THE NEXT PAPER WAS DATED 1907. THE ARTICLE SAID, "John Doyle turned eighteen and inherited the large farm he and his uncle live on and the old homestead from his deceased parents. He plans to put an orchard down by the old homestead and an asparagus field next to the orchard. He wants to honor his parents by continuing the farming practices of his late father. He is recently engaged and after the marriage, he and his wife will live in the farmhouse that John and his uncle currently occupy. His uncle has built a house in town."

❖

MOLLY WAS STUNNED. SHE SAT IN THE SHADE FOR A LONG time trying to figure things out, and then she gathered up the newspapers and went back inside.

"What do you have there, Molly?" asked Mom.

"Some old newspapers I found upstairs in the closet. You should look at them."

"Okay, put them on a chair. They're too dirty to put on the table," Mom said as she continued to sew.

Molly went upstairs to look at the other things. She got an old shirt out of Mom's box of old clothes and wiped the dirt off the picture she found. It was a studio photograph of a man sitting on a chair with his wife and two children standing next to him. The men wore suits, and the mother and daughter were wearing beautiful long dresses.

The mother was very pretty and the daughter resembled her. The daughter had curly long blonde hair. Her face was bright and happy. The father wasn't smiling, but looked pleasant. The son was frowning and looked very uncomfortable in his suit.

Maggie came upstairs and asked if there was anything good in the box.

"Yes, come see for yourself. I found three old newspapers, and I left them downstairs for Mom to read. Now I'm looking at this big picture in a fancy frame. I also found a big envelope full of pictures."

Maggie picked up the big picture and said, "Wow! There's Lucy or someone who could be her twin. This picture looks too old for this to be your friend. Let's take all these downstairs and spread them out on the table. It's too hot up here," said Maggie.

They left everything else in the box outside the closet door and went downstairs. They spread all the pictures out on the table and studied them. Nathan came in the kitchen and looked at the pictures and asked, "Is this Lucy and her family?"

Mary burst through the back door and shouted, "John is so mad! He told me he hates Molly and wants her to put the box back in the closet!"

"Now settle down, Mary. You're too excited over an imaginary friend," Mom said calmly.

"He isn't imaginary! He's real, and he's my friend, and

Molly is doing things he doesn't want her to do," Mary said as she tried to calm down.

"I'm looking at pictures. What's wrong with that, Mary? Look at the pictures. These are old pictures of a family who might be related to Lucy, because the girl looks just like her," Molly said as she pointed to the picture in the frame.

Mary walked over to the table and began to look at the pictures. "This is John!" she shouted. "This boy is John, my friend!"

"That's impossible, and John isn't real," said Nathan.

Mary started to cry and said, "Mom, he is real. You believe me, don't you?"

"Yes dear, I believe you, but before I can referee, I have to finish this part of Molly's dress and then I can put my sewing away. So, everyone, sit down around the table and calm down."

Molly asked Maggie to read the newspaper articles out loud so everyone could hear, so Maggie began to read about the fire. Mom was so enthralled by what she was hearing; she put her sewing down and turned to listen. After Maggie read all three articles, everyone in the room was very quiet.

"I think we need Grandma to help with this," Nathan said.

"Molly, is there anything else in the box upstairs?" Mom asked.

"Yes, some old clothes and a pair of old shoes and a book that could be a diary or journal."

"Bring down the book, and we'll see if there are any answers in it," ordered Mom.

"No, Mom, John said to leave the box alone!" shouted Mary.

"You calm down. I don't care what John said. I'm going to get to the bottom of this," said Mom trying to stay calm.

Mary ran upstairs and pushed the box back in the closet and closed the door.

Molly O'Neal 155

"Molly, Maggie, you two go upstairs and bring the book down. I don't know why Mary's so upset," Mom said.

While the girls were going upstairs, something started scratching at the back door. Mom and Nathan couldn't see anyone through the window, so Nathan walked over and cracked opened the door to see what it was. Swirl walked in and trotted upstairs as if she knew where she was going, so Mom let her go.

Molly was trying to pull the box out of the closet, when Mary ran at her and pushed her down into the closet and locked her in. Swirl let out a very loud scream, and Mary froze. Maggie opened the door and let Molly out.

"You brat! I bumped my head when you pushed me!" said Molly rubbing the top of her head. "What's wrong with you?"

With all of the noise and yelling, Mom came upstairs.

"Mary, downstairs, sit on the couch and don't get up until I tell you to! Let me look at your head, Molly," Mom said as she shook her head in disgust. "Maggie, get the book, and let's go downstairs."

Mom, Nathan, and Molly sat around the kitchen table, and Maggie picked up the journal and said, "It starts in 1900. I can't read it very well, because the handwriting is so bad, but I'll try. The first page says *Journal of John Doyle*. Maggie began to read the journal.

August 1900

Lucy is six now. I hate her. I'll have to walk to school with her. Ma and Dad love Lucy more than me. I wish I could take her and her stupid cat out in the woods and leave them to die. She named her cat, Agatha.

Pamela Gillette

What a stupid name. I call her Hagatha, because she's a hag and so is Lucy.

We had a picnic at some waterfall in the woods. The food was good, but Lucy kept seeing fairies. What a nut.

January 1901

Dad takes us to school in the wagon and picks us up, so Lucy won't get cold. He doesn't have anything better to do anyway. He picks up any other kids he sees walking. Ain't he just a holy man?

March 1901

I hate school. Lucy is the teacher's pet. I pushed her down at recess, so the teacher beat me with a switch. Some night I might go over to the teacher's house and scare her real good. I might break a window or kill her dog. I hate them all. I shoved Lucy in the mud on the way home, and got her shoes and coat all muddy. It was hilarious. She tried to get up and I shoved her face in the mud. She cried all the way home. Ma beat me with a switch and made me clean her highnesses shoes and do extra chores. Lucy's stupid.

August 1901

Ma and Dad gave Lucy another birthday party. She gets one every year. I wanted to push her face in the candles as she blew them out. She got a doll with a glass face. I bashed it against the wall the next day and broke the face. Lucy cried. I told her if she told Ma, I would kill her. She told Ma that she dropped the doll on the stairs. She's such an idiot.

October 1901

My friend Zach gave me some cigarettes. He stole some moonshine from his pop, and we drank it behind the barn the other night. He kept asking me to go get Lucy. I told him she was a tattle tale.

I had to beat Zach up, because he was going to tell his pop we burned down the old barn in the woods. I told him if he told on me, I would kill him. I told him I would kill him slow, so he would have to suffer for a long time. I'm sure he'll keep his mouth shut. He's a coward.

Dad caught me smoking behind the barn today. He yelled at me and made me do extra chores. I hate him. I'll have to smoke in my room when everyone is asleep.

November 1901

Ma made me talk to the preacher, because she caught me smoking in my room. It's none of her business what I do. The preacher talked and talked, but I didn't listen to a word he said. Ma already told me smoking is a sin.

February 1902

Ma caught me smoking in my bedroom again. Dad beat me with a switch again. Who cares? It don't hurt. I hate him and Ma, and I wish they were all dead. Someday I might get my wish and wake up and they'll all be gone.

I want to go live with Uncle Joe. He wouldn't care if I smoked.

March 1902

They don't make me walk to school with Lucy anymore. She meets up with other kids and walks with them. I wish a pack of wild dogs would come and kill all of them. Zach won't walk with me anymore. I guess he's afraid I might kill him.

August 1902

Little angel Lucy had her eighth birthday. Eight candles sure could have burned up all that stringy blonde hair.

November 1902

I'm quitting school as soon as I can. I don't need all this schooling to farm. I already know how to farm. All the girls in school are ugly and stupid anyway.

December 1902

I don't know how those two little kids fell in the lake. Yes I do. I pushed them idiots. The kid should have given me the marbles when I asked for them. Their parents should have taught them to swim. "Help me! Help me!" Why didn't she yell "Help US?" She pulled her own brother down trying to save herself. I guess the freezing weather didn't help. Oh Well, Ma had warm milk waiting for me when I got home. I wonder when the Charlins are going to miss those two kids.

"Oh my Lord," Mom interrupted. "Are there still any Charlins around here?"

"I don't know," Molly said.

"Well, something may come up about this in the future, but for now we'll concentrate on John Doyle. Maggie, go ahead and continue to read," Mom said.

"Okay, let me find my place here," Maggie said as she looked for the next entry.

February 1903

Well my stupid Ma went and got herself pregnant. She announced it today and was so happy. She'll probably have another kid just like Lucy. Pretty soon she'll be too fat to make me supper. I hate that baby already. I hope it dies. I wish Lucy was dead too.

May 1903

It's horrible living in this house with those holy people. Ma and Dad pray before meals, they pray before bed, and at church. Too much praying is bad, and Lucy is there praying along with them. Oh Lord, please bring the baby to us safe and healthy. How many times do they have to ask God for a healthy baby? I think they're crazy. They keep praying that I would quit smoking and come to the Lord. How dumb can you get?

June 1903

I tell everyone I was adopted. I wasn't of course. I look just like my stupid father. I tell my parents they lied to me, and I was really adopted. They never loved me like they do Lucy. She is such a goody two shoes. Ma makes her fancy clothes. I have to wear overalls all the time, because they work me like a dog. And now with the new baby coming, Ma is making little blankets and socks. It's sickening. Ma always tries to hug me, and her big belly touches me. I could throw up.

August 1903

I knew it. Ma has to rest all the time. Dad said she needs help around the house, and I should help out. I'm going to hang out at Uncle Joe's house more. They won't miss me. I wish I could live with Uncle Joe.

September 1903

Everyone was asleep but me. I decided to have a smoke. I thought it would be fun to burn the fringe off the rag rug in my bedroom and then I got a great idea. If I burned the house down, I could go live with Uncle Joe. I hurried up and pulled on my pants and shoes and started throwing my good stuff out the window. I'm glad I threw this book out the window. It's full of all my memories. I threw out my pillow and blanket just in case Uncle Joe didn't have any extra ones. I snuck downstairs and gathered up all my stuff and put everything in the barn. I heard thunder in the distance, so in case it rained, my stuff wouldn't get wet.

 I went back up to my room and lit a cigarette. Before I blew out the match, I set my mattress and rug on fire. I used the cigarette to set the curtains on fire. I can't believe how fast everything went up in flames. Pretty soon the fire was going up the wall between me and Lucy's room. Smoke was everywhere, and I figured I better get out of there. I left my room and started down the stairs when I saw Lucy open her bedroom door. She was coughing so bad, I knew she was a goner, and she was holding her stupid cat. The hallway was on fire, so I waved to her and ran down the stairs. Every man for himself.

 The fire was really going. I called for Ma and Dad and yelled, Fire! That's a lie, but it sounds good. At least I got out alive. I stood back and watched the fire blazing away. Then it started to pour down rain. It rained so hard it almost put the fire completely out. I was hoping nothing would be left, so I could start fresh. Ma and Dad never came out and Lucy didn't either. I had to think of a good story to blame Lucy for everything, so no one would blame me. I had to look pitiful, so I got all muddy, and I ran up to Uncle Joe's house so I would be out of breath. I left my shoes in the barn and all my other things. I knew I could get them some other day. I banged on Uncle Joe's door and screamed that the house burned down. I even cried. I told him I barely escaped with my life.

 I told everyone a whopper about how Lucy was a "bad seed," and she started the fire on purpose, and when she tried to escape the fire, she must have been overcome with smoke and died. I told them Lucy liked to start fires, and she hated me and Ma and Dad so much, she probably started the fire to kill us. I moved in with my Uncle Joe that night.

 Everyone felt sorry for me. They brought me food and clothes, and some people even gave me money. I put on a good show of fake crying, and all the neighbors *and relatives ate it up. This was one of the best things that ever happened to me. The preacher even said he couldn't believe Lucy would do such a thing, but if she did it on purpose, she would burn again in hell.*

I rode in the wagon with my dad's coffin and faked crying all the way to the cemetery. Now everything is mine. I'm going to burn this book before I die, but for now I'll keep it hidden, so I can read about my memories when I get old.

❖

Maggie finished reading the journal, and everyone around the table was quiet.

Nathan broke the silence, "What do you think it means, Mom? Who do you think this John Doyle is? Do you think he's related to Mr. Doyle, the landlord?"

"Give me the book. I'm going to discuss this with your father when he gets home. Molly, will you ask Lucy to come over? She might know the people in this book."

"Okay, Mom," said Molly as she and Swirl went out the door.

"Wait for me," said Maggie.

"Can I get off the couch now, Mom?" asked Mary.

"Only to go to the bathroom!"

"John Doyle was evil, or maybe he's still alive and might come for his book. He might want to burn this house down to hide the evidence," said Maggie as she and Molly walked out to the barn.

Molly, Maggie, and Swirl stood behind the barn and Molly began to sing. Soon they saw Lucy in the field walking their way. They started to walk to meet Lucy when a

Molly O'Neal

boy showed up behind her. She turned around to face him, and Swirl ran to be by Lucy's side.

"Who's that kid?" said Molly. She was surprised to see a stranger.

"Maybe it's her brother," said Maggie.

Molly and Maggie started walking their way. They couldn't hear what Lucy and the boy were talking about, but they could tell the boy was angry. They got closer to Lucy and Swirl, and the boy turned and ran back to Lucy's house. All three girls walked back to Molly's yard. Molly asked Lucy who the boy was, and she said in a sad voice that the boy was her brother.

"Did you find anything in the box?" asked Lucy.

"Oh yes, I found newspapers. The articles made us think a girl named Lucy was a *bad seed,* and she purposely killed her parents in a fire and accidentally killed herself in the same fire." Lucy began to cry as Molly spoke.

"Nothing else?" asked Lucy sounding defeated.

"Yes, I also found a journal written by a boy named John Doyle."

Lucy perked up and started dancing around. "Did he say he started the fire?" Lucy sang.

"Yes, it does say that," said Maggie.

"Oh, Agatha, we're free!" cried Lucy.

"What do you mean?" asked Molly.

"I am the Lucy you read about, and John is my brother. He was a horrible, mean boy. He knew he wasn't supposed smoke cigarettes. My Mom and Dad forbade it. He was always causing trouble and smoking and sometimes even drinking moonshine with his friends. The night of the fire, he was smoking in his room again and he got the idea that he would be better off without us, so he set his room on fire. His bedroom was next to my bedroom and right above Mom and Dad. Agatha was sleeping with me, as she always did. I woke up coughing. My room was full of smoke, and the wall between the bedrooms was on fire. I picked up Swirl and ran to my bedroom door. The doorknob was really hot, so I grabbed my robe and covered the doorknob so I could twist it. I opened the door, and the hallway was on fire. I saw John running down the stairs. I screamed for him to help me. He stopped, turned and looked at me, and smiled and waved. I started choking and then Agatha and I died. I didn't know what happened to Mom and Dad until I watched the funeral procession and saw the graves."

Maggie's eyes were bugged out. She began to back up and ran to the house.

Lucy continued, "I was so glad when you moved into the house, because I could tell you were sensitive to the spirit world, and I could get you to help me. I knew there was something in the house that would prove I didn't kill my parents. He shamed me and ruined my name. I can't pass over until my name is cleared. You have to tell a newspaper what really happened. Everyone must know John was evil. John's journal is all you need."

"Is John still alive? Will he be coming for the book?" asked Molly.

"John grew up and lived in your house. He got married and his wife supposedly ran off with another man a week after she gave birth to their only son, your landlord, Mr. John Doyle Jr. He hates the name John, so he goes by Paul. My brother, John, was killed by the combine about ten years ago. He was a mean father and cruel to Paul. At least Paul got to inherit all the land."

"I don't know what to say. I should talk to my mom. I wish Grandma was here."

"Her blessing is what protected you and your family from my brother. He could have terrorized your family inside the house. He did a pretty good job from outside the house. He realized your sister Mary was also sensitive to the spirit world, and he knew she was too young to recognize evil. He has been your sister's imaginary friend all this time. He watched you through the back window until your grandmother hung the sage on it. You can see him at night by the cigarette he always has in his mouth. He was the boy in the field who tried to stop me from talking to you. He's very angry now. Your sister must be told to never speak to him again. He is evil. We have to get him to cross over, even though he won't like where he's going."

"How can we get him to cross over?" asked Molly.

"Well, once the true story is out and everyone knows he's the one who killed me and Mom and Dad, he won't have a reason for staying here. He has protected the journal from being read. I've been waiting for someone like you to find the journal and expose him. Your family won't have any peace here until John doesn't have a reason to stay and then Agatha and I can cross over and be in peace. Agatha has been a *watcher*, protecting anyone who John wanted to harm."

"I'm having a hard time thinking my friend is a spirit and my cat is too. Is Sock a spirit?"

"No, Sock isn't a spirit. She's a good cat."

"I'm going in and talk to Mom about this. Will I see you again?"

"I don't think so, but we'll have to see what happens with the story and John. When I leave, you will hear me sing the Irish lullaby. My mother was from Ireland, and she used to sing it to me all the time. When I heard you sing it the first time, I knew you were the person who would find the truth and set us free. I love you, Molly. Listen for me in the wind."

Lucy turned and walked back down the field and disappeared.

Molly went into the house, and she and her mother had a long talk at the kitchen table. "I'm calling the local paper and having a reporter come out and read the journal and tell the story. I won't mention anything about Lucy or John. I'm going to ask your father to pick up Grandma and bring her here to stay with us for a couple of days until this is settled. Sound good?"

"Yes, that's sounds great, Mom."

❖

WHEN DAD CAME HOME, THE WHOLE FAMILY SAT DOWN for supper. After supper they had a long talk. Everyone, even Mary, rallied together, and once they knew the whole story, everything began to fall into place.

The next day Dad picked up Grandma bright and early. Mom called the paper, and they were going to send a reporter out as soon as possible.

Mom called Paul Doyle, and asked him to come over. She wanted to talk to him before the reporter got there. He showed up in about fifteen minutes. He came in the kitchen and couldn't help but look at all the pictures spread out on the table. He picked up one small picture in a cardboard frame and said, "This is my mother's picture. My father said she ran off with another man the week after I was born. He said she hated me, because I cried all the time. She couldn't wait to be free of me. Her mother, Grandma Campbell, raised me. She gave me a picture just like this one. She told me my mother would never have run off like that. These other pictures must be of my grandparents and the bad seed who killed them. I've never seen these before."

"Now, I want you to read these articles and then the journal. Here, have a glass of ice-cold lemonade, and please sit down, Mr. Doyle," said Mom as she pulled out a chair at the table.

Mr. Doyle sat down and read the newspaper articles. From reading the articles, he thought what his father told him about Lucy was true, but then he read the journal and learned the truth.

Mr. Doyle was very upset. He said, "My father always told me his sister was a bad seed, and she killed their parents in a fire, and he barely escaped. He had me so afraid, I never even went to the old house. For all I know, no one has been in there since the fire. Their old lane is only used to get to the fields. The barn fell down years ago, and the house has been overgrown with weeds and vines."

Mr. Doyle sat at the table and shook his head in disgust. He continued, "My father was never a loving dad. I thought it was because my mother ran away. Right after my mom left, my father took me over to my grandma's and left me. Grandma and Grandpa Campbell were the only real parents I ever knew. They tried to adopt me, but my father would never let them. When I was fifteen years old, he took me back to work on the farm. I stayed out of his way, and if he told me to do something, I did it, no questions asked. He would get drunk and rip off his belt and come at me. I slept many nights in the old barn. I had to work in the fields, and I missed a lot of school. He always said school didn't matter when you could be a farmer. That's why I don't farm now. As soon as my father died, I quit farming and leased the land out. I guess I really didn't like my father at all. He was such a liar. I had no idea he was so evil and that he killed his parents and his sister."

The reporter knocked on the screen door of the back porch. Mom answered the door and showed him into the kitchen. The papers, pictures, and the journal were spread out on the kitchen table. Mom introduced herself and Paul Doyle to the reporter. Mr. Doyle stared at the pictures while Mom filled the reporter in on the story. She kept out details about anything supernatural.

The reporters name was Scott Waters, and he was intrigued by the story.

He said, "My father was one of the men who went to the house to find and remove the bodies for burial. Finding the mother was especially devastating for the men, because they could see the fully formed infant still in her belly. It was a sad and gruesome sight. They kept looking and found the little girl who caused it all."

"Sit down Mr. Waters, and read the newspaper articles first, and then read the journal. Mr. Doyle and I will go outside and give you the time you need to go over the material."

Dad drove up with Grandma, and Mom filled them in on what was happening so far. Mr. Doyle and Dad walked over by the chicken coop and talked. Grandma and Mom went to the side of the house so they could talk. A breeze was kicking up, and it looked like a front was coming in. Mr. Waters took a good long time reading and taking notes. After about thirty minutes, he came outside.

"Mrs. O'Neal, Paul, I would like to go over to the house and look around. I have a story here and the name of a sweet little girl to clear. I want to see the place for myself. Let's go before it starts raining."

"I can take you in my truck, Mr. Waters," Paul said.

Dad told the older children to stay home and watch Mary. He drove Mom, Grandma, and Molly over to the burnt house. Doyle's lane, off County Road, had turned into nothing but a field road. The weeds were high, but farm machinery had knocked most of them down. It was nothing the station wagon couldn't plow through. They parked right next to the house, got out, and started looking around.

"Old John Doyle sure let this place go. He was probably racked with guilt," said Mr. Waters shaking his head in disgust.

"I never saw any sadness or heard anything loving about his parents or sister, or me, for that matter. I don't think he felt any guilt at all," Paul said sadly.

"I thought Lucy lived here," said Molly. "No one could live here."

"This was a very nice place in 1903 before John Doyle burned it down," Mr. Waters told Molly.

Dad and Paul were walking around the property. Mr. Waters, Grandma, Molly, and Mom trudged through the weeds and walked onto the porch. Only half of the house was standing, and it was charred and open to the elements. It had been fifty-eight years since the fire.

"This is where the kitchen was. This must have been the parents' room. Only one wall still stands. The bedroom above the parents' room was John's, and it's almost completely gone. All that's left is a partial wall," Mr. Waters said as he examined the house. "You can tell this is where the parents' bed must have been, so this is where they found their bodies."

"Look over here!" said Molly. "The outside wall is gone, but I can see into the room upstairs. I see what could have been a closet. It looks all black, but there are some bright colored clothes hanging in it."

"I'm going home to get a ladder. I want a better look at the closet," said Mr. Doyle as he jumped in his truck and left.

Mr. Doyle was only gone for about five minutes. He got the ladder out of the truck and set it up on the ground and leaned the ladder on what was left of the second floor.

"Be careful," said Mom.

"I'll hold the ladder for you, Paul," said Dad.

He climbed up the ladder and was astonished by what he saw. "This is impossible! I see little dresses in the closet. They look brand new. On the floor of the closet, I see some little charred shoes. This has to be Lucy's room, but how could the dresses be so clean and neat?"

Mom and Grandma looked at each other and spoke in Slovak. They turned to Molly and asked her to climb the ladder to see if she recognized any of the dresses in the closet. Mr. Doyle came down the ladder looking very confused. Dad held the ladder for Molly, and she climbed up far enough to get a better look at the closet.

"There's Lucy's pretty pink dress with the pearl buttons and the blue one with the yellow flowers, and her shoes are all burned. That's why she never wore shoes, Mom!"

"My father told me they found Lucy lying by her bedroom door holding a cat," said Mr. Waters. "He said they could tell it was her, because she was so small. I guess no one ever investigated the fire. Looking at this house, I believe the fire started in the boy's bedroom. I'm going to write a doozie of an article and exonerate Lucy. John Doyle was the bad seed."

Molly climbed down the ladder and was overcome with emotion. She ran into Mom's arms. "Those were the dresses she wore," Molly whispered.

Molly O'Neal 171

"I think she's watching us, and she treasures your friendship, Molly," whispered Grandma.

"Swirl was her cat. She had named her Agatha. She's with Lucy now, and I won't see them ever again," whispered Molly as she sobbed.

"I think I'm going to have this place bulldozed down," said Mr. Doyle.

"We have to get Lucy's dresses first," cried Molly.

"I can't believe my eyes. The dresses are gone! I must be seeing things," said Mr. Doyle.

"I saw the dresses in the closet," said Molly.

They all looked up at the closet, and all they could see was a couple of burned pieces of cloth hanging from hooks on the closet wall.

"Do you hear that, Mom? Do you, Grandma? It's beautiful. I hear Lucy humming. It's drifting in the breeze and getting louder."

"It's your song, Molly," said Grandma.

"I hear it," said Mom.

"Lucy said it's an Irish lullaby her mom sang to her all the time. She said I would hear her sing it when it was time for her and Agatha to cross over," Molly said.

"Her humming is beautiful, but she'll wait to sing the words when we need her for the last time," Grandma assured Molly.

"Lucy sounds so happy, Mom."

"She finally is," Mom said with a tear in her eye.

"Well, I have a story to write. It should be in the newspaper tomorrow," said Mr. Waters.

Mr. Doyle drove Mr. Waters back to the O'Neal's house to get his car, and Dad drove Mom, Grandma, and Molly home.

Mr. Doyle walked over to Mom and Grandma and said, "My father never even bought a suitable grave stone for his parents, and Lucy's grave is unmarked. I'm going to buy a nice big stone for my grandparents and a statue of an angel to place on Lucy's grave. I'm also going to get some men I know to get rid of the awful combine in back of the shed. We need to get rid of all traces of my evil father. I'm so grateful to Molly for finding the journal. You've been so good to me that I've decided to let your family live in this farmhouse rent free for as long as you like. I have a lot to think about. I would like to take the box of my father's things home. I'll go through everything and store it away in my attic. You never know when we may need to bring the awful journal back out."

Mom put all the pictures, newspapers, and the journal in the box, except for one picture. She asked Mr. Doyle if Molly could have the picture of Lucy sitting in a fancy, wicker chair holding Swirl. He told Molly she could have any of the pictures she wanted, but she only took the one. Before Mr. Doyle left, Molly asked him if there was a school on the big hill down the road. He told her there was a one room country school that closed around 1946, and only the stone chimney and some foundation stones remain. Mr. Doyle loaded the box in the front seat of his truck and thanked everyone again and drove home.

"Mom, so what do we do about Lucy's brother, John?" Anna asked.

"It's funny he stayed here as a child of fourteen instead of the man he grew up to be. I guess his life stopped being meaningful after he killed Lucy and his parents in the fire," Grandma said.

Mary ran out of the garage screaming, "He's going to burn our house down! Help me, Mom!"

"What were you doing in there? Nathan, Maggie, get out here!" shouted Mom. "You were supposed to watch Mary."

Molly O'Neal

"We were watching television," said Nathan as he and Maggie walked out the screen door. "I guess she snuck out."

"You two go back inside and don't come outside until I tell you to," Mom said sternly as she motioned them inside. "Mary, you stay with me. Give me your hand."

"Mom, I hope some of your gifts rubbed off on me. We have to face John Doyle," Anna said to Grandma.

"He's going to kill us, Mom! He's mad! He doesn't look like my friend anymore! He looks like a big black shadow!" cried Mary.

"I'm scared!" cried Molly.

"Charles, go in the house, and make sure the children don't come outside," said Grandma.

"Are you sure you don't need me?" he asked.

"The four of us can take care of this, Charles," Grandma assured him.

The wind was pretty strong, and dust was swirling around.

"There he is, Grandma!" screamed Molly.

A black shadow of what looked like a full-grown man, not a boy of fourteen, walked out of the garage toward Molly and her family.

"Everyone, hold hands," said Grandma in a calm voice. "Mary, you and Molly get between Anna and me." Grandma began to speak to the shadow in a calm but stern voice saying, "You have been found out. We know you killed your parents and Lucy in the fire. You blamed Lucy. She is free now. We know she is innocent and everyone will hear that you started the fire and saved your possessions and not your family. We saw your journal. Sing, Molly."

He was so close, they could hear him breathe, but as Molly sang, the shadow turned away from them and walked around the outbuilding and past the corn cribs. It stopped in front of the old combine. Molly, Mom, Mary, and Grandma followed the shadow continuing to hold hands and bracing against the wind.

"Lucy started the fire! She killed our parents and tried to kill me!" the shadow screamed.

"We know you started the fire. You're a liar. You must leave this place forever. You must go to your punishment," Grandma said calmly.

"Lucy pushed me into the combine! She killed me!" the shadow screeched as it began to change shape.

"You must leave. You have no reason to stay."

Molly continued to sing. Another sweet voice began to sing with her. It was Lucy coming to help.

The shadow became distorted and began to heave: first into a huge, round form and then pinched and twisted in the middle. It grew huge and round again and then pinched together like it was turning inside out. It got caught up in the wind, and it began to spiral and scream. It spun and contorted as though the evil inside was trying to escape. Mary tried to run, but Molly and Mom held on tight to her hands. Molly continued to sing.

"Tell him to go, Mary!" shouted Grandma over all the whirling wind.

"Go, John! You're horrible! You killed your Mom and Dad and Lucy! Go Away!" Mary shouted.

Another beautiful voice began to sing the same lullaby but in English. The shadow seemed to react to it and let out a deafening scream. And with that, the wind whipped the shadow into a tornado, spinning faster and faster, until suddenly, it was sucked into the ground.

"Continue to hold hands for a little while and be thankful that it's over!" said Grandma, looking very tired.

The wind died down. Molly finished her song, and Lucy's voice trailed off into the air. The third voice echoed on the last words "safe from all harm." The sun started peeking through openings in the clouds, and a cleansing shower began to fall.

"Run to the barn!" shouted Mom as everyone let go of each other's hands and ran for cover. Grandma sat down on a bale of hay and everyone was happy and laughing and talking. A great weight of despair was lifted off of the farm and the O'Neals. The rain stopped after a few minutes. The group looked out at the beautiful view of the rolling fields and the sun peeking through scattered clouds. It was a beautiful sight after what they had been through.

"Look, Mom, two rainbows," said Molly with a big smile.

Chapter Thirteen

The newspaper article came out, and Mr. Waters credited Molly for finding the journal, so she was kind of famous. He wrote how Lucy was the same age as Molly when she was killed and falsely accused of murder. It was such a great story, some big city papers picked it up. Mr. Waters got a lot of recognition for the story. Dad didn't like all of the attention put on the old farmhouse, because it was now known as the *haunted farmhouse*.

❖

Four children showed up at the O'Neal's back door. Mom answered the door and the oldest boy said, "Hi, we're the Campbells. Our father and Grandpa farm this land for our cousin Paul Doyle. We have the big farm over there," he said as he pointed east. "My name is Jake and I'm fourteen. This is, Jesse, and he's six. These are my sisters, Christy and Becky. Paul Doyle's mother was my Great Aunt Angela. He came over last night and told us some kids around our ages moved in the old farmhouse and we should come by and say hello."

"Let me get the kids." Mom went back to the kitchen and called, "Nathan, Maggie, Molly, and Mary, there are some neighbor kids out here to see you."

As soon as Nathan came out, Jake asked him if he wanted to move some hay with him and his dad. Nathan was happy to help. "Go back in and put on a long-sleeved shirt. I have an extra pair of gloves you can borrow," Jake said.

Mary walked up to Jesse and said hi and asked him if he wanted to go out to the barn and watch them load the hay. Christy and Maggie went out front to play jump rope. Molly and Becky took a walk and talked. Molly asked Becky if she rode the school bus. Becky told her she had always ridden the bus.

"I'm going into fourth grade. What grade are you going in?" Molly asked Becky.

"I'm going into fifth grade. I turned ten last week."

"I'll be ten in February, so we're not too far apart in age. Do you live in the big white house with the room on the roof?" asked Molly.

"Yes, the room is called a widow's walk. You should come over, and I'll show it to you," Becky said. "Christy, I'm taking Molly over to our house. I'll be back later and get Jesse."

The girls went inside so Molly could ask Mom if she could go over to the Campbell's. Mom thought their house was too far away.

"It's not too far, because we take the field road straight across. The field road at the end of your yard leads straight to our farm. It's only about a half a mile," said Becky. "We rode over in my dad's truck, but it will be full of hay now. We can walk over, and I'll bring Molly back later. When I come back, I'll pick up Jesse and take him home."

"Okay, Molly, you be careful. What's your phone number in case I need to call?" Mom wrote the number down and asked Molly to repeat her home number to make sure she knew it and off they went.

The walk was nice on the field road, because the road ran along a line of trees and was shaded. They walked onto Becky's property from the side. Molly was so surprised at how big everything looked. The huge barn was white and all the outbuildings were clean and white. The house was a mansion in Molly's eyes.

"We have lots of cows in the back pasture. My dad has two hunting dogs. We have two work horses that we can ride sometime and of course chickens, sheep, a few turkeys, some geese, and some goats. It keeps us busy. Come on in," Becky said.

They walked up the back-porch stairs into the mudroom and then the kitchen.

"Mom, this is Molly O'Neal, Adam's sister. We already know your brother. He works here and at my uncles' farms across the road."

"It's nice to meet you, Molly. Paul told us all about you and your family. This is my mother-in-law, Mrs. Campbell, and this little one is, Scotty, the baby of the family."

"Hello, nice to meet you all," said Molly shyly.

"I'm going to show Molly around, starting with my room and the widow's walk."

As they walked up the stairs, Becky said, "Grandma and Grandpa live with us, or maybe I should say we live with them. They have always lived here and had their children here. My great grandfather built the place a long time ago. The farm is too big for one man, so the whole family pitches in, but my father is going to inherit most of it. His brothers have the two farms across the road. Grandpa gave them their land a long time ago."

Becky showed Molly the big beautiful room she shared with Christy. The girls had canopy beds and old fancy

Molly O'Neal

dressers and night stands. The room had high ceilings and a glass chandelier.

"We have to go through Mom and Pop's room to get to the widow's walk."

Becky's parents' room was another gorgeous room. The door to the widow's walk was open. The girls went up the stairs into a room surrounded with windows and measured about ten by ten.

"Wow! This is great. I can see all the way around for miles!"

"We can see your house in the winter when the leaves are off the trees," said Becky. "It's really fun to come up here during a rain or snow storm. We put a small Christmas tree up here in December. I love this room." The girls went downstairs to the second floor.

"Do you have a bathroom up here?" Molly asked.

"We have two bathrooms up here. There's one in my parents' bedroom and one in the hallway for everyone else. This is my parents' bathroom," Becky said as she pointed to the bathroom door.

Molly looked in and couldn't believe her eyes. The bathroom was almost as big as Molly's bedroom. It had fancy wallpaper, beautiful tile floors with fuzzy rugs, and matching towels. Molly had never seen such a beautiful bathroom.

Becky showed Molly the bathroom in the hallway. It was smaller than her parents' bathroom, but still very nice.

"We have what my Mom calls a *powder room* down stairs. It just has a toilet and a sink. It's for guests, but we use it all the time. The bathrooms upstairs are too far away if you're in the kitchen or watching television," Becky said. Molly was in awe of Becky's house.

As Molly and Becky were leaving, Grandpa Campbell stopped them. "I heard you found that devil's journal. I want to thank you for clearing Lucy's name, and for exposing John Doyle for the S.O.B. he was. He always said my sister, ran off with another man. Angela wouldn't have left her baby. I don't know why my sister married that devil John Doyle. I don't know what happened to her. She was my older sister and my parents' pride and joy. It about killed my mom when John said that Angela had run off and left him and the baby. I wish there was something in the journal about Angela."

"I'm sorry, Mr. Campbell," said Molly.

"That's all right, Molly. I keep praying that someone will hear something about Angela."

"I'll pray too, and Mom wants Mr. Doyle to go through everything in the box. I only looked at a few things on top of the clothes. There might be something else mixed in with the clothes," said Molly.

"I'll call him right now and ask him to look. Bye, girls," said Grandpa Campbell.

Becky pushed her bike while the girls walked back to Molly's house. They talked all the way. Even though the girls had just met, they felt like they had known each other for a long time. Becky wanted to make sure Molly would save her a seat on the bus, so she gave her advice on how to catch the bus.

"The bus comes by at seven-fifteen, so be sure you're all up at the end of your lane a few minutes early, or you'll miss the bus," Becky said. "We're off tomorrow. I might be able to come over in the morning and play for a while, but in case I can't, I'll see you on Thursday. Save me a seat, okay?"

"That sounds great. If I don't see you tomorrow, I'll see you on the bus," said Molly. She was happy to have a new friend.

"I'm going to find my brother and take him home," said Becky as she began to walk to the barn.

Molly O'Neal 181

Molly went inside the house and saw Jesse, so she yelled out the back door to Becky, "He's in here watching television. I'll send him out."

After Becky left, Molly couldn't get Angela off her mind. She walked around outside trying to imagine Angela sneaking off and leaving her baby, and she couldn't imagine it.

Molly decided to talk to her mother about Angela. Mom was interested in the story, and she loved a good mystery.

"We should have gone through the box more thoroughly. There might have been more clues in it. I don't believe any woman would up and leave her family and baby," said Mom.

Maggie was listening to the conversation and said, "What if he killed her and buried her in the basement?"

"He was so evil, I wouldn't put it past him," Mom replied.

"Mom, do you remember the third voice we heard singing the Irish lullaby in English?" asked Molly.

"Yes, I do. That beautiful voice helped us banish John. I wonder if it could have been Angela. I didn't want to say anything, but before your grandmother left to go back home, she told me she felt a sweet but sad spirit outside. She doesn't think this is over yet, but she said we have nothing to fear from this one."

"I think we should ask Mary if she has seen any more of her *imaginary friends*," said Molly.

"Good idea," said Mom. She called Mary into the kitchen and asked her if she had seen anyone else outside besides John.

"No, not now, but when we first moved here and I saw John, a pretty lady came from the side of the house and told me to stay away from John. She told me he was mean and then John came running out of the garage with a frying pan in his hand. He ran after her, and she ran away. I never saw

Pamela Gillette

her again. When I get scared at night, I can barely hear a lady singing. I like the song. It sounds like Molly's song, but sometimes I can understand the words."

"Why didn't you tell us about the lady or that you heard someone singing?" asked Molly.

"I don't know," Mary answered.

"This lady must be the spirit Grandma sensed. We heard her the other day singing with Molly and Lucy," Mom said.

Molly's mom and Maggie loved to read murder mystery novels, so the O'Neal ladies decided to try to find out what really happened to Angela. Mom got out a tablet and pencil and began to write down a list of clues.

Clues

1. John killed his mom, dad, and sister – no remorse

2. Lady singing lullaby with Lucy and Molly, but in English

3. John – not imaginary friend – chased the lady away

4. Mary hears singing at night

5. John died before he could burn evidence in the box

6. Grandma senses another spirit

List of Strategy

1. Talk to anyone that knew Angela

2. Ask about lullaby

3. Have Paul go through the box with a fine-tooth comb or let us go through it

4. Get all the flashlights in the house and totally clean out the upstairs closet, on both sides

5. Check for loose floorboards upstairs and check pantry under the stairs for any hiding places

6. Treat like a murder

"That should keep us busy for a few days."

"Mom, I've heard the singing at night, but I thought it was the humming of the big fan," Maggie confessed.

"Tell me when anything out of the ordinary happens," Mom told the girls.

"Becky said she might be able to come over tomorrow," said Molly.

"Let's ask her grandfather to come with her. He was Angela's brother. We can ask him what he thinks happened to her. I'll call him right now and then I have to start supper," said Mom.

Mom called Mr. Campbell, and he was very anxious to come over. She asked him to bring Mr. Doyle and the box with him, and they could all go through it together.

❖

AFTER SUPPER MOM COLLECTED FOUR FLASHLIGHTS AND told Molly, Maggie, and Nathan to come up to the closet. "I realize this will be a dark and dirty job, so I want everyone to tie a handkerchief around your nose and mouth, so you won't breathe up dust. First, we'll take a good look to the left."

About five feet of closet space was over the stairs. The ceiling of the closet was only about four feet high, and then it slanted with the roof line. Mom shined her flashlight to the left. Nathan and Maggie ducked in and shined their flashlights into the space.

"Look! There's another box and some kind of blanket and some clothes," Nathan said.

"I think that's an old suitcase and some old purses. Nathan, crawl back there and pull some things out," said Maggie.

"First, let's move my box out of the way, and put it in the boys' room. That will give us more space, and we can start pulling things out," said Mom.

Nathan crawled into the closet and dragged a blanket out. He went back in and pulled out the clothes and handed them back to Maggie, and she handed them to Molly and Mom, who laid them out on the floor. When Nathan was finished with the left side, Mom said, "Take two flashlights back in and check the floor for anything small or shiny. Push on the boards to see if any are loose."

The big hall fan was on all the time to help pull out the dust and heat, but it was still stifling, hot upstairs.

"We'll take all this downstairs and out to the porch. We can put the clothes in this quilt and try not to raise too much dust," said Mom. She hollered down for Dad to come up and carry the heavy things.

Everyone cooled off outside and got a cold drink of water and then they went back upstairs to check the other side of the closet.

"Shine the flashlights, and let me see how far back this side goes," said Mom. "It looks like it goes all the way to the other side of the house. It lines the whole wall of the boys'

Molly O'Neal   185

room, but look, after about five feet it gets really small. I don't think we have to worry about the small area, but we'll look in there just in case."

Nathan crawled in and the others shined the flashlights for him.

"Here's an old Raggedy Ann doll," Nathan said as he tossed it backwards. "This looks like a jewelry box. It's open and a bunch of junk fell out. I'll put the stuff on one of these small blankets and you pull it out."

Maggie pulled the small blanket out and handed it to Molly, who handed it to Mom. She started spreading the items out on the floor so they could get a better look at them.

"Molly, go downstairs and get the clothes baskets out of the bathroom. Dump the dirty clothes on the floor. We'll use them to bring this stuff downstairs. Maggie, dig through these things and put the jewelry in the jewelry box," Mom said.

Mom seemed to be intrigued by all the personal articles they were finding. The last haul was a photo album and another small suitcase.

"Hey, shine the lights in here."

Some pieces of painted wood were crammed in where the ceiling height changed from about four feet to two feet. Nathan pulled the pieces out and tossed them back to Maggie. When he had gotten all the pieces out, he crawled out of the closet and cooled off a bit. After a couple of minutes, he took two flashlights back in and told the others to shine their two in also.

"I'm going to look in the small area for a dead body or something. I'll check the floorboards and then I'm done." Nathan was practically lying down on the floor to get a good look into the smallest part of the closet. "A skeleton!" he screamed as he tossed back what could have been a bone.

Maggie screamed, and Mom and Molly screamed, and Nathan started laughing.

Maggie looked down and saw what he tossed to her. It was another piece of the painted wood.

Nathan kept laughing while he checked the floorboards. He was very proud of himself.

"I hate you!" Maggie yelled as she threw the piece of wood at him.

"Stop clowning around," Mom said very sternly. "Check all the corners and look closely for more jewelry."

Mom told Maggie and Nathan to lock the closet door when they were finished and bring the pieces of wood downstairs. She told them to bring down whatever she and Molly couldn't carry. "Once we get everything laid out on the porch, we can put things in order."

Molly found all of the jewelry she could and put it in the jewelry box.

"Look, Mom, these old purses are empty, but this one has a pair of gloves, a compact, lipstick, and even a coin purse," Maggie said. She opened the coin purse to see if there was any money in it, but it was empty.

"It's getting late and everyone needs a bath. Nathan, you go in first, and clean the tub out when you're done," said Mom as she sorted through some of the things.

Dad came out and tried to hold the pieces of wood together. He thought it looked like parts of a cradle. He also said someone had smashed it apart with a hammer.

Maggie had her turn in the tub and Molly was next. Mom swept up the dust upstairs and ran a mop over the floor. When she was finished, Molly and the girls came up to go to bed.

"We'll go through everything tomorrow. We have lots of new clues. You girls need to get some sleep now," Mom said

Molly O'Neal

as she kissed each girl on the cheek. "Good night."

Mom came downstairs and put the mop and bucket away and sat down at the table and added to her clues list.

> 7. Found clues in the closet that prove she did not run off with another man
>   a. Jewelry box
>   b. Purses
>   c. Clothes
>   d. Empty suitcases
>   e. Four pairs of shoes
> 8. Looked like her things were just thrown in the closet. Nothing was neatly placed. Jewelry box was tossed in and contents were scattered.

"Anna, your turn in the tub," said Dad.

The next morning Dad left for work, and Mom, Molly, and Maggie started going through Angela's things.

"Girls, I'm taking this old quilt to the clothesline. Bring these baby blankets. They're crocheted, so Angela probably made these. This quilt design is called *Wedding Rings*, and look, in the corner she embroidered her name, Angela. This quilt was beautiful. It's too bad parts of the fabric have rotted. It's very fragile. She must have quilted this with her mother and maybe her grandmother, to have after she was married. We know she was a romantic person and very talented to make a quilt like this. She was so young when she got married: only seventeen, I think," said Mom sadly.

They shook out the crocheted baby blankets and hung them over the line. They went back to the porch and started sorting through the box of clothes and shoes. They neatly placed the shoes together and the purses together.

"Mom, I'm sure she would never have left her purse behind," said Molly as she opened the purse to look inside. "Mom, look, Maggie missed this when she looked in the purse. There's something at the bottom. It's a letter to Mrs. Campbell."

"Open it, Molly, and read it to us," Maggie said. Mom nodded that it was okay, so Molly opened the letter and read it out loud.

Dear Mom and Dad,

I'm sorry John didn't let you see me when you came over. Ever since I got pregnant, he's been mean. I don't think he loves me anymore. I had the baby by myself. He didn't help me. He left me alone and went off in the wagon, probably to get moonshine. I was so afraid, and then a pretty little girl walked in the bedroom and asked me if I needed help. She said she heard me crying in pain. She told me her name was Lucy.

The little girl knew just what to do. She sang the lullaby you sang to me when I was little, but she sang it in Irish. I told her I knew the song, and she told me to sing with her. Pretty soon the baby boy was here, and she cut the cord and everything. She took care of the baby and wrapped him in one of the blankets you made for him and gave him to me. She began to sing and we fell asleep.

I woke up the next morning, and John had never come home. When he finally got home, he wouldn't even look at the baby. I'm writing this letter hoping that I can give it to one of the farm hands to take to you. I am having a very hard time here. When you get this letter, please come and get me as soon as you can. I have to leave John. I think he will hurt the baby.

All My Love,

Angela

p.s. I named him Paul, after Grandpa.

"Oh my goodness, she was never able to get the letter to her mom. This is getting sadder by the minute," Mom said.

"Look through the photo album," said Maggie.

"Mom, the little girl that helped her was Lucy. I know John killed Angela," said Molly. "If she named the baby Paul, how did he end up John Junior?"

"That's something Mr. Doyle can find out on his birth certificate. This has got to be Angela and John's wedding photograph. She's smiling, and she's beautiful. He looks like a normal person there, but he's frowning," said Maggie.

"This must be Angela's family. I don't know who any of these people are," said Molly as she looked through the album.

"Look at this fancy mirror with a silver back and handle and a matching brush. These things are nice," Mom said. Mom shook the dust out of some of the dresses. "Look how tiny she was. Angela must have barely been one hundred pounds."

Mom went in the house and called Mr. Doyle. She asked him to bring a copy of his birth certificate. He was sure he had one, but he would have to look for it. He also said he had a surprise for Molly.

About an hour later, Mr. Doyle and Mr. Campbell drove up. Mr. Campbell told Molly that Becky couldn't come over, because she had chores to do. Molly was a little sad. She was hoping to play with Becky.

"I have something that will cheer you up, Molly," Mr. Doyle said. "I have a surprise for you." They walked to the back of the truck, and he got out a shiny new bike.

"I got this bike for you, and it's bright green to match your eyes. I'm sure you'll let Maggie ride the bike sometimes, won't you?"

"Sure, when I'm not riding it! Wow, thanks! This is the best present I ever got. Thank you, Mr. Doyle! May I ride it now?"

"Sure, it's yours."

"Mrs. O'Neal, I hope you don't mind. I am just so grateful."

"I don't mind. It's a wonderful gift. I wanted to show you and Mr. Campbell the things we found in the upstairs closet. I want you to brace yourselves. I don't believe Angela ran off with another man. We have a lot of evidence here that proves she didn't. I think John Doyle killed her and hid her body. I don't know how or where, but if we put our heads together, we may be able to figure it out. Did you go through the box yet, Mr. Doyle?"

"No, I wanted to wait and go through it with Henry."

Mom brought out the evidence list she made. She showed them the quilt and baby blankets, and the clothes, shoes, jewelry box and jewelry. She told them how everything looked like it was thrown into the back of the closet.

"If she left with another man, she would have packed

clothes in a suitcase and taken her hair brush and shoes. She wouldn't have left her purse."

Henry was looking through the jewelry box. "This was our mother's necklace. She would never have left this. Mom died four years ago, and she never believed Angela ran off. I feel ashamed. I never listened to her," said Henry with tears in his eyes. "Angela was my sister. I should have had more faith in her."

"Mr. Doyle, I want you to read this letter Molly found in Angela's purse. It's very sad. You should read it out loud so Mr. Campbell can hear it," Mom said.

"Please, Mrs. O'Neal, would you read it. We're too upset," said Mr. Doyle.

Mom read the letter and both men got very angry. Mr. Campbell said if he had known any of this, he would have killed John Doyle himself.

Mr. Doyle pulled his birth certificate out of his pocket. His father had registered his birth two weeks after he was born. The father's name on the certificate was John Doyle Senior and for the mother he put, Angela.

"He named me John Junior, but my grandma always told me that she knew my mom wanted to name me Paul, after her grandfather. He heaped on so much disgrace. I'm going to have my name legally changed to Paul Campbell. I hate my father, and I won't have any part of his name."

Mr. Doyle was terribly upset and excused himself. He walked around to the side of the house to be alone.

"Maggie, fold the dresses and stack them in a pile. Check the suitcases and make sure they are completely empty. Check all the purses for anything that might be hidden in them. Mr. Campbell, shall we go through the box in the truck. I don't think Mr. Doyle is up to it," Mom said.

Pamela Gillette

"Yes, we can put the newspapers, journal, and pictures to the side and take everything out piece by piece. Be sure to check the pockets in the clothes," said Mr. Campbell as he began to remove items from the box.

Nothing else in the box seemed to be important. It was just some old clothes and two pairs of shoes from John Doyle's childhood. Mr. Campbell put all the old clothes and shoes back in the box.

He was about to put the large framed photograph back in the box, when Molly ran up to the truck and said, "Mom, I just got a feeling. I don't understand it. There is something behind the picture in the frame. Look behind the picture."

"Okay, Molly," Mom said. "Mr. Campbell, would you like to take the back off of the picture frame?"

"Oh yes, behind the picture. Why didn't we think of it?" Mr. Campbell pried off the backing. "What is this?"

Mr. Campbell found some handwritten papers. John Doyle had written his thoughts down, and they were very well preserved between the thick photo and the frame backing. He took them out and handed them to Mom.

"I'm too upset to read these papers, and Molly is too young to be burdened with all of this, so will you please read them out loud. I'll get Mr. Doyle so he can hear this too," said Mr. Campbell.

Mom told Molly and Maggie to go inside while she read the papers. They all went under the shade of the porch and Mom began to read what John Doyle wrote.

❖

I WOULD LOVE FOR EVERYONE TO KNOW MY ACCOMPLISHments in life, but not until I'm dead and had a wonderful funeral. When I was a kid, I wrote in my journal about the fire. That was a stroke of luck. I'll burn my journal when I get old. I want to keep everyone guessing about that time of my life, but I want to take credit for the most brilliant scheme I ever pulled off.

I don't know who I was when I was courting Angela Campbell. I pretended to listen to her. I even brought her wildflowers I had picked. All I knew was that I was turning eighteen and I would inherit this big farm. Uncle Joe would be moving out, and I needed someone to cook and clean. Uncle Joe's girlfriend came over and did all that, and she said when Joe left, she wouldn't ever come back here.

I needed a woman, and Angela was right across the fields. We got married, and she moved in. She wasn't a good cook yet, so I informed her she better learn quick. She thought I was teasing, but I wasn't. Then she up and got herself pregnant. She wanted me to help her with laundry and cleaning. I don't do women's work. She cried all the time. She was good for nothing. She reminded me of my mother when she was pregnant with Lucy. One day, I caught her singing a sickening song to her big belly. My mother used to sing the same song to Lucy. I told Angela I hated that song. I slapped her in the face, but I wanted to punch her as hard as I could in the belly. I'd a loved to kill the brat. That night, she started screaming like a banshee, "Help me, John. The baby's coming." I didn't want anything to do with it, so I took off in the wagon to play poker and get drunk. I came home the next afternoon, when I thought it would be all over. I figured her and the baby would be dead, but she was in bed with a screaming brat by her side. She told me the baby was a boy, and she wanted to name him Paul. I told her, no one cares and that I was hungry. I told her to get up and make me some food.

The next week was hell, with a screaming baby. Angela wanted me to get her mom and dad or take her to their house. I was too busy to bother. I only came home for meals. The final straw was when I came in for supper, after a hard day in the field, and Angela was sitting on a chair in the kitchen, nursing the brat. She was singing again. I told her to shut up. I looked at the stove, and no food was cooking. I grabbed the iron skillet and walked slowly over to her. She looked up at me like I was going to hit her or something. She gave me a great idea. She pulled the baby close to her, and I bashed the top of her head in with the frying pan. Blood splattered everywhere and all over the screaming kid. I thought up such a great story about how she ran off with some other man. I thought it was a great story and so believable, but I had to make it seem reasonable, so I decided not to kill the boy.

I thought he might make a good, free farm hand one day, but until then, I had to get rid of him. He was covered in blood, so I put him in the kitchen sink. I took Angela outside so she could bleed in the grass. I used towels to clean up the floor and the wall. I took off the boy's clothes and washed him in the sink. I left him in the sink while I took all the evidence out to the burning barrel. I hitched up the horse and wagon and wrapped the screaming brat in a towel and took him over to the Campbell's. I told them I came out of the fields and the boy was in his cradle, screaming. I actually cried when I told them Angela left me a note on the table saying she left me for another man, and I was to take the baby to them. I added some hope for her parents. I told them the note also said she would be back for the boy someday. Hope is like torture with no end.

I couldn't fake cry anymore, so I yelled at them to take the baby, and then I whipped the horse like I was really mad and left. They bought the whole story. I'm such a good actor.

I had to deal with the body. After I took care of her, I took all of her things and threw them in the back of the closet. I didn't have time to burn them. I knew no one would look up there. I took the skillet and bashed up the baby's cradle. I'll never need a cradle. They can keep that kid. It's been five years now, so I got away with murder. I might put this in my will, so everyone will know how gullible they were.

❖

"This is too much for me to take in right now. I have to go home and think about this for a couple of days," said Mr. Doyle, visibly upset.

"This is just too much evil to understand," said Mr. Campbell. "Let's pack up all of Angela's things and put them in the back of your truck. I'll take you home, Paul, and I'll take Angela's things to my house. You take your time and decide what you want and what we're going to do about this."

Mom got the quilt and baby blankets off of the clothes line, and Paul packed them in the truck. Molly and Maggie got the laundry baskets and put them in the house. Soon everything was packed and the men drove off.

"Mom, what do you think he did with Angela's body?" asked Molly.

Mom looked at the house and said, "I don't know, dear."

Everyone in the family was stunned when they were filled in on the confession of the murder.

Molly found it very difficult to sleep that night. She had to sing her lullaby to calm the house. Maggie swore she heard some humming along with Molly, but she dismissed it again as noise from the fan. She knew it was humming, but she was too terrified to deal with it.

Chapter Fourteen

Mom started calling children down at five-thirty the next morning. Adam was first in the bathroom and everyone else had their scheduled time. Mom made lunches for Molly and Mary, because their school didn't have a cafeteria. Molly and Mary had book satchels to carry their lunches, paper, pencils, and anything else they needed for school. The older children were going to public school, so they ate in the cafeteria. Adam worked and paid for his own lunches. Dad gave Maggie and Nathan lunch money. Adam's car wasn't running, so he had to ride the bus to school. All the O'Neal children had to walk to the bus stop.

The school bus drove by their lane and went down School House Hill and over two creeks. It turned around in Jacobson's farmyard. By the time the bus got back to the O'Neal's lane, it was about one-fourth full. Adam and Nathan headed for the very back of the bus. Molly and Mary sat in one seat and Maggie sat opposite them. The next stop was the Campbell's lane. Becky got on and squeezed in by Molly and Mary. Christy sat by Maggie, and Jesse asked if Mary would sit by him. The bus driver picked up children all along County Road. When they got to town, the bus was almost full. The first stop to drop off children was the elementary school. All the O'Neals stayed on the bus, but Becky and Jesse got off there. The next stop was North Junior. Maggie, Christy, Jake, and Nathan got off and were told to go to the gym and find their grade section on the bleachers. Molly and Mary got off the bus and were ushered to the gymnasium and told to sit on the bottom bleacher in the corner and wait until the teacher on duty called the Catholic school bus number, which was bus number seven. Molly and Mary were the only two children waiting to catch the Catholic school bus.

When their bus was called, Molly and Mary went out and saw that the bus was cram packed with kids. They had to squeeze in three kids to a seat, so they sat opposite each other, with strangers. Someone on the back of the bus called Molly's name. Molly looked back and saw Jan, one of her friends from school.

Finally, the bus pulled up in front of Molly's school. Molly felt right at home. All the children could play on the playground until the bell rang. When the bell rang, Nuns came out of the building along with lay teachers to get their students. Numbers of each grade were painted on the parking lot and each student was to find their grade number and make a line. Molly found Paula, and they hugged and got in the fourth-grade line together. They were very excited to see each other after the long summer break.

"I read about you in the newspaper," said Paula excitedly.

"You did?"

"Everyone read about you and the guy who used to live in your house."

The principal, Mother Innocence, blew her whistle for everyone to be quiet.

"We'll talk at recess," Molly whispered.

The principal welcomed all the children back to school, and each grade, starting with the first grade, went single file into the school and to their classrooms. The fourth grade went into their freshly painted classroom. Mother Theresa introduced herself and told the children to pick a seat for the first day. Paula and Molly sat next to each other in the second row. Molly was so happy, she could burst. Mother Theresa said she would probably arrange the desks in alphabetical order in a few days.

"Put your things in your desk quickly. We only have five minutes before we leave for Mass."

The children lined up for Mass and walked down the hallway to the side entrance of the church. The fourth grade sat in their pews waiting for Mass to begin. Paula already had her veil on. Molly forgot her veil, so Mother Theresa handed her a tissue and two bobby pins. Molly had to pin the tissue on top of her head. She would have felt silly, but she wasn't the only girl with a tissue on her head. She looked across the aisle and saw Mary with a tissue on her head too.

❖

During lunch the children sat at their desks and ate. The school had little milk cartons delivered fresh every day for the children. Each child paid two cents for white milk and three cents for chocolate. Molly always asked for chocolate milk. Molly and Paula were able to talk quietly during lunch. After lunch the children lined up and went to the playground, which was the parking lot, for recess.

Molly and Paula had so much to catch up on. They told each other about their new houses, and Molly told Paula some of the things that happened to her, but nothing scary.

She knew Paula would never believe her. They picked up right where they left off in May.

When the school day was over, Molly picked up Mary from the first-grade room to make sure she made it to the bus. The bus filled up fast, and the driver didn't waste any time leaving the school. Running for the bus was a far cry from talking to friends after school and walking home as she did last school year. The bus pulled into North Junior's driveway and had to squeeze past all of the public-school buses lined up in front of the school. Molly and Mary and two other children got off their bus and had to go between two parked buses to get to the sidewalk. The two other children walked home, and Molly and Mary went in the gym and sat in their place on the bleachers.

They were the only two children in the gym until the bell rang. Soon the bleachers filled up with children waiting for the teacher to call their bus numbers. Everything was very organized. Molly saw Nathan come in and go to the top of the bleachers, and Maggie and Christy came in and sat by Molly. The teacher called one bus number about every two or three minutes, so the children would file out and get on the correct bus. After a while hardly anyone was left. The County Road bus picked up at the high school first and then it went to the elementary school, before ending up at North Junior, so it ran later than the other buses. Finally, the teacher called bus number twenty-five, and the small group of children who were left on the bleachers got up and boarded the bus. Becky had saved Molly a seat, Christy and Maggie sat together, and Jesse had saved a place for Mary. Nathan sat in the back with Adam and the Campbells. It was a long ride home. It seemed even longer because of all the stops along the way. Adam got off the bus at the Campbell's

Molly O'Neal

lane. The next stop was the O'Neal's. The bus dropped the children off at their lane around four o'clock and then they had the long walk home.

Molly and her brother and sisters finally walked in the kitchen door and were greeted to homemade cookies and a glass of milk.

"You only get two cookies a piece so you don't spoil your supper," said Mom. "How was school?"

"I love it, Mom. I saw Paula, and I love my new teacher. The bus ride is too long, and the walk down the lane is too long, but I had a good day," Molly said.

"It was all right," said Maggie. "I like North Junior, because the library is right inside the school."

"How about you, Mary?" Mom asked.

"The bus ride was a little scary. I'm glad Molly was with me all the time. I met new friends, and my teacher is nice."

"It was school," moaned Nathan. "I hate how late we get home, and I hate the long walk down the driveway."

※

ON THE BUS THE NEXT DAY, BECKY TOLD MOLLY ABOUT Paul Doyle coming over to her house and talking to her grandpa.

"They've hired a lot of people to meet over at your house tomorrow to look for my Great Aunt Angela. Can I come over tomorrow morning and watch with you?"

"Sure, Becky, I'll tell my Mom tonight. She might have some ideas about where to look," said Molly.

"Paul also said he had an appointment today to get his name changed to Paul Campbell. He said he's gone by Paul all these years, so now he's Paul Campbell, not John Doyle

Junior. He said he has a surprise for everyone too. I have no idea what it is," Becky said.

❖

WHEN MOLLY GOT HOME FROM SCHOOL THAT EVENING, she told Mom what Becky said. Mom already knew lots of people were coming over on Saturday.

"Mr. Doyle, or should I say, Mr. Campbell, called and told me about it. I called Grandma, and she said you could save those men a lot of time. She said Angela was so mistreated in life, that she's a timid spirit. Grandma wants you to start in the kitchen. She said to sit at the table and sing the lullaby. If you know it in English, then sing it in English. If you don't hear anything, go outside and stand by the back door, and sing very quietly and listen. I'll keep all the children inside and quiet."

Molly followed Grandma's instructions. She sat at the kitchen table and started singing softly. She got up and walked outside, continuing to sing. She stood outside by the back porch and stopped singing and just listened. She heard someone humming the lullaby. Molly looked to the right and saw a beautiful young woman standing by the corner of the house. She looked more like a mist than an actual person. The woman began to sing in a beautiful soft voice that was almost a whisper. She walked to the side of the house, and Molly followed her. Molly softly hummed the song and watched as the woman stopped and sat down on the concrete slab covering the old cistern. She was cradling a Raggedy Ann doll in her arms and singing the haunting lullaby.

She finished the song and looked up at Molly and whispered, "He threw me in there." She pointed down at the concrete. "I've been waiting all these years. Thank you, Molly. Tell my boy I've always loved him, and I would have never left him." She blew Molly a kiss and faded away.

    Molly stood very still. Mom came around to the side of the house and asked Molly if she saw anything. Molly turned and faced her with tears running down her face. Mom ran to her and Molly said, "I saw her, Mom. I saw Angela. She was singing the lullaby and holding a Raggedy Ann doll. She told me she's under the concrete, and she said to tell her boy she has always loved him and would have never left him. She thanked me and blew me a kiss, and she faded away."

    "Mom, she's in the cistern," Molly said as she pointed to the old cistern.

    "Oh honey, it's sad. It's just so sad," Mom said as she hugged Molly. "Let's go in, and I'll call Mr. Campbell."

    Mom called Paul Campbell and began to explain to him that Molly had special gifts, and he interrupted her and said, "I know she does. I could tell when we were at the old farmhouse and Molly recognized Lucy's clothes in the closet. I knew she was blessed with special gifts. Has she spoken to my mother?"

    "Yes, Molly knows that your mother's body is under the concrete on the side of the house."

    "The old cistern. It hasn't been used ever since I can remember. When I was a teenager, I remember the hole being covered with pieces of wood. It was very dangerous. He put the concrete slab over the cistern the same time he had the well in the front yard covered. It must have been around 1950. I mowed the grass for several years and mowed around those boards, and to think my mother was there all the time. The plans are changed for tomorrow.

We don't have to look for my mom, Molly found her," Mr. Campbell said with a shaky voice. "Tomorrow we'll recover the body. I'm calling the funeral home, police, and coroner. We'll be out as early as possible."

"Mr. Campbell, I have to tell you something," Mom said, interrupting him. "Molly said your mother sent you a message I know you'll want to hear. She said, 'Tell my boy I've always loved him, and I would have never left him.' She didn't desert you. She loved you Mr. Campbell. She was cradling a Raggedy Ann doll like the one we found in the closet, so you might want to keep the doll, because it was special to her. I'm sorry, Mr. Campbell," Mom said with tears in her eyes.

Mr. Campbell broke down and cried. He tried to regain his composure and said, "I can't thank you and Molly enough. See you tomorrow," he said as he hung up the phone.

All of this was too much for Molly. To cheer Molly up, Mom got out Adam and Nathan's sleeping bags and some quilts to make the living room a slumber party for the girls. Mom closed all the windows and pulled all the shades. She put towels over the windows in the kitchen so the girls couldn't see out, especially the back-door window. The boys were scared too, so they slept in the kitchen. No one wanted to sleep near the side of the house with the cistern.

The next morning finally came, and all kinds of official cars and trucks showed up. Mr. Waters, the reporter, walked around the yard asking questions. Paul Campbell came on a tractor and Henry Campbell, Angela's brother and Becky's grandfather, brought a long chain. He and his son Harris attached the chain around the concrete slab.

Mom and Dad made the kids stay in the house. Becky came with her dad and grandpa, but she had to stay in the house too.

The chain was ready and attached to the tractor. Paul Campbell pulled the slab off of the cistern. He moved the slab to the side, and the men took crow bars to pull the old boards off of the hole. The cistern was dry and only about ten feet deep. Paul stepped back and told the coroner to look first. The coroner shined his flashlight down the hole and took a look.

He turned to Paul and said, "I see bones, sir. We'll carefully bring them up and place them on the table I set up in the tent. I will do a preliminary examination to try and establish cause of death. With your permission, I'll send down my assistant to collect all the bones. Then he'll take down a metal detector to check for jewelry. We'll be very careful."

"Yes, please start," said Paul. He and the other men stepped to one side to observe the proceedings.

Harris and Henry's wives were standing by their car, and several other Campbell relatives were there for support.

The coroner's assistant was lowered into the cistern on a rope. He carefully placed the bones in several cloth bags and put them in buckets. The buckets were pulled up, and the bags were given to the coroner. He placed them on the table, as they were given to him, and laid them out as an intact skeleton. One of the last bags to come up was the skull. The top of the skull was missing. The assistant sifted through the few inches of dirt, which had accumulated at the bottom of the cistern, and he collected all the pieces of the skull, along with other small bones.

The coroner pieced the skull together and counted the bones to make sure his assistant did a thorough job. They sent down the metal detector and found a wedding ring and a small gold necklace with a cross attached.

"We know how he killed her, because we have his written confession, but what do you say?" Paul asked the coroner.

"First off, it is the skeleton of a woman, and I don't see any other trauma to the bones except for the massive blow to the head. When he dumped the body in the cistern, it must have been in use and had several feet of water in it. That would explain why she didn't have any other broken bones. I've counted all the bones and we have all of them. We know the cause of death. I think we can release her to the mortuary now."

Paul and Henry were very upset but very grateful for all of the support they received. The mortuary staff backed their hearse up to the tent and very discreetly took Angela away. With the help of some men, Paul was able to move the concrete back over the hole. Everyone who came to help, or support the family, began to leave. Becky left with her mom and dad.

Paul came to the back door to talk to Mom and Dad. "I'm going to drive Henry's tractor back to his house and get my truck, and I'm going to go home to sort a few things out and make some calls. I'll be back later to talk over a few things with you."

"Yes, that will be fine. We're so sorry, Paul," said Dad.

"I know. Your family has been great. I'll be back."

※

"Charles, we can't stay here. The children are afraid of this place, and I don't blame them. We haven't been here very long and so much has happened," Mom said.

"I'll start calling around and try to find us another place to rent. I'll tell Paul when he comes back to talk to us," Dad said.

A couple of hours flew by and Paul came back to talk to Mom and Dad. They invited him in, and they sat around the table to talk. Paul brought a notebook with a list of things he wanted to discuss.

He began, "Well, Mr. and Mrs. O'Neal."

"Please call us Charles and Anna."

"All right, Charles and Anna, I know you are going to have to move out of this horrible place, and I don't blame you. I'm getting ahead of myself here. I have asked my long-time girlfriend to marry me. After all that's happened, I realize life is short, and I don't want to have any regrets. She said yes, and we're going to get married in a couple of days. She has a very nice house in town, and we plan to live there. So, that's were your family comes in. I am offering you my house across the road. My cousins are, at this moment, moving me out. Five men and six strong teenage boys, one of them being your son Adam, are across the road loading up trucks. They'll have me moved out in no time. They are all willing to come over here and move your family across the road this afternoon."

"It's an answer to prayer, Charles," Mom said.

"I had the house built after I got out of the service. It has a big kitchen with a laundry room, full basement, nice and dry, and four bedrooms. It also has two bathrooms. I also have window air conditioners in some of the rooms. I hooked onto city water a couple of years ago, so you won't have to worry about the wells. The same deal applies, free rent for as long as you want to live there," Paul said.

"Thank you, Paul. We'll be very happy to move. The children are very unsettled here," said Dad.

"I understand. We've all been traumatized the last few days. It's the least I can do for all the help your family has given me. Little Molly has changed my life forever. Now my grandparents, Aunt Lucy, and my precious mother can rest in peace. We are going to have a ceremony at the grave site for my mother in about a week. First, I'm having my father exhumed and moved out of Campbell Cemetery to an unmarked grave in the City Cemetery in the next town. Campbell Cemetery is taken care of by the Campbell family. It's right down the road on the Campbell farm. Family and neighbors have been buried there for about a hundred years, so John Doyle has no place there."

Paul got out a handkerchief and wiped his face, and continued, "I should also mention that I'm leaving my freezer in the basement for you to use. I am leaving the side of beef and several pounds of pork in it for your family. I won't need it. I filled up my future wife's freezer last month. Her name is Joan by the way. Well, what do you say?"

"It sounds wonderful," said Mom with tears in her eyes. "Thank you, Paul, but isn't it too much?"

"Charles, your family deserves it. The kids have been through too much, and it's my crazy father's fault. It's the least I can do. I'm going to have this house burned down and leave some of the outbuildings standing. I'm going to sell the farm to my cousins. I have a job in town anyway. Eventually, I'll sell the house across the road, probably to my cousins, but I'm in no hurry. You can stay for years if you like.

"I took the liberty of bringing a bunch of empty boxes for you to start packing. You don't have to empty dresser drawers with all these strong guys helping. They'll have you moved this afternoon."

Molly O'Neal

"Okay, Anna, let's start packing," said Dad. He was overjoyed, because they had a nicer house to live in, and it wasn't haunted.

Mom and Dad didn't know the kids were listening on the stairs. They ran into the kitchen screaming with happiness. In a couple of hours, six trucks pulled up and eleven men helped the O'Neals move. They were all packed up and moved out in one trip.

"Take one last look, don't forget anything, and come out to the station wagon," Mom said.

"The upstairs is empty. I'm not even checking the closet," said Molly.

"I got your box of old clothes out, Mom," said Nathan. "It was packed into a truck. Adam and Sam got the chicks."

"Maggie and Molly, will you go out to the barn and look for Sock?" said Mom as she checked the kitchen and bathroom.

Mary went along with Molly and Maggie. The girls were giggling all the way to the barn.

"Sock, here kitty kitty," Molly called. Sock came out from behind a stack of hay. Molly picked up Sock and said, "We're going to have a new home, and you're coming with us."

Dad honked the horn, and the girls ran to the car. Molly and Mary sat in the third seat of the station wagon facing backwards. They never intended to go in the farmhouse again. As they drove down the lane, Molly and Maggie stared at the old house.

"No more evil imaginary friends for me!" Mary said.

"Just think everybody!" Molly shouted. "Two bathrooms!"

Chapter Fifteen

The O'Neals had moved into their new house on County Road. The whole family was overjoyed with two bathrooms and air-conditioning in most of the rooms. The house was close to the road, so they only had to walk down the short driveway to get the mail or catch the school bus. The house was a lot bigger than the old farmhouse and more modern. This house had a laundry room on the first floor, by the kitchen, with a washer and dryer. Nathan and Adam still shared a bedroom, and Molly and Mary shared a bedroom. Maggie got to have the smallest bedroom all to herself. The girls were assigned to the upstairs bathroom, and the boys shared the bathroom downstairs with Mom and Dad.

Mom took a walk around the new place to check things out. She went in the outbuilding Paul had called a barn, and she was surprised to see it had a concrete floor, a big utility sink, some cabinets and counters, and finished walls and ceiling. It was more like an apartment than a barn. She thought that with a few chairs and some curtains it would make a great little beauty shop. She was so happy they had such a great place to live.

Since Monday was Labor Day, the O'Neals were going to Grandma and Grandpa's house in Coaltown. Molly and

Maggie were hoping to see Doris and Gail Riker. They hadn't seen them since July.

"We can give Doris and Gail our new address again. I wrote and gave them our farmhouse address a month ago," Molly said.

"I know. Thank goodness we were able to move out of that horrible, creepy place. Our new house is so much nicer and bigger. We're still way too far out in the country, but we have the Campbells down the road, and I have a library at school," Maggie said.

❖

Labor Day came and the O'Neals, including Adam, loaded in the station wagon to spend the day at Grandma's. Dad pulled up to Grandma's back garden gate and parked behind Uncle Tim's car. Aunt Veronica, Aunt Julie, and Grandma were preparing lunch, and the men were in the living room talking. Grandpa was in his favorite chair smoking his pipe. Dad, Adam, and Nathan joined the men, Mom joined the ladies in the kitchen, and Molly, Maggie, and Mary stayed outside just in case the Rikers came home. There was no sign of the Rikers, so eventually, the girls went inside. Molly walked into the kitchen and could smell the wonderful meal Grandma prepared and the smell of cherry tobacco from Grandpa's pipe.

Molly, Cousin Chris, Mary, Cousin Jimmy, and Maggie ate lunch at the children's table in the kitchen. All the adults ate at the dining room table, and Nathan and Adam used TV trays and sat in the living room to eat. Grandma had made her spectacular stuffed peppers and homemade sweet bread, slathered with real butter. The adults had tea and coffee, and the children had Kool aid. The children fought over which aluminum cup they could drink from. The girls' favorite cup was the purple one. Maggie usually got the purple one, and Molly settled for the pink cup.

After lunch Molly and Maggie went over to the Riker's and knocked on the back door. No one answered, so they went back to Grandma's and asked if they could go over to the school playground. All the children went over except for Adam. He thought he was too mature to go to a playground. Molly and Maggie pushed Jimmy and Mary on the swings and then ran to the big slide. Between playing on the merry-go-round and the slides, they gave the little ones an occasional push on the swings. Nathan climbed up one of the tubular fire escapes to see if the door at the top was unlocked, but it wasn't.

Molly got on a swing next to Mary and twisted in circles a few times. Soon she was getting a bit bored, so she went over to the well and pumped until some water came out. She turned and looked toward the road and saw a man standing on the sidewalk looking at her. He was wearing dark pants, a working man's jacket, and a dark cap with a brim. It was at least eighty-five degrees and sunny, so he looked overdressed. Molly ran back over to the swing sets and asked Chris to look for a man standing by the road. Chris ran completely around one of the buildings and came back to the swings. He hadn't seen anyone by the street.

"I guess he left. He looked odd wearing a coat in this weather," Molly said wondering who he could have been.

"Let's go back and have some of Grandma's poppy seed bread," Maggie suggested.

"I could go for some lemonade," Chris said.

The group walked down the sidewalk in front of the

Riker's house and into Grandma's backyard. Grandma didn't want the children to cut through the Riker's backyard. She thought it wasn't polite, so they never cut through.

Back at Grandma's, they were happy to see ice-cold bottles of cola waiting for them. The children hung around Grandma's backyard and talked until it was time to go home.

Uncle David had parked in the front of Grandma's house, so everyone went to the front yard to say their goodbyes. They all stood by the sidewalk and waved as Uncle David, Aunt Julie, and Chris drove away. When Uncle David's big fancy car drove past Mrs. Skora's house, Molly saw the overdressed man again. He was standing inside of Mrs. Skora's picket fence, and he was waving at Molly. She thought he had to be a friend of Mrs. Skora's. She noticed he had gloves on and it looked like he waved with a fist. She couldn't see his face because of the shadow cast by his hat brim. Molly waved back at him. She thought her family was behind her, but she turned around and saw that they were already in the backyard. She heard Grandma's front porch chimes, and she remembered what happened earlier in the summer. She quickly turned back to the man, and he was still waving. She felt a rush of adrenalin and ran to the backyard and joined the others.

"Are you all right, hon, you look a little pale?" asked Grandma.

"I don't know, Grandma," Molly said as she was interrupted by Aunt Veronica.

"We're going now, Mom. Let me give you a hug. Jimmy, hug your grandma goodbye."

"We're going too, Mom," said Anna.

They all walked through the backyard to the back gate. They loaded up in the cars, and Mom took a head count, and off they went. Molly, Mary, and Maggie were in the third seat facing backwards waving goodbye until Grandma and Grandpa were out of sight. Maggie read a book, and Mary and Molly counted station wagons. Nathan and Adam were in the middle seat talking about sports. All the car windows were down in an attempt to keep cool, but it was a long hot ride home.

"Should I turn left here?" Dad said as they came close to their driveway.

"No!" yelled everyone in the car.

"Up a little bit and turn right!" yelled Nathan.

As they got out of the car, Mom told Molly not to forget to feed Sock and make sure she had fresh water, and she told Nathan to take care of the chicks.

"I'm going to call Sam to pick me up. I'll be home early," Adam said.

The O'Neals were on the same party line they had at the old house, but instead of two short rings, the new ring was one long one. They had only been in their new house for three days and already everyone felt comfortable and right at home. Mom especially loved the washer and dryer, the city water, and of course the freezer full of meat.

❖

Catching the school bus was so much easier. They loved not having to walk the half mile down the old farmhouse lane. The bus picked them up on the way to the big hill. Molly got to see School House Hill and the two bridges over Big Pine Creek and Little Pine Creek. When the creeks flooded over their banks, they basically combined into one huge creek and ran together to the Mississippi. After crossing the two creeks, Molly saw a small place at the foot of a big hill. The pasture and farmyard were lined with white fences to match the white barn and house. Beautiful ponies were grazing in the pasture. It all looked so serene. Then the driver drove up another big hill and turned around in the Jacobson farmyard. Two high school girls and one junior high school boy got on there. The bus went back down the hill to pick up two boys, about seven and eight years old, standing at a crossroad near the pony farm. The bus crossed over the two bridges and trudged up School House Hill. Near the top of the hill, the driver had to downshift to get enough power to continue up the hill. Molly looked to the right and saw what was left of the old school house. All she saw was a stone chimney and some stones.

The bus made it up the hill, and on the right was Charlin Road. A few families lived on the road, but it was a dead end, so any children who lived on Charlin had to wait for the bus at the intersection with County Road. Only two small children got on there. The bus buzzed along all the way to the Campbell's bus stop. On the way, Molly glanced over and saw the spooky old farmhouse they moved out of and she shuddered.

Becky got on the bus and sat by Molly. She told Molly that her cousin Paul got married in a quiet ceremony on Labor Day, and they had a big party for him and his new wife. Becky said she was happy he finally got married.

Becky got a serious look on her face and said, "Next Saturday we're having a big ceremony at our cemetery for placing the new stones for Lucy and her parents and a funeral for Angela, Paul's mom. He ordered a big stone for her, but it won't be delivered for a couple of weeks. Your whole family is invited to come, and after the funeral, we'll go back to our house for a big party. My grandpa says a nice party will celebrate their lives."

"I'll tell my mom," said Molly.

"My mom is going to call her today. My family loves you guys for what you did for Paul and his mother and his grandparents. They especially love you, Molly," Becky said.

Molly smiled and didn't know what to say. She wanted her life to be a little normal for a while.

❖

MOLLY AND MARY FOUND FRIENDS TO SIT WITH ON THE crowded Catholic school bus, but they still stayed close together. Molly made sure Mary got off and on at the right places.

Molly remembered to put her little chapel veil in her satchel to wear at Mass. She also remembered to bring extra bobby pins in case Paula lost hers. Right after Mass, it was time for Catechism. Molly loved to hear the Bible stories. She enjoyed anything that had to do with school.

During recess, Molly and Paula met up with two other girls to compare or trade holy cards.

"My parents read about the lady they found in the cistern at your house," one of the girls said. "My parents said that you helped them find the lady. They said you had a feeling she was in the cistern. Is it true, Molly?"

"Well, I did have a feeling, and that's where they found her. It's too sad. I don't want to talk about it, okay?"

"Let's compare our holy cards," Paula said.

The children received holy cards for different occasions or for getting an *A* on an important assignment. Molly and Paula each had quite a collection. The girls were trying to spread some of their cards out on the church steps, but the wind was too strong. They picked up their cards and went into the girls' bathroom. Molly ended up trading her two doubles. She traded one of her baby Jesus cards, for a Saint Jude, and her double of Saint Frances, for a Moses and the Ten Commandments. Soon the end of recess bell rang. The girls stood against the wall in the hallway and waited until their class came by and joined the line to the classroom.

Occasionally, Molly and some of her friends hung out in the girls' bathroom at recess. Mostly when it was too cold or they had a lot to talk about. The bathroom had six stalls and four sinks, and it was spotless. A large wired and glazed window ran across the wall near the high ceiling. The plumbing was exposed against the wall. One small pipe ran sideways along the wall from the back of the sinks to the radiator. It stuck out about three inches. Molly liked to stand on it and bounce up and down.

❖

THE NEXT MORNING, RIGHT AFTER THE BUS PICKED UP the Campbell's, the bus stopped abruptly. It wasn't a normal bus stop, so the children stood up and looked out the front window of the bus. They saw that someone's cows got out and wandered onto the road. The driver honked and honked, and they wouldn't move, so he slowly moved the bus forward as the cows lazily walked off the road.

About a half mile up the road from the cows, the bus stopped to pick up a small group who hadn't ridden the first three days of school. Two redheaded boys got on. Molly thought they were twins. They sat in the middle of the bus, not in the back with the other high school boys. Then a high school girl got on. She had dull brown hair and a dingy wrinkled white blouse and dark blue skirt. She wore loose fitting flats with no hose or socks. A little boy got on after her. He had longish messy blond hair, and he wore overalls with no shirt. The overalls were split so low on the sides it was obvious he wasn't wearing any underwear. His shoes were too big for him and all scuffed up, and he wasn't wearing any socks. No one moved over in their seats to let them sit down. The bus driver, told them to sit down in the front seat by the door. Nobody ever wanted to sit there. He asked the girl if she wanted to open and close the door, when other students got on, so she and the boy would feel like they belonged and were welcomed. She smiled and nodded, and they sat in the front seat.

Becky whispered, "Those boys are the Sherman brothers. They're twins but not identical. Nobody likes them, because they're pretty mean, and they poach deer out of season on other peoples' land, including our land. Every so often, we lose a lamb or one of our chickens disappear. We can't prove it, but we think it could be them. My father caught them, a couple of times, fishing in our lake without permission. They're trouble. The girl's name is Cathy. My Mom says she had to grow up too fast. The little boy is Johnny. He's ten years old, and he's very shy and never talks. He lives with his mom and Cathy, his cousin. His Mom is the boss of all the relatives who live back there in some sheds."

"He looks hungry, and he's not carrying a lunch. I doubt if he has money for the cafeteria," whispered Molly.

"He doesn't. He sits with a couple of kids during lunch, and everybody gives him the food they don't want. He gets a lot of food, but a lot of the same things, like six apples or four pieces of bread and butter. It has to be embarrassing," Becky said with a sigh. "His mom doesn't accept charity from neighbors. My mom tried to give her some clothes for Johnny, and she refused them and got insulted, so what can you do? Oh, here's my school. Bye, see you later."

"Bye, Becky," Molly said as she pondered Johnny's situation. She watched him from the bus window, and as he walked toward the school, he stepped out of one of his shoes.

Molly wondered what people thought of her. She wore a white ironed blouse and her navy-blue uniform, which was too small. It was tight, short, and uncomfortable. Her saddle oxfords were old and scuffed, and her anklets were too small, so they slid down into her shoes at the heels. She figured she looked poor too, but at least she had socks and underwear, and she combed her hair. She also thought she had parents and grandparents and sisters and brothers who would be there if she needed them. After counting her blessings, she was ready to get off the bus with Mary at North Junior to wait in the gym for the Catholic school bus to take them to St. Patrick's.

❖

When Molly got home from school, she told Mom about the little boy on the bus. She also told her how she felt about her own appearance.

"As soon as I can, I'll get Adam to take me to a store where I can get some new socks. I can't buy you a new uniform, because next year the school is switching to pleated skirts, and I can't afford a new one," Mom said sadly. Your Aunt Veronica has friends at her church. I'll call her and see if anyone she knows has old uniforms that will fit you. In the meantime, I'm going to try to cut down Maggie's old uniform from last year. I can take it in and hem it, and we'll see how it looks."

"Can we polish the white part of my shoes without getting white on the black part?" Molly asked. "I hate these saddle oxfords. They're too tight. I wore these last year, and they hurt my feet."

"I really can't get you any new shoes right now. Let's polish your old shoes, and I'll go upstairs and get Maggie's old uniform. We'll try it on you and pin it up, and I'll work on it tomorrow," Mom said.

"Can you make an extra bologna sandwich tomorrow, so I can slip it to Johnny?"

"Yes, I would be happy to make an extra one."

※

THE NEXT DAY WAS THURSDAY, AND MOLLY GOT ON THE bus with her bologna sandwich in her satchel and an extra lunch bag in her hand. Mom also put three cents in Johnny's bag for chocolate milk. Molly and Becky were in the third seat right behind Mary and Jesse. When Cathy and Johnny got on the bus, they sat in the front seat so Cathy could work the door handle. Molly tapped Mary on the shoulder and told her to give the bag to Johnny when Cathy was opening the door for students. Mary waited until Cathy's back was turned, and she slipped Johnny the lunch bag. Johnny hurried and put it in his overall pocket. He nodded a thank you, because he didn't dare let Cathy know he was given a lunch.

※

FRIDAY WAS SIMILAR TO THURSDAY. MARY PASSED JOHNNY a bologna sandwich and three cents. The bus driver watched Molly and Mary through his rear-view mirror and smiled.

The bus driver's name was Pete. He worked as a janitor at North Junior during the day. All of the bus drivers did double duty as janitors for the school district. The men wore tan uniforms with brown ties and brown shoes. They had uniform jackets, coats, and hats. Pete was a very nice man and a hard worker. He got to know each child on the bus by name and all the children, even the high school students, respected him.

❖

Saturday morning came, and it was time to go to the funeral. All the O'Neals dressed up in their Sunday best. They drove over to the Campbell's and followed them down a field road and came up along the side of the cemetery.

The cemetery had about one hundred tombstones. Paul Campbell made sure his Aunt Lucy's angel statue was big and noticeable.

Molly got out of the car with her family, and they joined all the Campbells and their friends and neighbors at the grave of Angela. A man in a kilt was standing a short distance from the grave playing *Amazing Grace* on the bagpipes.

A preacher led the memorial, and Henry Campbell, Angela's brother, gave the eulogy. He talked about how Angela was her parents' pride and joy: so beautiful, and sweet. He said he was very young when she was killed, and he grew up believing that someday she was going to come home.

Henry said, "Over fifty years have passed and a little girl named Molly O'Neal, with the help of her mother, found out what really happened to my sister, and we are forever grateful. Now Angela can rest in peace, and we can rest in the fact that all our questions have been answered. She is home safe with her family now."

A tear ran down Henry's cheek. Everyone in the family, and Molly and her mother, were given a rose to put on the casket.

"I would like for everyone to see the new stones I had made for my grandparents and the beautiful angel statue for Lucy. Angela's statue will be a little different than Lucy's. It's in the process of being engraved," Paul said. "Everyone here is invited to the celebration of the lives of my mother, grandparents, and my Aunt Lucy at the Campbell farm. I hope to see you all there."

As everyone was slowly leaving, the bagpiper began to play again.

❖

THE CAMPBELLS HAD A LARGE BUFFET STYLE LUNCH SET up on the front lawn. Pictures of Angela, as a child, were displayed on a table. Paul and his new wife, Joan, greeted all the guests. He introduced Joan to Molly and her family. Joan told Molly she was very happy to meet her, and she had heard so much about her. After all the formalities, everyone had lunch.

After lunch, Becky and Christy showed Mary and Maggie the widow's walk and their gorgeous bedroom. Molly went with them. She looked down at the gathering on the front lawn, from the widow's walk, and she marveled at how small everyone looked. Maggie and Mary loved the whole house.

"I would love to sit in the widow's walk and read books, especially when it's raining. What a great room," said Maggie.

The next day Molly's family had a nice, quiet Sunday.

Chapter Sixteen

On Monday morning, the bus picked up the O'Neals right on schedule and headed down the road. Several stops later, Johnny got on the bus with Cathy and the Sherman brothers, Molly noticed he was wearing a dingy white sleeveless t-shirt under his overalls. Molly thought his mother might have gotten a note from the teacher saying that Johnny had to wear a shirt under his overalls. He still wore the big shoes and no socks. Molly gave the lunch bag for Johnny to Mary, and Mary passed it to him when Cathy wasn't looking.

After the bus picked up all the children, Mrs. Campbell drove over to the O'Neal's. She knocked on the back door. Mom came to the door and invited her in.

"Would you like some coffee, Mrs. Campbell?"

"Please call me Joyce, and I'll call you Anna if that's all right. I would love some coffee. I've been meaning to stop by and ask you if you would like to go grocery shopping with me. I go every Thursday."

"I would love to go and give Adam a break on Saturdays. That would be wonderful," Anna said with a big smile.

"I was noticing your hair always looks so nice. Where do you get it done?" Joyce asked.

"I do it myself. After high school, I graduated from

Beauty College."

"It would be great if you could do my hair. I would pay you the going rate. I could wash my hair at home and drive on over."

"The kids are back to school now, and I think it would be good for me to have a little side job. I had a small beauty shop in my old house, and I kept my equipment."

"How about tomorrow then, say ten o'clock?"

"That sounds great," Mom said.

"Thanks for the coffee. See you tomorrow," Joyce said as she walked out to her car.

Anna was excited at the thought of being able to fix an adult's hair for a change. She was also excited about having a friend.

❖

The next Friday evening, Dad took Mom and all the girls over to Aunt Veronica's house. On the way to town, Dad dropped Nathan off at his friend Kim's house. Nathan spent some Friday nights and Saturdays at Kim's house, when he wasn't working for the Campbells. Sometimes he took the bus home with Kim, so he wouldn't have to bum a ride back into town.

Aunt Veronica lived on a very steep hill near downtown. Dad pulled up in front of her house, and Uncle Tim gave him instruction on how to park up a steep hill. "Turn your front tires out so the back of the tire will bump the curb."

When Uncle Tim turned back to go on the porch, Dad said, "I guess he thinks I've never driven a car before."

The ladies and Cousin Jimmy sat on the front porch and talked.

"Would you like some homemade ice cream?" Aunt Veronica asked.

"Yes," all the girls yelled.

After they ate the ice cream, Aunt Veronica asked them if they wanted to go for a walk down to the river.

"It's a short walk past some stores and over the railroad tracks. We'll sit on a park bench by the river for a few minutes. We'll be back before dark."

"I would love to go for a nice walk," Mom said.

"I haven't seen the river up close," Molly said.

They walked down the big hill and crossed Bella Street.

"Bella means beautiful," Maggie said.

They walked two and a half more blocks past stores with mannequins in the windows. They walked past a restaurant, and Maggie read the sign, "Marco's Restaurant. Looks like a fancy place to eat."

They crossed some railroad tracks, and came to the small park. Maggie stood and watched people going in and out of stores, and Molly sat and looked at the river.

"On the way back, we'll stop off at the library. I have my library card with me, so we can check out some books," Veronica said.

"Can I check out a book or two?" asked Maggie.

"If we have time. Let's go now before it gets too late," said Veronica.

As they were leaving, Molly noticed a woman sitting on one of the benches. She waved at Molly, and Molly waved back.

"Mom, I know its summer, but why was that lady wearing a swim suit?"

"What lady, Molly?"

"The lady over there," Molly said as she pointed back to a bench by the river.

"Mom looked at Veronica and asked, "Do you see a lady sitting on one of the benches?"

"No, is she still there, Molly?"

"She's waving at me," Molly said as she waved back.

Veronica tried to get Molly's mind off the lady. She said, "Come on, Molly. We better get to the library. It's getting late."

"Just think, you only live a couple of blocks from a huge library, Aunt Veronica," Maggie said excitedly.

"The children's library is in the next block," Aunt Veronica said.

Maggie pulled Molly back a few feet as they were walking and whispered, "If we ever became orphans, I have dibs on Aunt Veronica. I could put up with Uncle Tim if I lived this close to a library."

Molly laughed and whispered, "Not me. Not after the time he put his glass eye in his mouth and pretended to chew it up."

"Here we are. Catch up girls," said Mom as she held the library door for them.

Maggie went up to the desk and asked, "Do you have a children's section?"

"We have a very small section over there. Most of our children's books are in the children's library."

"Thank you," Maggie said. She walked quickly over to the section the lady pointed out and started looking at chapter books. She quickly found two books from an author she liked, and took them up to the front desk to wait for the others to choose their books.

Mom brought up two mystery books, and Molly and Mary had each picked out one book. They placed their books on Aunt Veronica's stack to be checked out.

As they walked back to Aunt Veronica's, they passed Uncle Tim's hardware store and then they trudged up the steep hill.

"You girls were gone pretty long. It's time we were getting home," Dad said.

Before they left, Veronica pulled Anna aside and said, "You do know Molly was serious when she asked about the lady sitting on the bench? After all that's happened this summer, you know Molly has inherited the *gift* from Mom's side. Molly sees more than we do. Don't make a big deal of the things she talks about. Let her be a little girl as long as possible."

"I wish Mom lived closer," Anna said.

"We'll talk," said Veronica as she waved goodbye.

❖

Molly had an uneventful weekend for a change. She did chores on Saturday morning, and she rode her bike to Becky's house in the afternoon. Sunday was church and a day of relaxation.

❖

Monday morning came too soon. On the bus, Molly and Becky noticed that Johnny didn't get on with Cathy, so Molly was stuck with two bologna sandwiches for lunch. Becky asked Cathy where Johnny was, and she said his sister came home and took him back to New Mexico with her. Cathy sat in the front seat all by herself, opening and shutting the door for students.

When Molly got to class, her teacher said, "Children, we'll line up for Mass in a minute. Right now, I want to introduce you to Diana McKinney. She moved to Laton last week. I want everyone to make her feel welcome. Now, everyone, line up for Mass. Diana will be first in line today."

Molly noticed how pretty Diana was. She had long light brown hair that went all the way to her waist. Her uniform fit perfectly and her blouse was immaculate. She also had saddle shoes, but not the big orthopedic kind. Her shoes were the smaller more stylish kind, and they looked brand new. All the boys in the class wanted to be second in line. She put on her full-length veil for Mass. Molly's was a little, round circle of lace for the top of her head.

Molly got in line with Paula and said, "She sure has pretty hair."

"Yes, she does," sighed Paula.

At lunch, Molly was sure glad she had the extra sandwich, because her two admirers, who usually shared their dessert with her, were busy fawning over Diana. The boys acted like Molly wasn't even in the room.

※

A COUPLE OF DAYS WENT BY, AND WHEN MOLLY AND HER classmates got to school on Wednesday morning, there was an envelope on everyone's desk. Molly opened hers, and it was an invitation to Diana's birthday party on Saturday. Everyone in the class started buzzing about the invitation.

"May I say something, Mother Theresa?" asked Diana.

"Yes, you may, Diana."

"I know the invitation is short notice, but I just moved here, and Saturday is my birthday. It will be a good way for us to get acquainted, and there'll be pony rides," Diana said.

Molly O'Neal

She got a lot of, *I'll ask my mom*, but everyone in the class was excited.

"I want to go. Do you, Paula?" Molly asked.

"I sure do. I can't wait to ride a pony."

"Everyone, line up for Mass," said Mother Theresa.

Today the girls wanted to be in line by Diana. She was instantly the most popular girl in the school.

When Molly got home, she showed the invitation to Mom.

"Can I get some new shoes, dressy ones, not saddle oxfords? I'll wear the new dress you made for me to wear to church. Can we go to the store tonight?"

"Let me ask Adam if he'll take us. I think this is an emergency."

Adam agreed to take them right after supper. Mom had to get some money from Dad. They got Molly a pair of slip-on black patent leather shoes. Molly felt secure that she was going to look nice enough to go to a birthday party. Adam suggested getting Diana two of the latest music records, so he helped Molly pick them out.

❖

Saturday came, and Mom washed and rolled Molly's hair. Molly sat under Mom's hair dryer, just like Mrs. Campbell did every week. Molly's hair turned out lovely, and Mom surprised her with a new cancan to wear under her new dress. She felt like a princess. Mom had wrapped the records in white wrapping paper with a purple ribbon. Molly was ready to go to the party.

Dad drove Molly to the party. Directions to the house were drawn on the back of the invitation. They drove into town and followed the directions down a street and up to a guard house and gate. A man in a uniform came out and asked Dad, "Who are you visiting today?"

"The McKinney's house," Dad said.

"That would be the McKinney birthday party. Turn left from here and follow the road to number 310. You can't miss it. The ponies are in the yard. Have fun," the guard said.

"Thank you," Molly said.

Molly was in awe of all the big gorgeous homes. They came to number 310, and Dad turned in the large half circle driveway and lined up behind a few other cars dropping off children. Diana was waiting at the front entrance to show everyone to the backyard where the party was all set up. Molly thought the house was a castle. It was made of stone and even had two turrets. The front entrance had a staircase on both sides and a covered porch sheltering the huge ornate wooden doors.

"Dad, it's a castle!" Molly exclaimed.

"I think it is, Molly," Dad said.

"Don't forget to be back by four o'clock. Bye."

Molly jumped out of the station wagon and trotted up the stairs to join her friends.

Diana's mother came out and told all the children, who had gathered at the entrance, to follow her through the house to the backyard. They walked down a wide hallway to a large living room. Molly was amazed at all the beautiful things. They walked out two glass doors and onto a large stone patio and then to a lush green lawn decorated with crepe paper, balloons, and flowers. It looked like a carnival. Banquet tables were pushed together to make one long table in the center of the yard. The table was decorated with a white table cloth and small vases of flowers every foot or so.

About thirty folding chairs were lining the table. A pretty bow was attached to the back of each chair. A two-tiered birthday cake was sitting at the head of the table.

"Play all the games you want, and ride the ponies. Diana will join you as soon as all the other children arrive," Mrs. McKinney said.

There were several adults manning the games, and several children were already playing games or riding the ponies. Molly saw Paula in line for a pony ride, so she ran over to get in line with her.

Soon Diana came with the last group of children and joined the party. Diana got in line behind Molly for the pony ride.

Four ponies were tied to a circular horse walker with two attendants helping the children get on and off the ponies. Molly looked over at a truck with a large horse trailer parked in the yard. The address on the truck said County Road. She knew these had to be the ponies from the farm down by the two bridges. The ponies had long manes, and their tails almost touched the ground. The saddles and halters were very ornate and the saddle blankets were beautiful colors.

Molly turned so her back wasn't to Diana. She marveled at the beautiful dress Diana was wearing, and she loved the beautiful crown of real flowers she had in her hair. Ribbons were flowing from the back of the crown all the way to Diana's waist.

"I love your hair, Molly," Diana said.

"Thank you. I love the flowers you have in your hair, and your dress is beautiful," Molly said, trying not to stare."

"Thank you for asking us to your party," Paula said.

"Thank you for coming."

"Your house is beautiful. It looks like a castle," Molly said. "I love it here. It's a lot bigger than our old house. It's our turn to ride now," Diana said as she motioned the girls to the ponies.

One of the attendants helped Molly onto a tan pony with a blond mane and tail. This was the first time Molly had ever ridden a pony. After Diana had a pony ride, her mother called everyone over for a game of musical chairs. After musical chairs, they played pin the tail on the donkey. Two clowns were entertaining the children as they waited for their turn in the games. After about an hour of games, one of the clowns put on a magic show and then it was time for everyone to take a seat at the huge table. Diana's mom had lit the candles on the beautiful cake. Diana blew out the candles, and everyone sang to her. Diana's mother cut the cake and helpers made sure every child had a piece of cake and a drink. After they had cake, it was time for Diana to start opening her huge pile of gifts. The party was magical for Molly. She rode on the ponies two more times, and one of the clowns made her a balloon giraffe. All too soon, it was time to go home. Cars were lined up in the driveway and down the street. Diana's mom supervised an orderly departure from the front entrance.

Molly was quiet on the way home. She had such a wonderful time, and she wondered what it would be like to live in a castle.

❖

THE NEXT DAY, DAD TOOK MOM AND THE GIRLS TO church. He picked up Nathan at his friend's house on the way. Molly wore her new dress and her new shoes. Her hair had lost its curl, but she still felt like a princess anyway. As they sat in the pew before Mass started, Molly whispered, "Mom, will you teach me how to put curlers in my hair?"

"I have brush rollers that will make it easy to roll your hair at night, but you'll have to sleep in them. By morning your hair will be dry."

"Won't it hurt to sleep in the rollers?" Molly asked.

"You have to suffer if you want to be beautiful. Now shh, Mass is starting."

Dad was about ten minutes late picking them up from church.

"Where were you?" Nathan asked.

"At the office," Dad answered.

"The parking lot is empty," Maggie said disgustedly.

After Mom got in the front seat she said, "I may as well announce it now. Mrs. Campbell has been giving me driving lessons. She is going with me tomorrow to take my driving test. If all goes well, I should have my license soon."

"Then she can haul you kids around wherever you need to go," Dad said.

"That's wonderful!" the girls squealed.

"It's about time," Nathan said.

After lunch, Adam's friends picked him up, Nathan took off on his bike, and Dad went fishing. Molly got out a pen and paper to write to Doris about Diana's birthday party. She went upstairs to get her address book out of her dresser. She stopped and looked out the bedroom window that faced County Road and the old farmhouse. She saw a few people moving around by the house and barn, so she went downstairs and told her mom what she saw.

"It's probably Mr. Doyle. I mean, it's probably Mr. Paul Campbell and some other people who have permission to be back there. You know, I have some binoculars I've had for years. Let me get them and let's be nosey," Mom said as she went into her bedroom. "Here they are."

Mom and Molly went upstairs to get a better look at what was going on. "There are people there," said Mom. "There's Mr. Campbell's truck turning in the lane. I wonder if he knows who those people are. I wonder if they're going to burn the house down today. No, they wouldn't do it on a Sunday."

All the men went behind the house, so they couldn't see anybody. There wasn't anything interesting to watch, so Mom went downstairs while Molly kept watching the house. She saw several men walking around the pigpen. The weeds were too high, so she could only see their heads. It looked like the men were chopping down the weeds. Then she saw Mr. Campbell's truck coming up the lane. She looked down into her own yard and saw Mom standing near the road waving for him to come over. Molly ran downstairs and out the back door as Mr. Campbell was pulling into the driveway.

"Hello, Anna. I saw you waving. Is there a problem?"

"Molly and I noticed all the men over at the old farmhouse, and we were curious. Are they going to burn down the house?" Mom asked.

"A woman named Rita called me. She read the article about finding my mother in the cistern, and she had a hunch John Doyle could be connected to the disappearance of her father, two brothers, and two uncles. They were migrant workers who worked for John Doyle in 1936. None of her relatives ever came home that year. I told her she and her family could look around all they want, dig up anything, or cut down anything they want to. Right now, they have

Molly O'Neal   235

sickles, and they're cutting down some of the weeds in the pigpen. They even have a man with a metal detector trying to find any trace of the missing men and boys. It should take them a couple of days to go over the pigpen and barn."

"Do you remember any of the migrant workers?" Mom asked.

"The first year I had to go back and live with John Doyle, I remember men came seasonally to work in the orchard and during the harvests. I can't call John Doyle my father ever again. Anyway, we had land in the west section planted in fruit trees. I didn't pay much attention to the workers. They camped out on the property and kept to themselves. I do remember two boys a little younger than I was, but we never hung around together."

"How did she know her father worked for John Doyle?" Mom asked.

"She recognized John Doyle's name and the farm on County Road. Rita's mother gave her the last letter her father, Carl, had sent home. She told Rita to find out what happened to her father and brothers. The letter told her they were working and camping on the Doyle farm, and the farmer wouldn't pay fair wages."

Mary had been listening and said, "I didn't tell anyone, but I used to see two boys about as big as John, my awful friend, getting drinks at the well in the front yard when we lived there. John told me to stay away from them, because they had knives in their pockets, and they would stab me."

"Why didn't you tell us?" Mom asked.

"I thought they worked with the farmers who came through the yard all the time. One time I heard an older man, who was standing in the pigpen, yell at the boys to get to work."

"Oh no," said Molly. "I'm so glad we don't live there anymore."

"Rita wants to meet me at the farm, and tell me about the men who disappeared," Paul Campbell said.

"I tell you what, if you call Rita up and she wants to come out and talk, we'll walk across the road and talk to her in the lane. I don't want the girls to go near the house again. We'll be here all afternoon, Paul."

"See you soon," said Paul as he left.

Paul left and went to the Campbell's house and called Rita. She was very anxious to come out and said she would meet him on the lane in thirty minutes. He called Mom and told her when he and Rita would meet on the lane.

Mom walked across the road with Molly and Mary. They walked down the lane a few feet to Paul's truck. Another car pulled into the lane and parked behind Paul. A lady and a man got out of their car and she said, "Hello you must be, Paul. I'm Rita and this is my husband Franklin."

"This is Anna O'Neal, and her daughters Molly and Mary."

"Hello. I read about you and your daughter Molly in the newspaper. I thought since you found the lady in the cistern, you might be able to find out something about my father, my two uncles, and my two brothers. We were living in Texas in 1936. The men left to go north for seasonal work. I was eighteen, so I remember them vividly. My poppa last wrote my mom and said they were working on the Doyle farm on County Road, just outside the town of Laton. He said Doyle was an S.O.B., but they needed work. That was the last my mom heard from him. When he didn't come home, she said she felt they were all dead, and she wanted answers. She went to the police in Texas, and they communicated with the police here. The police telegraphed back and forth. She was given some of the telegrams. I have them here. This one says the Laton police have put a man on the case to investigate the Doyle farm, and they will send news of the five males."

Rita continued, "The next telegram says they thoroughly investigated John Doyle and searched the farm for any trace of migrant workers. It also says, Doyle told them he paid the workers cash three weeks earlier, and they left in their truck, and he never saw them again. The police said Doyle suggested they check northern towns with farms and orchards."

"I remember the police coming here and combing the outbuildings. They took their cars down the field roads and searched the woods on Doyle's property," Paul said. "The police even brought out search dogs."

"Those men at your farm now are my sons and nephews. We traveled up here together to search for the remains. We know there is no way the men wouldn't have come home if they were alive. We want to find them and bring them home to Texas for burial."

"May I look at the telegrams?" asked Molly.

Rita handed Molly the telegrams and a necklace and said, "This was my father's St. Christopher medal. He was never without it. He wore it on this chain, but for some reason he didn't bring it on the last trip."

Molly took the necklace and put it around her neck. Mary came over to Molly and held her left hand and Mom's right hand. Molly read the last telegram to herself.

"This is all wrong!" Molly cried. "The pigs, it was the pigs!" Molly dropped the telegram and took the necklace off and handed it to Rita.

Molly grabbed Mom's waist and hugged her tightly. "John Doyle killed an older man with a pitchfork and threw him in with the pigs in the barn. I want to go home!"

"I'm going to take the girls home now. This mystery has to be solved. Your boys are looking in the right place," Mom said as she began to leave with the girls.

Rita was so upset she had to sit in the car for a while. Paul talked to her husband.

"I'll cooperate with anything you want to do to the place to find any remains of her father and the others," Paul said.

"We have to find them. Today is a good start," Rita's husband said.

When Molly got home, Mom sat the girls down and told them they didn't have to be involved with anything that had to do with the farmhouse or John Doyle.

"I wanted to help, but it was too horrible. It was like when I wake up from a dream when someone is trying to kill me," Molly said as she shuddered.

Mom and the girls sat on the sofa and Mom turned on the television. She sat with them, and they watched a game show. Mom thought it would get Molly's mind off the missing men. Paul called Mom later in the day. He said the men were going to tear the pigpen apart looking for any trace of their relatives.

"We have to remember John Doyle was an evil man and very clever, and he got rid of your mother's body the easiest way he could," Mom said to Paul.

Maggie was listening to the one-sided conversation. "Mom wants to solve this mystery," Maggie whispered to Molly.

Paul said, "I remember the day John Doyle told me the migrant workers left. I remember it, because there was still a lot of work to be done, and while he was talking to me, blood was oozing through his pant leg. He told me he fell on a pitchfork in the barn and then he limped into the bathroom. A few minutes later, he came out of the bathroom and got in his truck and left. He probably went to his girlfriend's place. I went in the bathroom, and there were bloody towels on the floor. It was a mess. I filled a wash tub with water and put the towels in it, and I went over to the Campbell's to spend the night."

"Do you remember his girlfriend's name? Did you know her very well?" Mom asked.

"Oh yes. Her name was Frances Carpenter. She was a divorcee, and she was perfect for John. She had a steady job as a cook in a diner at the edge of town. John ate there all the time. She came out to the farm to clean or do his laundry a couple times a week. She was his girlfriend until the day he died."

"You and Rita have to find her, and see if John ever told her anything. He was a drinker, right?"

"They're talking about John Doyle's girlfriend. I can't believe he had a girlfriend," Maggie whispered.

Molly motioned a shh, and they continued to listen in.

"Hold on a second. I'm going to look her up in the phone book," Paul said. He looked Frances up and wrote down her number and address. "I'm going to call her and see if she'll talk to me, and I'll call you back."

"Okay, I can't wait to hear if she'll talk to you," Mom said.

Paul called Frances, and she remembered him from when he lived with John.

"I read about your mother in the paper. I would like to talk to you if you have the time, and call me Fran."

"I would love to talk. When is good for you?" Paul asked her.

"Come over right now. I live at the corner of Fourth and Cherry Streets."

"I'll see you as soon as I can get there, and I may be bringing a friend, if you don't mind."

"Who is it?" she asked.

"I might be able to bring Mrs. O'Neal with me."

"Can I trust her to be discreet?"

"Yes, she will be very discreet," Paul assured her.

Paul hung up the phone with Fran and called Anna back. He asked her to go with him. She couldn't wait to meet Fran and ask her some questions.

Dad walked in, and Anna filled him in on most of what was going on. "I have fish to clean, or I would like to go too. Go ahead and go, and I'll watch the kids."

When Paul and Mom drove up to Fran's house, she was waiting on the front porch. After Paul introduced Anna and the pleasantries were over, Paul got right down to business.

"Do you remember the night my father went to your house with a wound on his leg?"

"I sure do. What I'm about to tell you needs to come out for the families of those poor migrant workers. He came over with a lot of bandages he bought on the way over to my house. He made me remove the old rags he had on his leg and clean the wound and bandage it up. The wound wasn't too bad, but I thought he should have gone to the hospital and got some stitches at least. He told me he fell on a pitchfork in the barn. He blamed you for it, but I thought it looked more like a knife wound. I took him at his word that he fell on a pitch fork, but after a couple of months when the police started searching the farm, I started to wonder."

Paul shook his head as Fran continued.

"He never talked about why they were searching his place until one spring about thirteen years later. He started to complain about all the work on the farm, and he was drinking even more than he usually did. After you went into the military, he sold all the hogs, which should have lightened the workload, but he still complained. Then you got home from the military, and you built the house across the road. You helped him as much as you could. He was mad because you got a job in town. Anyway, one night he came over already drunk. He brought more whiskey and insisted that I drink with him. He started to tell me the story about the migrant workers. There were five of them. The man named Carl had two boys working for John, and the other two men were Carl's brothers. It was like he wanted to brag or something. He wasn't sorry for anything he did.

"John told me Carl came in the barn when he was feeding the hogs, and he wanted all the back-pay John owed them, and he wanted it in cash. John said he didn't have any cash on him and he would go to the bank the next week. Carl said, 'I know you have our money, and I want it now.' John said Carl pulled a knife out of his pocket and started cleaning his fingernails. John knew he wanted to use the knife on him, so he reached over and got his pitchfork. He said the man lunged at him and tripped and fell on the pitchfork, but I know, no one would start a fight with only a pocket knife against a man with a pitchfork. John stabbed him in the chest with the pitchfork. He said he had to think fast before the others came back from the fields. He picked up Carl and pushed him over the railing and into the pigsty. He had some very mean hogs, and they began to devour Carl. He didn't want to watch too long, so he went to the porch to wash up at the well.

"The two other men and the two boys came back from the fields, and John told them to wash up at the pump in the front yard. The two boys went in the front yard, but the older men stayed behind and asked John where Carl was. John told them Carl had left in a truck with some men to go work north of there. He said he had paid Carl in full, and they better catch up with him. He told them to pack up their camp. He didn't need them anymore. The two men couldn't believe Carl would leave and not tell them. They walked to their camp and started to pack up their truck and noticed Carl's things hadn't been touched. Carl's brother, Juan, found John on the back porch and asked him what he was trying to pull. He said Carl's things were still at the camp. He asked John where Carl was, and he reached in his pocket and pulled out a knife and flipped it open. John had anticipated trouble, so he had his shotgun leaning on the porch wall. He reached for his shotgun, and he asked Juan if he was going to pack up and leave quietly or cause trouble. John told me Juan reared back to throw the knife, so he shot him in the chest. Juan had thrown the knife, and it hit John on the side of his thigh. That's when he got the wound.

"I don't remember the other man's name, but he heard the gun shot and left the boys by the well. He ran around the house and saw his brother half blown apart. He cradled Juan like a baby and cried. He asked Doyle why he did it. John acted righteous and said Juan had pulled a knife on him. He said he had no choice but to shoot him. When he was telling me this, he was actually smirking and mocking the men."

"Oh, Lord," Paul said.

Frances continued, "The man pleaded with John to call the police. John said they didn't have to bother with

Molly O'Neal

the police. It was clearly self-defense. The man told John he was crazy and then he heard a ruckus in the pigpen. He looked over and saw two hogs fighting over a pair of dark pants. The boys came around to the back of the house and yelled that the pants looked just like their father's.

"John looked at me and said, 'I told those fools that Carl probably fell in with the hogs. I told them I have some real mean hogs, and they're hungry all the time.' John said it. His words, not mine.

"John also said that Carl's brother was stupid and laid Juan down and started bawling like a baby. He screamed at the boys to run, because he knew John was going to kill them. Well, John said the man attacked him, so he had to blow him away. He couldn't have witnesses, so he calmly reloaded and went to the side of the house where the boys were. They saw him and began to run, which started the thrill of the hunt. John said one barrel was for the boy on the left and the other, for the boy on the right. He said they died close to the well in the front yard."

"He was a cold-blooded killer," Mom said.

"Yes, he was," Fran said as she continued. "He went in the house and tore up a sheet to bandage his wound, and he came back out and hobbled over to the boys using a mop as a makeshift crutch. John said it was getting late in the afternoon, and he knew you would be coming back from the fields soon, so he had to get rid of the bodies fast. He pushed the wood cover off the well and pulled the boys over one by one and dropped them in the well. He said he had to get a souvenir from each boy, so before he pushed them in, he took the left shoe from one boy and the right shoe from the other. The well was an easy way to dispose of the bodies. He pushed them in and pulled the well cover back over the hole.

"John had to get rid of the men, but first, he needed two more souvenirs. He took their belts off of them and picked up a rib from each man. He said it was hard to tell which rib was from which guy, but he took two ribs anyway. The men were heavier and harder to handle, so he dragged them, one at a time, to the barn and pushed them over into the pigpen. He was afraid the hogs weren't hungry enough to eat two more men, so he made sure you didn't go into the barn for a couple of days. He cleaned up the bloody mess next to the porch by throwing buckets of water on the grass. He didn't know what to do with their truck, so he hid it in heavy brush by the creek. He knew no one would come looking for the men for at least two weeks or more."

Anna was speechless.

"Why did you stay with him after he confessed to the murders?" Paul asked.

"I tried to break it off with John several times. He threatened me and my family, and I knew he was capable of anything. I was actually visiting him the day he died. I was in the house cleaning. He was bored, so he said he was going out to work on the combine. I snuck out to see what he was really doing. I was standing by the side of the outbuilding, looking through a window. The big doors were open, and I could see him. The combine was parked a few yards from the building, and he was actually working on it. He turned it on to see how it was running. I was about to go inside, when I watched as a young girl, with long red hair, walked up to him and started talking to him. I couldn't hear them, but I could tell he was yelling at her. He looked really mad. She hit him and ran near the building fairly close to me. I ducked down under the window. I could hear him yelling at her. He called her all kinds of names, and he told her to go home and never come back, or he'd kill her. I peeked through the window again. I had to see what was going on. He pushed the girl to the ground and turned and went back to the combine. She got up and let out a blood curdling scream. She ran at him and push him in the combine. The poor girl couldn't have been more than fourteen. I must have screamed, because she spun around and looked at me. She just stared at me. I ran in the house and got my purse and keys and took off. I never told anyone about the poor girl. She did us all a big favor killing him," Fran said.

"I'll never tell about the girl, but I do have to tell Carl's daughter that I think John killed her father and brothers. Is it all right?" Paul said.

"Yes, he told me the story years after it happened, and if the authorities want to talk to me, I'll tell them I thought it was a drunken lie. Truthfully, until I saw the article in the paper about how they found your mother, I thought he was exaggerating. I would appreciate it if you wouldn't tell them about me at all," Fran said.

"Now we know what evidence to look for and where to look. We can tell the story from what we find and what I remember of that day. We won't bring you into it. Do you happen to know where he would have kept his souvenirs?" Paul said.

"Yes, as a matter of fact, one day I saw him putting something up in the rafters of the back porch near the well. There's a little cubbyhole there," Fran said.

Paul and Mom left Fran's house. Back in the car, they discussed what Paul could tell Rita. They decided he should tell Rita her family should keep searching the pigpen, especially where the pigs were fed in the barn.

"I'm going to get some people out to get whatever is left of the boys out of the well. They'll have to pump it as dry as they can get it. I'll tell Rita I have a hunch the boys are in the well, because my mother was in the cistern. It was an easy way for John to dispose of the bodies. We won't ever mention Frances or the redheaded girl."

"Okay, as long as we're on the same page," Mom said.

"When all of this is over, I'll have dump truck loads of dirt hauled in to fill the dry cistern and the well, so no one can ever use them again. As soon as they're finished searching for any trace of the men, I'm having the house burned down. The Campbells are getting all their hay out of the barn and it will be burned soon after the house. Any remnants of the house will be bulldozed into the basement and covered with dirt. If you see a lot of trucks in the yard this week, it will be the coroner and others getting those poor boys out."

"When will this ever end?" Mom sighed.

❖

BY THE TIME MOLLY GOT UP FOR SCHOOL THE NEXT DAY, the old farm was crawling with people.

"Mom, from my bedroom window I can see a lot of cars and people across the road."

"All those people are looking for the men who worked on the farm," Mom said.

"Are you going over there and watch?"

"No, I think I'll watch from afar."

"I left the binoculars by the window," Molly said.

"Okay, have fun at school," Mom said as everyone filed out the door to catch the bus. Dad was driving a company car now, so Mom had the station wagon to use. Now that she had her driver's license, she felt very independent. She was also doing the hair of three more ladies, and dreaming of making part of the outbuilding into a little beauty shop.

    She didn't have any customers that day, so she went upstairs to look out the window. She could see people standing around the well. She guessed it would take a while to drain it. Mom was intently watching the men in the pigpen, when the phone rang. It startled her, but she recognized her one long ring, so she went downstairs to answer it. Paul called her from the Campbell farm to ask her if she would like to see what *souvenirs* are in the rafters of the porch. She was curious about everything, so she told him she would meet him at the farmhouse in about twenty minutes.

    Mom got ready and drove over. She was amazed at all the people milling about. The Campbells were loading a huge wagon with hay, and men were pumping the well dry. Rita was standing by her husband watching the search being done in the pigpen. Mr. Waters knew the event would make a great story for the paper, so he was there talking to people and taking notes.

    Mom was walking toward the back porch, when Paul came around the side of the house and called to her, "Mrs. O'Neal, I'm glad you're here. This is Sheriff Carlyle, and he's here to start looking for the *souvenirs*."

    Rita and Franklin Jenkins joined them on the porch. The sheriff and Paul were examining the ceiling of the porch and poking at the boards. In the corner, close to the well, a section of the boards was loose. Paul brought a ladder and climbed up and removed four boards. He saw a space that could fit the description of a cubby hole.

    "Does anyone have a flashlight?" Paul asked.

"I do. Just a minute," said the sheriff as he went out to his car.

He brought back a flashlight and handed it to Paul.

"Oh my Lord!" Paul said as he almost fell off the ladder.

"I'll take it from here, Mr. Campbell," Sheriff Carlyle said.

The sheriff went to his car and got some plastic bags and rubber gloves. He put the bags down and climbed the ladder and shined the flashlight in the hole.

He came back down the ladder and said, "I think it would be a good idea if Mrs. O'Neal and Mrs. Jenkins left the area. The articles in the ceiling are pretty gruesome."

"I must see what happened to my father and brothers, Sheriff. I must stay," Rita said as she took her husband's hand.

Mom decided to wait in the car.

"All right, let's remove these things," the sheriff said as he climbed back up the ladder.

"I'll hand you down the items, Mr. Campbell, and put each item in its own bag. Here's the first skull."

Rita gasped.

"The next skull has parts missing."

When he handed down the third skull, Rita said, "That's my father. I recognize his three gold teeth. He had two on the top and one on the bottom. My poor father didn't deserve this!" Franklin took her to the car to sit down.

"There are two more bones up here. I would say they were rib bones."

The sheriff handed the bones down and then the two belts. He handed down a left shoe and a right shoe, which were different styles and sizes. He handed down an iron skillet, two pocket knives, a mitten, a bag of marbles, and a long piece of braided red hair.

Molly O'Neal

"This hair still has the roots connected. This braid was yanked out. Sick. Did your mother have red hair, Mr. Campbell?"

"No, but he killed her with the skillet. I'm sure of it," Paul answered.

The sheriff put the bags in his car. He told Rita's husband the skulls would be released to her as soon as possible for burial.

Mom called to Paul that she was going home and would come back later.

Soon after Mom left, the men working at the well found the skeletal remains of two humans. They collected all the bones and noticed that some of the bones were shattered. The coroner wanted to examine the bones further. He told Rita he would release the bones to her after the investigation was over. Rita was going to take all of the remains back to Texas to be buried with other family members.

By mid-afternoon, Rita's boys and other family members excavated inside the barn and found a large bone under several inches of dirt. The men felt they had found everything they possibly could and the search was over. They were convinced all three adult males were eaten by the hogs.

Mom came back to the farm around three o'clock, and Paul filled her in on all they found. She was especially intrigued by the red braid.

"Didn't Frances say the girl who pushed Doyle into the combine had long red hair?" Mom asked.

"Yes, she did. I wonder who she was, or is."

"I'm glad my girls are in school and didn't have to witness any of this."

When the kids got home from school, they asked Mom what happened at the old farmhouse. She told them John Doyle had indeed murdered the farmhands, and the authorities are taking care of things.

"Is it over, Mom?" Molly asked.

"I'm not sure," Mom answered shrugging her shoulders.

Molly went upstairs and looked out the window with the binoculars and only saw a couple of trucks still parked at the farmhouse.

"Now just burn it down," she said to herself.

❖

After supper, Molly helped Mom and Maggie with the dishes. When the dishes were done, Maggie went upstairs to read, and Molly went up to look out the window at the haunted house again. She suddenly had a gnawing feeling and went downstairs and found Mom in the living room and said, "Mom, we have to go to the old house on Bellum Street. I have an awful feeling. We have to go get Chester."

"Well, hon, are you sure?'

"Yes, Mom, we have to hurry and go now. Mary has to go too."

"Did you say something about Chester?" Mary asked as she came in the living room.

"Yes, we have to go get him," Molly answered.

"Can we take him?" Mary asked.

"Yes, we probably always could have, but we thought we had to leave him with his grave. I say we can get him now. He needs us," Molly said confidently.

"Let's go, Mom," Mary said.

"Okay, get in the car."

"Wait, do I want to go?" Maggie asked.

"We're going to get Chester," Molly said.

"This could be interesting. I'll go."

They drove to town, and Mom parked in front of the house they used to live in on Bellum Street. A *For Sale* sign was in the front yard of the house with a smaller *Sold* sign next to it. The old man who lived next door and his wife were sitting on their front porch. As soon as Mom parked the car, Molly jumped out and ran to the backyard. Mary wasn't far behind. Molly ran to the dog pen and called Chester's name. At first, she didn't hear anything. She called him again, and she heard whimpering coming from the doghouse. Molly knelt on the ground and looked in the doghouse, and Chester bounded out into her arms and started licking her face. Mary was next to Molly by then, and Chester jumped over to Mary. He jumped and barked with happiness.

"Come on, Chester. We're going home," Molly said as she picked him up.

While the girls were in the backyard, the old man who lived next door saw Mom waiting by the car. He came over to her and said, "Mrs. O'Neal, we haven't seen you around here for a long time."

"It's been a couple of years," Maggie said as she got out and stood by Mom.

"Yes, it has been a long time," Mom said.

"It's funny. Bridget was the only child who ever had a dog in this house. Remember the little girl who had polio?"

"I remember you telling me about her," Mom said.

"It's funny you should show up tonight. The house has been sold, as you can see by the sign. The new family moving in has a big dog. I talked to them yesterday. They said their dog will be in the pen during the day while they're at work and their children are in school. They told me they're bringing a bigger doghouse. Anyway, they're moving in tomorrow, so it's a good thing you showed up tonight," the old man said as if he knew why they were there.

The girls ran to the car and Molly was visibly holding something. Molly and Mary were laughing and talking as they got in the back seat of the station wagon.

"Well, bye, ladies," said the old man as he went back up to his porch.

"Nice seeing you again, bye," Mom said as she got in the car.

"I can't see anything," Maggie said.

"Chester's here with us," Mary said.

As they drove away, Molly saw the neighbor and his wife waving, and she read their lips. They were saying, "Bye, Chester."

Molly and Mary introduced Chester to his new home. He would sleep in the girls' bedroom and wait for them to come home from school anywhere he liked. He was welcome. His new home was with the girls, where ever they lived.

Chapter Seventeen

The next day, as the O'Neals waited for the bus, they saw a big truck, pulling a trailer, turn down the lane to the old farmhouse. Molly hoped they were going to burn the house down. Soon the bus came, right on schedule. They got on and sat in their regular seats. After a few minutes they came to Becky's stop. She got on the bus and sat by Molly.

"Guess what? Johnny's back. I heard my mother talking about it. His mother wants to talk to my mom and your mom about something. I don't know what. My mom stopped talking when she realized I was listening."

"I wonder what she wants to talk to my mom about," Molly said.

Johnny and Cathy got on the bus along with the Sherman twins. Poor Johnny was limping and had a big bruise on his cheek. He was wearing the same awful overalls, but this time he had on a large dress shirt under his overalls. He had on the same scuffed shoes, which were too large for him, and no socks. He and Cathy sat in the front seat. He seemed very sad. Molly felt bad, because she didn't have an extra sandwich for him. The children on the bus were very quiet that morning.

❖

Joyce Campbell had called Anna and told her Mrs. Lambert wanted to talk to both of them. Joyce said she would pick her up as soon as possible. She was ready to go by the time Joyce pulled in the driveway. Anna got in Joyce's car and drove over to Johnny's mother's house. *Keep Out* signs were on some fence posts and on some of the trees as they drove into Lambert's farmyard. Johnny's mother, Mrs. Sadie Lambert, was the matriarch of the family. She lived in a small white two-story house. Some other family members lived in two other houses, which were basically outbuildings, and one other small pink round trailer. They had two big barns and a lot of expensive farm equipment.

"Sadie Lambert has a fairly large farm. She keeps family around to do the farming for her. Her husband was gored by a bull and died about three years ago," Joyce said.

As they parked, they saw a woman, wearing a robe, standing at the open door of the little pink trailer. A big man pushed by her and stood outside the trailer and stared at them. Mom felt uneasy and had a bad feeling about those two.

They knocked on the door and Sadie answered. They went in, and Joyce introduced Anna to Sadie. She offered them coffee and told them to sit at the kitchen table.

"I asked you two here because I think we may be having some problems. My Sarah is back from New Mexico, and she brought her awful friend she calls, Clive. She's trouble, and I can tell he is probably even more trouble. Joyce, I know you're more familiar with the situation than Mrs. O'Neal."

"Please call me, Anna."

"Okay, Anna. Did Joyce tell you anything about my, Sarah?"

"No, she hasn't told me anything."

"Well, I had Johnny when Sarah was fourteen. Sarah always carried him around like he was her doll or something. I think she thought she was his mother. She always told me I was too old to have a baby. I was only forty-five. I'm not too old to raise him. I do have to admit though, that I have a hard time running the farm ever since my husband was killed."

"That was a sad time," Joyce said.

"Sarah has always been strange about Johnny. She's taken him before, and she brings him back in a week or two. She stole him from me when she took him to New Mexico a couple of weeks ago. Now she's back, and she brought that awful man with her. I think Clive was the one who beat up my poor Johnny. I hope and pray she wasn't the one who put all those bruises on my poor boy. I keep telling her Johnny is her brother, not her son, and she has to stop taking him, or I'll call the police. Well, she just laughs and says he can stay with me. She says it like she is giving me permission to take care of my own son. She's going to stay in the trailer as long as she likes. She makes Clive sleep in the barn. I'm afraid of her, and there's something about Clive that seems so evil. I can't put my finger on it."

"Maybe you should tell Anna about the odd things Sarah used to do as a child," Joyce suggested.

"That might help paint a picture," Sadie said. "Sarah has always been fascinated with witchcraft. It all started when she was about six or seven. I hate to say it, but my own mother encouraged her. As she got older, she would check out all the books she could find on witchcraft and spells and things from the library. She would never return them. I had to search for the books and try to return them. The library refused to lend her any more books, so she started to steal them. She hid them in the barn and in the crawl space of the house.

"The way the road turns, our land actually butts up to the back of the Campbell property. She used to walk over to the Campbell's waterfall in the woods, and read her books and God only knows what else. She refused to go to church after she turned eight years old and made fun of us for going. She had a favorite cat, but hated all the other animals. One day she actually hung her brother's puppy."

Anna was starting to put things together with what Sadie was saying and Molly's nightmares about the witch named Sarah. She started feeling uncomfortable.

Sadie continued, "I thought Sarah was becoming deranged, because she kept talking about fairies at the waterfall. She said they didn't like her to come around their home. They said she was intruding. My husband and her older brother thought she had lost her mind. She was such a beautiful girl. Here I'm talking about her like she's dead, and she's right outside there."

"It's hard when it's your daughter," Joyce said.

"My husband was embarrassed by her when he found out she had been seen and heard running through the woods screaming like a banshee. She was only twelve at the time. We sent Sarah away to live with my husband's sister in Chicago, but she sent her back in about six months. His sister said she was too mean and wild. We hated to send her to school, because the teacher and principal said she cursed all the time and tried to put spells on other children.

"She had beautiful long red hair, and one morning when she was fourteen, she came in for breakfast, and she had a bald spot where she usually wore a long braid in her hair. I asked her about it, and she just laughed it off."

"Oh no, this can't be. She's the Sarah from Molly's dreams! And the braid!" Anna cried.

"Paul told me they found a long braid of red hair among John Doyle's things. I thought you should know, Sadie," Joyce said sadly.

"I don't trust her. She scares me, and her boyfriend is horrible. There is something really wrong here. I might send Johnny to live with my mother in town until Sarah goes back to New Mexico. Sarah wouldn't dare try to take Johnny from her," Sadie said.

"We should go now, Joyce. I have to go home and call my mother. I really have to talk to her about this," Anna said as she stood up to leave.

❖

Mom called Grandma as soon as she got home. Grandma said she had been calling for the last hour and was getting worried. Grandma said she had a horrible dream and needed to come over as soon as possible. She said Julie was picking her up the next day, and they would be there by one o'clock.

Mom was very nervous about what Sadie told her and wondered about Grandma's dream. She had to calm herself down, because she had an appointment to cut, color, and set a client's hair. The lady coming over was Mrs. Jacobson from the farm down by the two bridges. Mom heard Mrs. Jacobson was a talker, so she kept the conversation light.

While Mrs. Jacobson was under the dryer, Mrs. Leslie Campbell came over. She was Joyce Campbell's sister-in-law and lived at one of the farms across the road from the big Campbell farm.

"We don't know how you can take all the suspense. Joyce has been keeping me informed of all the awful things that have been coming to light across the road," Leslie said. "I washed my hair at home. I just need a trim and a set today, Anna."

"I'm very nervous about what they found over there. I can't wait until the place is burned down," Mom said.

"I can't hear you too well under here, but I thought you said they're going to burn the place down. Do you know when?" Mrs. Jacobson asked.

"The men over there today are salvaging all they can from the barn, and I'm pretty sure tomorrow the house is going to be burned down. Paul is filling in the cistern and the well today. It's a shame it was a nice dry barn," Leslie said.

"That is too bad," said Mrs. Jacobson.

When Leslie was ready for the hair dryer, Mrs. Jacobson was ready for her comb out. Mom enjoyed talking to the ladies. It got her mind off her worries. It was a little awkward doing the ladies' hair in the dining room, but Mom had plans. She was planning on turning part of the outbuilding into a small beauty shop when things calmed down.

Later that afternoon, the kids got off the bus and ran in the house. Molly noticed that Chester didn't greet her at the door.

"Mom, where's Chester?"

"You know I can't see him."

Molly heard some whimpering behind the couch. She looked back there and saw Chester all curled up in a ball.

"Come here you silly dog," Molly said. He came to Molly, and she picked him up. "Mary, do you think he looks okay?"

Molly O'Neal   259

'He looks a little scared."

Mom heard the conversation and it just added to her worries.

"Grandma is coming tomorrow to stay for a few days," Mom said. "I wonder if it has anything to do with the full moon this weekend."

"I've been having dreams about being outside at night and looking up and seeing a full moon," Mary said.

"Do your homework girls," Mom said nervously.

Chester never left Molly's side the rest of the evening.

❖

When Molly got up the next morning, she noticed almost the entire old barn was taken apart. All that was left was a pile of boards no one wanted. As she rode by in the school bus, she watched a firetruck driving down the lane. She was sure the old farmhouse was finally going to be burned down.

She brought a lunch bag with a peanut butter and jelly sandwich and three cents for Johnny. She had it on the seat next to her until Becky got on the bus and then she put it on her lap.

❖

That afternoon, Grandma, Grandpa, and Aunt Julie finally came over. Mom couldn't wait to hear what Grandma had to say.

"Anna, I have been having awful dreams. They have been about a witch named Sarah. Molly had a bad dream about Sarah when she was at my house this summer. In my dream, I'm watching Sarah walking through some woods. She is calling the fairies to come out and play. She is very pretty, but she is also very ugly when she shows her true colors. She is evil. Somehow Molly's involved, but I don't know how yet. The urgent problem is the full moon this weekend. I have had several dreams of your home and the surrounding farms being stalked by a large wolf-like creature. I have a book here about werewolves."

"It's in Slovak, Mom," Anna said.

"Actually, it's Magyar. We lived close to the Hungarian border when I was growing up, so we could understand them perfectly. You can just skim the book."

"You think there'll be a werewolf in the area this weekend because of the full moon?" Anna asked.

"Yes, I do. It fits with my dreams. We have to warn your neighbors to bring in their dogs and take precautions this Saturday, Sunday, and Monday. We may have things under control by Monday. I'm hoping, but I can't be sure," Grandma said looking very worried.

"I'm scared," Anna said.

"Dad can stay at my house tonight, and I'll bring him back tomorrow, Mom," Julie said.

"That's good. Bring the rollaway bed with you tomorrow. We'll need it. Tonight, I'll sleep on Anna's couch. Right now, I'm very anxious to do an extreme house cleansing and blessing. I'll also do the out buildings and walk around the whole yard. I wish Molly and Mary were home. I could use their help," Grandma said.

"While Mom does the cleansing, I think we should go to the grocery store and stock up on food. We don't want anyone to have to go out after dark this weekend," Julie said.

When they got back from the grocery store, Julie and Grandpa left. Aunt Julie had to pick her son up from school.

Molly O'Neal 261

❖

Grandma had finished blessing the house and perimeter, just as the school bus dropped off the O'Neal children.

When Molly got off the bus, she heard tiny voices saying, "Help us, Molly."

"Do you hear the voices, Mary?"

"No, I don't, but look in the field across the road. Can you see all those glittering little lights? They look like fairies or something."

"I see them. They're going back to the woods. I wonder if those are the fairies Lucy saw," Molly said as she felt the beryl stone on the necklace Lucy gave her.

Chester met them on the driveway, and they went inside.

Molly was very happy to see Grandma. She ran up and gave her a big hug. She told Grandma and Mom what happened on the bus.

"Mom, a scary looking lady got on the bus with Johnny today. Pete, the driver, asked her if he could help her, and she told him she wanted to make sure her brother was safe on the bus. She said she had heard some little girl was giving him dirt in a bag and making fun of his clothes. She handed Johnny his lunch bag, and she looked at Mary and then at me. Her eyes seemed to flash, and she said to Johnny, 'Here, don't forget your bologna sandwich and milk money.' She walked back to my seat and practically sat on me. Becky and I scooted over as far as we could. She stared in my eyes like if she was trying to figure me out or something. She asked me what was in the bag I had on my lap, and I told her it was my lunch. I hurried and shoved it in my satchel. She handed me a lunch bag and told me it was a little dessert she cooked up for me since I'd been so generous to Johnny. She whispered, 'Enjoy it, honey.' Then she got up and walked off the bus. I looked out the window with Becky, and we saw a really mean looking man wearing black leather clothes standing by an old rusty ambulance. Cathy shut the door of the bus, and Pete took off. Seconds later Becky screamed and yelled that the bag was moving. Pete stopped the bus and came back and took the bag from me. He opened the bag, and a giant beetle with huge pinchers crawled out!"

Molly was too excited to finish the story. She sat down at the table, and Maggie finished her story.

"Pete actually yelled and dropped the bag on the floor. The beetle hung on his tie for a second until he knocked it off. We couldn't see too well, because all the kids were standing up watching. I did see him stomp on the floor and open the bus door and kicked it and the bag out. It was creepy, and the woman was creepy too. Christy told me it was Sarah Lambert. She said Sarah thinks she's a witch, and the spooky thing they drove up in looked like a hearse," Maggie said.

"I thought it was an ambulance," Molly said.

"There wasn't a light on the top of it, and it was black, so I thought it was a hearse," Maggie said.

"She wants trouble," Grandma said. "She's going to get it."

"I can't believe she had the nerve to give you a creature. I have a lot to tell you girls about Sarah. We'll all talk about it, as a family, this evening," Mom said.

※

AFTER SUPPER, MAGGIE AND MOLLY CLEARED THE TABLE and everyone stayed seated for a family meeting. Mom told everyone about Sarah. She told them Sarah was a witch, and she threatened Molly. Grandma talked to everyone about her dreams and how they match up with this weekend and had something to do with Sarah and her friend. They realized Grandma, Molly, and Mary, for that matter, knew what they were talking about, and they should take the warning seriously.

"Do you think it would be a good idea for me to go over to Sam's house tonight? We were planning to go to the movies," Adam said.

"Would it be too terrible if you stayed home this weekend? I would be so worried every minute you were gone," Mom said.

As they were discussing the matter, the phone rang one long ring. Adam answered the phone thinking it could be Sam.

"Hello. Is Molly there?" a woman asked.

"It's for Molly. It's some woman, Mom," Adam said.

"Give me the phone. Hello, who is this?" Mom asked.

"It's me. I wanted to know if Molly liked her dessert."

Mom was visibly shaken as she hung up the phone. "It was Sarah. She asked me if Molly enjoyed her dessert."

"I'll stay home tonight," Adam said. "What's on TV?"

Everything was quiet the rest of the night. Grandma assured everyone her *blessing* on the house was sufficient to keep them safe.

❖

SATURDAY MORNING STARTED WITH A BIG, HEARTY breakfast. Everyone was pretty quiet and seemed a bit worried.

"Do what you normally would do today, but don't leave the yard," Grandma said.

"I was supposed to work at the Campbell's today," Nathan said.

"Me too," Adam said.

Grandma tried to explain her concern. "Let me show you what I'm talking about. This is a chart showing the phases of the moon. Today the moon is at 99 percent. A werewolf can turn at that percent and it doesn't have to necessarily be dark. Tomorrow the full moon will be at 100 percent, and Monday back at 99 percent. I don't think we should risk you being killed. The Campbells will have to do without you two this weekend."

"I want you boys to use the day to clean up the shed. Sweep and then wash the floor. Wash the windows, and clean out the sink and cabinets. Bring your radio in there. It'll help time pass, and all this will be a big help to me," Mom said.

The boys did as Mom asked and were busy all day.

❖

AFTER SUPPER EVERYONE IN THE HOUSE WAS ON EDGE. As they were discussing the matter, someone knocked at the kitchen door. Everyone at the table just looked at each other. Dad got up and answered the door. It was Paul and Henry Campbell, along with Henry's son Harris, who is Becky and Christy's father. Henry brought his other two sons, Beau and Chad, who have farms across the road. Some of their sons were standing out by their trucks. Dad introduced everyone to Grandma.

"Becky and Christy told us what happened on the bus. We know all about Sarah Lambert, and we came over to tell you we are here to support your family," Henry said very sincerely.

"Thank you," Charles said looking very worried.

"I think Sarah is the cause of all of this, but I think the

man she brought back from New Mexico is big trouble. What kind of message is he trying to send driving a hearse?" Henry said.

Mary ran down the stairs, "Has anyone seen Molly?" she asked.

"Everyone, start looking for Molly!" Mom said in a panic. "Did she say anything to you?"

"She did say she heard voices calling for help when she got off the bus, and I saw fairies in the field across the road," Mary whispered to Mom and Grandma, "And Chester is gone."

"Oh my God, help us! Where could she be?" cried Grandma.

"In one of her dreams, she saw a waterfall," Mary said.

"It could be the waterfall we went to with Lucy," Nathan said. "Lucy was looking for fairies there."

Earlier when Dad answered the door, Molly had gone upstairs to get Chester. She couldn't find him, so she went outside and looked around the yard. She saw Maggie hiding behind the shed reading a book.

"What are you doing out here?" Molly asked.

"What does it look like I'm doing," Maggie smirked back.

"Aren't you afraid to be out here?"

"I'm in the yard. I need some peace and quiet."

"I'm looking for Chester."

"Haven't ever seen him," Maggie smirked.

Molly ran around to the front of the shed. Chester barked at her as he stood by her bike. He turned and ran down the driveway and across the road to the old farmhouse lane. She got on her bike and rode after him. She peddled down the rocky lane. She saw him run onto the field road. He had sparkling swirls around him. She heard a voice say, "Molly go to the waterfall. Only you can save us."

Her peddling was suddenly easier, and the ground was smoother. She looked down and saw fairies sparkling around the wheels and peddles of the bike. She was going very fast down the field road. When she came to the break in the corn, Molly jumped off her bike and ran through the cornfield and into the dark woods. She yelled for Chester, but he kept running. She ran through the woods with fairies swirling around her. She was getting close to the waterfall.

❖

BACK HOME, MOM TOSSED DAD THE KEYS TO THE CAR and said. "Hurry, drive us to the waterfall. Nathan will show us the way." They all ran for the car.

"We'll go too," said Henry. Paul and all the Campbells and Adam loaded in the trucks and took off.

They all drove down the field roads until they saw Molly's bike. Dad couldn't drive through the cornfield with the station wagon, so Henry told Mom, Grandma, and Mary to get in the cab of the truck. Dad and Nathan jumped in the back, and Henry drove through the cornfield. Henry's sons took their trucks right through the cornfield behind him. Nathan, Adam, and the younger men, jumped out of the trucks and ran into the woods.

❖

MOLLY GOT TO THE WATERFALL, AND IT SEEMED LIKE hundreds of fairies were flying around. One fairy flew up to Molly's face and said, "She is trying to control us and steal our power."

Molly O'Neal

"This is like my dream!" Molly cried.

"Only you can help, follow me."

With Chester by her side, she followed the fairy over to a large stone near the waterfall. The fairy flew behind the waterfall and came back with a tiny glowing ring. She placed it on the stone.

"That's mine!" screamed Sarah as she came from behind a tree. She was wearing a black cloak. She took the cloak off and let it drop to the ground. Her golden dress glowed as she walked toward them.

"That's Sarah! Molly, hurry take the ring and put it on!" said the fairy.

"No, it's mine!" screamed Sarah. "I've waited all these years for the ring!"

As Molly reached for the ring, Sarah spun her around, and Chester started barking.

"The ring is mine!" Sarah said as the fairies began to encircle her. She lifted an iron rod into the air and swiped at the fairies, and the fairies backed away. Sarah laughed and glared at Molly. She raised the rod again, but this time to kill Molly. Molly could hear the boys calling her. Nathan and the others came running near the waterfall. Some fairies flew over to them and froze them in place, so they wouldn't get involved. They couldn't move, but they could watch what was going on.

Sarah looked toward the path, and when she was distracted, dozens of fairies totally encased her arm holding the iron rod.

"Get the ring, and put it on, Molly!" the fairies were screaming.

Molly grabbed the ring and put it on, just as Sarah was lowering the rod onto her head. Molly jerked the rod out of Sarah's hand and flung it to the side. Molly was surprised, because the rod twirled through the woods until it disappeared.

Sarah came at her, with her hands going for Molly's throat, and Molly yelled, "NO!" Sarah flew backwards several feet.

"I'll banish your dog to hell," Sarah screamed. She came at Molly again screaming, "Give it to me!"

She reached down for Chester, and Molly yelled, "NO! He's mine and so is the ring." Sarah flew backwards again but this time far into the woods. She got up and ran for the Lambert farm.

When Sarah was gone, the boys watched Molly talking to someone they couldn't see.

"Molly, you don't need the beryl stone to see us. You never did. Sarah has been trying to control us ever since she was a little girl. The ring has great power, but not for evil. Since you're so young, put the ring on this gold chain, and wear it close to your heart always. Never take it off. When you get older, you can wear it on your finger. If we need you again, the ring will glow. If you need us, touch the ring and call my name, Euphemia. Sarah will always be after the ring, as long as she's alive. Your grandmother and sister are almost here. We have to hide now. Never take it off. Take care of your friends and family during the full moon. He is very strong and almost indestructible."

"Who is he?" Molly asked.

"The one they call, Clive," Euphemia said as she disappeared.

As soon as the fairies hid, the boys were free and all the others made it to the waterfall.

"Molly and Chester!" Mary screamed. "You're all right!"

"The woman from the bus tried to kill Molly with a big iron rod, but Molly kicked her butt!" Nathan yelled.

"She flew backwards!" Sam said.

"She came at Molly again, and Molly must have hit her again, because Sarah flew backwards and ran home!" Adam said.

"I'm never messing with, Molly," Nathan said.

"Yeah, don't make her mad," Adam said as all the guys patted her on the back.

"That's my girl," said Dad.

Molly was still pretty stunned. She ran up to Mom and hugged her. "She tried to kill me, Mom. The fairies saved me."

"Next time bring me," Mary said as she took Molly's hand.

They all started walking back to the trucks.

"Listen," Grandma said as she stopped for a second. "We must hurry. Sarah has made it home. Listen to the horrible howling. It has to be Clive."

"We've got shotguns in the trucks," said Henry.

"We have to get back home quickly. Clive is mad, and I'm sure Sarah's not finished with us," Grandma said.

Molly picked up Chester and was carrying him out, when Mary said, "I'll carry Chester for you, Molly."

"That's okay. He's not heavy."

"Who's Chester?" Paul Campbell asked.

Mary looked at Mom. Mom raised her eyebrows and nodded her *you know what to say look*.

"Chester is our imaginary dog, Mr. Campbell," Mary said.

"Oh, that's nice," he said.

It was a long walk out of the woods. When they got to their trucks, everybody got in the truck beds except Grandma and Mom. They rode in the cab with Henry. He dropped them off at the station wagon.

"Look, Dad," Nathan said. "What happened to the car?" The front right fender had huge deep scratch marks about two feet long.

"It was Clive. Get in the car, and let's go home," Grandma said.

The Campbell men came back to the O'Neal's to bring Adam home and make sure everything was all right. Before they left to go home, Grandma gave them all warnings.

"Everyone, stay home tonight, and take care of your families. Bring in your dogs and cats if you can find them. Don't let your children out of your sight."

Julie and Grandpa were waiting by the back door. Uncle David and Chris were in the house.

"We were so worried. It's getting dark," Julie said.

"Oh, Julie," Grandma said as she gave her a big hug. She hugged Grandpa and said, "We had a big scare this evening, but everything is better now."

"You missed it. Molly had a fight with a witch in the woods," Nathan told Aunt Julie.

"What?"

"I can't tell you about it now. You really must go. It's getting dark. Oh, did you bring the camera I asked for? We need all the cameras we can get our hands on," Grandma said.

"Yes, it's inside."

"I'll find it. Goodbye," Grandma said as she kissed Julie on the cheek. Uncle David and Chris came out of the house, and Julie told them they had to go, so they got in the car left.

As they were turning on to County Road, a blood curdling howl could be heard from the woods across the fields.

"Make sure all the outside lights are on," Grandma told Dad."

"Maggie's upstairs. She's mad at you guys for leaving her," Grandpa said.

Molly O'Neal

"Oh my gosh, we forgot Maggie in all the excitement. Where was she anyway?" Mom said as she ran up the stairs. Maggie was laying on her bed reading.

"You guys left me. I was reading in back of the shed, and the ugly guy who was at the bus stop with Sarah, walked up to me and asked me if I was Molly. I told him no, and I got up and ran to the house, and no one was there. I locked the back door and looked out the window. He was standing in the field by the shed. I saw him throwing clods of dirt at some kind of invisible wall. He charged it at one point, but it was like he hit glass he couldn't break. I knew it had to be Grandma's shield, so I felt better. Then Uncle David drove up, and I unlocked the door for them."

"Phew, that was a close call. Come downstairs and join the family," Mom said.

Downstairs, the phone was ringing. Nathan answered and yelled, "She kicked your butt! No, you can't talk to her!" Mom ran over and hung up the phone.

"This is not good," Grandma said.

Molly asked Grandma to come in the living room. She showed her the ring on the gold chain around her neck and whispered, "A fairy named Euphemia gave this to me. This is what saved my life. She told me to never take it off. It fits my pinky finger, but she told me to wear it on this gold necklace. Sarah wanted it."

"Oh, Molly, this ring is precious. You have a wonderful gift. It will grow as you grow. Do exactly what the fairy said," Grandma whispered. "Now, hide it in your shirt."

Dad and the boys were locking all the windows and doors and closing all the curtains. Grandpa got out a deck of cards and started playing solitaire.

"Turn on the television, Anna," Dad said. "Let's carry on as normally as possible."

"Good idea."

Mary and Molly got in the same bed and started reading comic books.

"Can I get in with you guys tonight? I don't want to be by myself." Maggie asked her sisters.

"Yes," Mary said. "Let's push the beds together."

Mom heard the noise upstairs, so she and Grandma went up to the girls' room to see what was going on. Grandma saw that all three girls wanted to sleep in the same room, so she called downstairs, "Can a couple of you big strong men bring up the rollaway bed and, Stefan, come here."

Adam and Dad brought up the rollaway, and Grandma told them to put it up in Maggie's room for her. She told Grandpa he'll be able to sleep on Maggie's bed. In Molly and Mary's room, the two beds pushed together made the girls feel safe.

"I don't know if we're going to get any sleep tonight, but this works out fine," Grandpa said.

The girls stayed upstairs reading and talking.

"Don't worry. Chester is watching out for us. He'll bark if there's anything outside," Molly told her sisters.

Grandma and Mom came upstairs after an hour or so and told the girls to say their prayers. Grandma said a prayer over the girls and then she and Mom went downstairs to keep watch with the rest of the family. All the lights were on in the out building, and the big light on the driveway was on. The lights by the back door and the one next to the front door were on. The full moon was bright and the sky was clear. Anyone or anything lurking around the yard would be seen. About eleven o'clock, Mom and Grandpa took watch while the boys went to bed. Dad fell asleep in a chair, and Grandma laid down on the couch for a nap.

Around two o'clock in the morning, the phone rang. Mom was sitting at the kitchen table with Grandpa playing cards. The ringing startled everyone. Dad woke up and ran for the phone.

It was Harris Campbell and he said, "Something awful has happened to our sheep."

"Tell them not to go outside, Charles," Grandma said very seriously.

"Don't go outside. Joanna is sure it's not safe. You don't want to get killed," Charles said as he handed the phone to Mom and went over and opened a window.

He could hear sheep screaming in the distance.

"Hey, what's going on? This is Stan Charlin. We're on your party line, and when the phone rings at two o'clock we answer too. Anyone need help over there?"

"Stan, don't go outside. If you can, bring in your dogs, shut and lock all your windows, turn on all the outside lights, and tell your neighbors to do the same. If you see anything suspicious, call the police," said Harris. "Call me tomorrow, and I'll fill you in. We called the police, and they should be here soon. I wanted to warn you. I have to go now," Harris said as he hung up.

The phone rang again about an hour later. This time Grandma answered the phone.

"Hello, Sarah," Grandma said very calmly.

"Who are you?"

"I know all about the werewolf, Sarah. I know he killed some sheep tonight. Do you think you may be next, Sarah?"

"Me, oh no," she laughed. "Maybe everyone in your house will be dead by morning. He likes to hide in closets or behind shower curtains. Have you checked on Molly lately? You know second story windows won't stop him, or me."

Grandma motioned for Grandpa to check upstairs. She handed him his rifle to take with him.

"Sarah, I think a storm has just moved in." Grandma began to speak in Slovak. Sarah started screaming so loudly everyone in the room could hear her through the phone.

Grandpa went upstairs and everyone was fine and awake. The girls and Mom were looking out the bedroom window.

"Grandpa, look, there's something in the field running our way," Molly said.

"Heads up downstairs, something is running toward the front of the house!" Grandpa shouted.

Grandma came upstairs and said to Molly, "Hold the ring, honey, and think clouds and heavy rain. Mary, come here and hold our hands. Think lightning to strike the creature."

As they followed Grandma's orders, a loud lightning bolt hit near the road. Mom and Maggie and the boys screamed.

"Boys, come here and put a hand on Molly's shoulder," Grandma told them. "We're safe in the house. The storm will weaken him."

They were looking out the window when lightning flashed, and they could see the creature lying in the field right across the road. In another flash they could see a hooded person standing over it.

"Mom, I think Sarah's out there with the werewolf," Molly said.

"Get away from the window!" Mom yelled.

"They ducked just as a ball of lightning exploded about twenty feet from the window. It was not able to penetrate the shield Grandma had placed on the house and yard.

Molly O'Neal

"I'm going downstairs with Dad," Adam said.

"Me too," Nathan said. "I would rather hide in a closet, but I guess I'll go downstairs."

"You're safe with us," Grandma said to Nathan and then she whispered to Molly, "Especially with you, Molly, and the fairies' ring."

Dad and Grandpa were standing guard downstairs with rifles. Dad didn't know Grandpa's rifle had silver bullets in it.

"Is everything all right, Anna?" Dad yelled.

"Yes, Charles," Mom said as she and Grandma looked out the window. Grandma closed her eyes for three seconds and a long lightning flash lit up the field and showed them that Sarah and the wolf were gone.

"Everyone can go to sleep now. They're licking their wounds, but they'll be back tomorrow night. I'm sure of it," Grandma said.

Grandma reassured Dad and Grandpa that it was safe to sleep now.

Chapter Eighteen

About eight o'clock the next morning, the phone started ringing. First it was Aunt Julie and then Aunt Veronica. Grandma assured everyone the problem was being taken care of, and she would tell them the whole story when it was over.

Henry Campbell called to check in. "As far as we can tell, we lost two sheep last night to whatever it was. We should meet up and talk about this," Henry said.

"You should really talk to Joanna and Stefan. They seem to know how to handle the situation," Dad said.

"We'll come over to your house about one o'clock, if it's all right with you."

"Can you make it two o'clock? They're going to late church, so lunch will be a little later today," Dad said.

Everyone was tired that morning, but Mom and Grandma would never miss a Sunday Mass.

"Are you sure you don't want to go to church, Charles, especially after last night?" Mom asked.

"No, I'll keep watch here. I have my rifle if I need it."

"Use mine if you need to," Grandpa said. "It has silver bullets in it."

Adam drove Nathan in his old car, and Mom drove Grandma and Grandpa and the girls. Grandma tried to keep the conversation light on the way to church. Mom pulled up and parked next to Adam in the parking lot. They all got out of their cars and as they were walking toward the church, they were approached by Sarah and her friend. She walked right up to Grandma, and her boyfriend stayed back a few feet and stared at Molly.

"I didn't know you could go to Mass, Sarah," Grandma said very calmly as she held Molly and Mary's hands.

"I'm not here to go to church. This isn't my kind of church," Sarah smirked. "Hmm, looks like everyone is here. Oh, except Molly's daddy. Home alone huh?"

"He's well-armed and you know the house is protected. Did you like the storm last night? Are those burns I see on Clive? He should probably go to a doctor or better yet a veterinarian," Grandma mused.

"I even think that's funny. You're quite witty, aren't you, Granny?" Sarah said smiling. "They can't cure what's wrong with him, unless they give lobotomies." Sarah turned to Molly and said, "Sweet little, Molly. Where's my ring?" As Sarah spoke, she stared into Molly's eyes. Molly and Mary stared back at Sarah. "Such pretty little yellow-eyed girls," Sarah sneered.

"You can't put a spell on those girls, Sarah," Grandma said smiling.

Sarah gave Grandma a dirty look and turned back to Molly and said, "You're not very bright, are you? Kinda like my friend Clive here. I don't see you wearing your ring, Molly."

"I would appreciate it if you wouldn't speak to my children," Mom said sternly.

"Listen to the mother hen. Bak bak baak," Sarah said as she bent her arms and flapped them like chicken wings. She turned to Clive and said, "Don't you get a kick out of her, Clive? Speak, Clive, speak," Sarah said mockingly.

"Uh, yeah, Sarah, anything you say," Clive mumbled.

"Anyway, isn't Becky Campbell your little friend? There's no "blessing" on her house. Who you kidding old lady with that *blessing* stuff? I'm surprised you three can even walk in the door of any church and not get struck by lightning."

Molly touched the ring through her dress.

"That's where the ring is!" Sarah said laughing. Sarah suddenly began to choke.

"Apologize," Molly said calmly.

Sarah's boyfriend began to laugh as Sarah choked. Soon his laughter changed to screams as his burns from the night before began to sizzle and smoke. He screamed, and Sarah managed to hoarsely whisper an, "I'm sorry."

"Thank you, Molly," Grandma said.

The choking and the burning stopped. Sarah and Clive ran to their hearse and drove away.

"I'm going to have to do a blessing at Becky's house later today. Let's go. Mass is about to begin."

Adam and Nathan were stunned. "Yeah, run away. You're the chickens," said Nathan. Adam remained very quiet.

They all walked in and dipped their fingers in the holy water and made the sign of the cross. There was no lightning strike.

※

AFTER LUNCH, PAUL WAS THE FIRST CAMPBELL TO SHOW up. Grandma met him at the door and invited him in and told him to sit at the table. She wanted to talk to him before the other Campbells got there.

"I know we can talk to you about Sarah and Clive."

"Do you think she and her friend killed the two sheep?" Paul asked.

"Yes, I do," Grandma answered.

"Harris counted the sheep this morning, and they're missing two. They only found one, and it was torn to shreds, and they found its head on the back-porch stairs," Paul said.

Molly came into the kitchen and said, "He ate the other sheep in the field across the road."

"Before the others come, is there anything I should know about this guy?"

"I have no doubt Sarah is a witch, and she seems to be fairly powerful. Clive, on the other hand, is a werewolf and extremely dangerous, and Sarah controls him."

"If it were anyone else telling me this, I wouldn't believe them, but I know I can trust you and Molly," Paul said.

"And Mom and Mary," Molly chimed in.

"Yes, those two also," Paul said. "What can we do to get rid of her and Clive?"

"Ideally, kill him, but since the police would never believe it was self-defense, we have to get them to go back to New Mexico and never come back. There's nothing to keep Sarah here. I don't think she cares about her mother or brother at all," Grandma said.

"Her mother wouldn't want her if she knew what she did," Mary said.

"What do you mean, Mary?" Grandma asked.

Mary looked at Molly and took her hand and said, "Sarah told Johnny to go in the bull pen. Johnny was only about seven. She told him to go in and pet the bull. He said he didn't want to, and his papa always told him to never go near the bull. She said if he didn't go in and pet the bull, she would whip him with a switch. She opened the gate and pushed him in. Then Sarah started to scream for their father. She screamed that Johnny was in the bull pen. Their father came running out of the barn. He opened the gate and went in with Johnny and the bull." Mary looked at Molly and asked her to finish the story.

Molly said, "The bull was starting to charge Johnny, so his father picked him up and ran for the gate. He yelled for Sarah to open the gate. She smiled and held down the latch. The bull was charging them, so Johnny's father tossed Johnny over the fence. Just as he did, the bull gored him. Sarah started screaming and calling Johnny a killer. She kept telling Johnny he had killed his own father."

"Poor Johnny thinks he killed his father, and I think his mother thinks so too," Paul said.

※

HENRY AND THE OTHER CAMPBELL MEN CAME TO THE door. Mom invited them in, and Paul did most of the talking.

"We should probably tell the police we don't know who or what attacked your sheep. We should get more proof before we blame Sarah and Clive. We'll tell them it could have been a pack of wild dogs or coyotes. We'll go over to the Lamberts and confront them and see what happens. I have reason to believe Sarah plotted the murder of her own father, by using her brother. We should go over and talk to Johnny. I think he was old enough to remember what happened. Sarah blamed the poor kid for their father's death. If we can prove she killed her father, we can get rid of her and Clive."

"Why isn't he telling them Clive is a werewolf, and he'll be back tonight?" Mary asked.

"Shh, honey," Mom said as she escorted Mary to the living room.

Paul knew that unless they saw Clive as a werewolf, the Campbells would never believe it.

"We have to set a trap and get pictures and confront them about all of this," Henry said.

"That will be the plan for tonight, but first I think we should go over to Sadie's house right now and talk to Johnny," Paul said.

"Who should go? We don't want to scare the kid," Henry said.

"Who can safely go?" Harris asked.

"I'll go with Anna, Molly, Mary, and Paul," said Grandma. "I think we can make Johnny feel comfortable talking about what happened."

"Are you sure?" Dad asked.

"Yes," Grandma said confidently.

"The police have been around the area all morning investigating all the complaints from last night. If they come around here, we'll send them to the Lambert farm to nose around," Harris said.

"Okay then. We're going. I'm sure when we go over to the Lambert's, Sarah will confront us," Paul said.

Before they left, Molly pulled Grandma to the side and asked, "Grandma, is it okay if I call Euphemia and have some fairies come with us?"

"That's a wonderful idea." Molly touched the ring and whispered Euphemia's name. As they were getting into the car, Molly and Mary saw a cluster of fairies swirling around the car.

On the way over, Grandma told Paul that if Sarah confronts them, to let her do the talking. He was happy to oblige. They drove into the farmyard and parked by Sadie's back porch. Sadie walked out her back door and waited for them to approach her.

"What are you doing here?" Sadie asked in a surprisingly sharp tone. She looked over at Sarah and Clive, standing by the trailer, and she motioned for them to get inside and she yelled, "Get in the trailer you two fools!"

"I think Clive is some kind of demon or something," Sadie said right off the bat.

"Well, we would like to figure out a way to get them to move back to New Mexico permanently or to get them put in prison," said Paul.

"Oh, really," Sadie said gruffly.

"Sadie, this is Anna's mother, Joanna."

"Sadie, I want to talk to Johnny. Could you get him for me please?" Grandma asked.

"He's upstairs in his room. I'll call him."

"Well, I guess you should all come inside. Whose little girls are these?"

"This is Molly and Mary. They're Mrs. O'Neal's girls," Paul said.

Sadie called Johnny, and he and Cathy came down to the kitchen. Johnny saw everyone and looked down and started to turn away.

"And who is this girl?" Grandma asked nicely.

"That's, Cathy. She's my granddaughter. Her father's in the military, and her mother thought it would be better if she stays with me," Sadie said.

"I think it would be best if just Johnny, Sadie, and Paul were in the kitchen while I speak to him," Grandma said.

"Anna, take the children in the living room. Turn on the television if you want to," Sadie said.

"Johnny, I'd like for you to sit down at the table by me and your mother and Paul."

He sat down, and the others left the room.

"Your mother loves you with all her heart. You know that don't you?"

"Ahuh," he said without looking up.

"Now I want you to look at me and don't be afraid. We're on your side. I know what happened the day your father died."

"It wasn't my fault!" Johnny cried.

"I know, hon," Grandma said calmly. "I know what happened, but I want you to tell me and your mom what really happened."

"How would you know what happened that day? He decided to play in the bullpen, and he got his papa killed," Sadie sneered.

Grandma took Johnny's hands and asked him again, "What really happened, Johnny?"

"Sarah told me to go in the bullpen and give him a carrot. I was afraid to, because he was a mean bull. She said I had to show her I was a man or she would get a switch and whip me until I did. She said if she whipped me in front of the bull, all the noise would make him mad, and he would charge the gate. I didn't want to make the bull mad. Sarah opened the gate and pushed me in. Then she started screaming for help. Papa ran around the barn and got in the pen with me. He yelled for me to run to him. I ran to Papa, and he pulled me to the gate. Sarah held the latch down, so we couldn't get out. Papa picked me up and threw me over the gate. I looked back and the bull was goring him! He threw Papa around like a rag doll!" Johnny began to cry uncontrollably.

Sadie was speechless. She went over to Johnny and hugged him just as Sarah and Clive walked in the door.

"What lies have they been telling you?"

"Just the truth about how you plotted to kill your own father," Grandma said.

"How could you? He loved you!" Sadie said as she hugged Johnny and cried. "Look what you've done to Johnny."

"My father didn't love me. He loved Johnny more. He was so happy to have a boy to help him on the farm. To him, girls were useless. It was a great idea to use my own brother to lure him into the bull pen."

"Liar! You're nothing but a liar!" Sadie said.

"Me, a liar? What kind of game are you playing?" Sarah screamed at Sadie.

Sarah turned to Paul. "All you men are alike. Women are only good for cooking and cleaning. You've heard what a stellar citizen John Doyle was. Did you inherit any of his wonderful traits? I hated him. I saw him burying a body in the woods one night when I was fourteen. I asked him who it was, and he ran after me and pulled out my braid. He told me, if I told anyone, he would kill me. He got his, soon after that."

"As for me killing my own father, no one would believe Johnny. He wandered in the bull's pen. Don't blame me for something a stupid kid did," Sarah said glaring at Sadie.

Clive smirked and said, "Good one, Sarah."

"Shut up you idiot. I have to do everything," Sara said as she picked up a skillet and walked toward Grandma. "Hmm, I guess you're going to fall down the steps as you're leaving and crack your skull old lady, and Paul will fall down the cellar stairs or maybe get caught in a combine. Mom will vouch for me. She always has."

"Not this time Sarah."

Paul stood up, and Grandma motioned for him to stay calm. "We can take care of this, Paul."

"Girls come here," Grandma said calmly.

Mary and Molly ran to Grandma's side.

Sarah stopped in her tracks. "Clive, help me!"

Mom and Cathy came around the corner just in time to see Clive turn into a werewolf. Mom ran to Grandma's side, and Cathy started screaming and ran upstairs.

Grandma stood up and took Mary's hand and said, "Molly, the ring."

Molly touched the ring and the fairies encircled Sarah's arm and caused her to hit Clive on the head with the iron skillet. He ran outside, and she followed him screaming and hitting him. Paul kept everyone else in the kitchen and called the police.

Clive picked Sarah up and threw her across the farmyard. She got up and ran into the trailer she was living in and slammed the door. Clive tore the door off the trailer and went in. The screaming and the growling sounds coming from the trailer were horrendous.

"This was inevitable. He was going to turn on her sooner or later," Grandma said.

The police were in the area, so they got there within minutes. Clive came out of the trailer covered in blood. He had turned back into a man, but still had a wild look in his eyes. The fairies froze him in place until the police could get handcuffs on him. The police called for backup. One of them went in the trailer to investigate and quickly came back out and threw up. Paul and Sadie went out to talk to the police. Grandma and Mom stayed back and made the children stay in the house.

"Molly, did we do a good job for you?" Euphemia said.

"Yes, you saved our lives again," Molly said.

"We love you Euphemia and all your friends," Mary said.

"We do love you all," Molly said. The fairies encircled Johnny and Cathy and then went out and swirled around the trailer for a few seconds before they disappeared.

"Mom, isn't there something you can do for Cathy and Johnny to help them forget what they saw?" Anna asked Grandma.

"The fairies already did it. All they'll remember is Sarah attacking Clive. They won't remember seeing him as a werewolf, and they never saw the fairies."

Mr. Waters showed up and asked Paul what happened.

"Sarah Lambert brought this man into our area. He mutilated two of the Campbell's sheep last night and scared the farmers on County Road. I believe he's criminally insane, but I'm not a psychiatrist," Paul said.

"I see the O'Neals are here," Mr. Waters mentioned.

"They were here to talk to Sadie and her son when those two started fighting," Paul said as he pointed to Clive and the trailer.

"I think this guy has a cracked skull," said one of the policemen. "The ambulance should be here soon."

"Make sure at least two armed policemen never leave his side," Paul advised.

"I'm calling for the coroner. I assure you, after what he did, he'll never be free again," a policeman said.

After the coroner left, a clean-up crew went in to gather up all they could of Sarah. Sadie told them to call Cole Funeral Parlor to collect the remains.

"I won't even ask you Campbells if I could bury Sarah in Campbell Cemetery. I wouldn't want to desecrate the land,"

Sadie told Paul. He nodded in agreement.

"Well, Anna, we don't have to worry about him or her anymore. She's dead, and he'll be in prison for the rest of his life," Paul said. "I'm sure we can leave pretty soon."

Mom asked one of the policemen if they needed to ask them any questions, because they had to get the children home. He took everyone's names and addresses and said if he had any more questions, he would contact them.

"Can you call me when he's in a secure cell?" Paul asked the policeman. "Seriously, he is the strongest man I've ever seen."

The policeman told Paul he would give him an update later, and he could take the O'Neals home.

On the way home Grandma said, "I'll be happy when I know he's in a secure cell. He can change at any time. I doubt they'll be able to keep him. If he escapes, he won't be coming back here. He is wanted for murder and the only tie he had here was Sarah."

"I can't believe I saw a werewolf," Paul said. No one spoke the rest of the way home.

When they got back to the house, Grandma called Aunt Julie. She told her all about the murder and that she wanted to stay until Tuesday. She wanted to make sure Clive was gone, and she wanted to stay until the full moon was over. She told Julie to call Veronica and fill her in on the news.

About an hour later, Paul called and talked to Grandma.

"I got a call from the policeman we spoke to earlier. He said the ambulance had left Lambert's and was going down County Road. Two policemen were in the ambulance guarding Clive. They said he turned into some kind of animal and broke the handcuffs like they were nothing. He smashed through the back door of the ambulance and took off running across a field and into the woods. They shot at him and one policeman swore he hit him, but he kept running. So that's where we are now. He's free," Paul said.

"I'm staying here until Tuesday with my husband. Our rifle is loaded with silver bullets. Stefan brought a dozen or so extra bullets just in case. We can spare some if Henry or Harris have the same type of rifle and want to borrow them. Hopefully, he'll keep running, but you never know, he may want some kind of revenge and go after you or us, Paul," Grandma said in a worried tone.

"I'll call Harris, and I'm sure he'll come over and borrow some bullets from Stefan," Paul said before he hung up.

"Anna, Clive may want revenge on us for the lightning burns from last night and the scene at Lambert's farm. We should still be on our guard," Grandma said.

"I want all my children in the house. No reading outside. Your father will take care of the chickens and make sure they're locked in the chicken coop early this afternoon. Your grandma and I are going to make an extra special supper tonight. Absolutely no one is going to school in the morning unless we get word that Clive is either recaptured or dead. Sock still has to be kept inside all night. If I think of anything else or anyone else thinks of anything important, say it. Am I forgetting anything?" Anna said.

"No, I think you covered everything for now, Anna," Grandma said.

"How about a game of rummy? Get the cards, Maggie," Dad said.

Nathan, Adam, Dad, and Maggie played several games of rummy. Molly and Mary went upstairs and played with their cut-out dolls and other toys. Grandpa watched television and Grandma and Mom made supper.

After the wonderful roast with potatoes, carrots, lots of gravy, green beans, and buttered bread, Henry and Harris came over with their rifles to see if the silver bullets were the caliber they needed. Luckily the bullets were, and they borrowed six bullets.

"I don't know, but the cows seem pretty restless to me, and the sheep are making a lot of noise. We're going to lock the cows in the barnyard and bring up as many sheep as we can and lock them in the equipment sheds for the night. We can get a good shot from the second story windows if something gets in with the livestock," Henry said.

"We better go, Dad, if we want to help Chad and Beau round up the sheep and cattle. We'll give each of them one silver bullet for their rifles," Harris said.

"I'm sorry I don't have more, but there never really was a need for them in Coaltown," Grandpa said.

As the men stood outside and talked, they could hear the bloodhounds hunting Clive in the distance. Police and volunteers came from all over to hunt down the man who tore Sarah Lambert to shreds.

Molly and her sisters went up to bed about nine o'clock. The beds were still pushed together and Grandma and Grandpa were going to sleep in Maggie's room again. Maggie was reading by lamplight, and Mary and Molly were just about to doze off, when Molly heard whispering in her ear. She sat up and listened.

It was Euphemia, and she said, "Molly, your family and friends don't have to worry. We are taking care of Clive. Sarah put a curse on him and turned him into a werewolf. She controlled him and made him do evil things. He met her in New Mexico when he was playing in a local band. He fell in love with her. He didn't know she was a witch until the night she cursed him. He's only nineteen and he doesn't reason very well."

"The police are searching for him," Molly said.

Mary sat up and said, "Who are you talking to?"

"Euphemia is telling me about Clive. Speak to both of us. Mary isn't asleep."

"No one saw us, but after Clive killed Sarah's body, her spirit slithered out of the trailer right into our waiting arms. We brought her back to her beloved waterfall and encased her in a flat stone on the path just outside the waterfall, so visitors will surely step on her. She will be encased there forever. Now, Molly, will you go and get your grandmother?"

"Okay," Molly said. She turned on the bedroom light and went downstairs.

"Grandma, no one has to worry. The fairies have Clive, and Euphemia wants to talk to you."

Grandma hurried upstairs to the girls' bedroom.

"Joanna, Clive was a victim of Sarah, and I think we should break the curse. It should be very easy to do now that Sarah is encased in a stone," Euphemia said.

"I was wondering if we'd seen the last of Sarah," Grandma said. "What do you need us to do?"

"We threw the police and the dogs off the scent by dragging Clive's shirt through the woods and fields straight north. We planted sightings of him two hundred miles north of here. The police had been looking south, but they were too close to us. We changed their course. Call Henry Campbell and tell him about the sightings. The word will get around, because every time a phone rings around here, the people on these party lines pick up quietly and listen in. The full moon is tonight, so we'll keep him confined and safe. Tomorrow morning, about ten o'clock, come to

Molly O'Neal 291

the waterfall. Bring Molly of course, and Mary and Anna," Euphemia said.

Maggie was watching while Grandma and the girls talked to the air.

"I'm not even going to ask what you guys are doing," Maggie said as she turned off her lamp and pulled her covers over her head.

Euphemia continued, "Charles should go to work and Nathan, Adam, and Maggie should catch the bus like any other Monday. See you ladies at the waterfall tomorrow at ten." Euphemia fluttered away.

"Grandma, she told me Clive fell in love with Sarah, and she cursed him to use him for her dirty work," Molly said.

"Tomorrow you'll be able to fix this problem, Molly."

"With a little help from me and you, Grandma," Mary said.

"Yes, with a little help from us. Now you two go to sleep. We have a big day tomorrow," Grandma said as she tucked the girls in.

Mom, Grandpa, and Dad were standing outside the bedroom door listening. They all said goodnight and went back downstairs.

"Do you think it's safe?" Dad asked.

"I trust Euphemia. She saved our lives once already and Molly's life twice," Grandma answered.

Everyone got a good night's sleep.

❖

THE NEXT MORNING, MAGGIE AND THE BOYS CAUGHT THE school bus. Becky and Jesse asked where Molly and Mary were, and Maggie said her mom wanted them to rest after the busy weekend. Johnny and Cathy didn't go to school either. Johnny's sister had been killed, and poor Cathy saw too much.

❖

Some strangers pulled up at Sadie's house and knocked on her door.

"Are you, Mrs. Lambert?" they asked.

"Yes. Who are you?"

"We are June and Ira Miller. We're looking for our son, Clive Miller. We found this address in his old apartment in New Mexico. We were letting him live in one of our apartments so we could keep an eye on him. One of his friends told us he had a girlfriend named Sarah. They said she was a lot older than him, and she bossed him around."

"Clive was temporarily staying in the barn, and my daughter was staying in the trailer over there. Are you two werewolves like your son?" Sadie asked.

"I don't know what you're talking about. Our Clive has always been sweet natured. We have to take care of him. He's an innocent."

"Well, he killed my Sarah in the trailer over there. She was no angel, but he ripped her to shreds," Sadie said as she began to cry.

"There must be some mistake. Our Clive is a gentle soul and very gullible. We tried to keep an eye on him and then he got a girlfriend. We think she was a bad influence on our boy. We found horrible huge shackles in his apartment, and everything was a filthy mess," June said.

"Go in the barn and get his things out. He was staying where he belonged: with the other livestock," Sadie said as she slammed the door.

"Where is he? Do the police have him?" cried June to no avail. Sadie wouldn't come back out to talk to them.

"I'll go to the barn. You get in the car, and see if you can get any news on the radio," Ira said.

Ira gathered all the clothes in the barn, and he put them in the trunk of their car. He walked past the pink trailer, and he noticed the door was mangled and propped up on the side of the trailer. He looked in and saw blood spattered all over the walls.

"Something horrible happened in there. We have to get out of here, June."

"Do you have everything? Check the hearse for his instruments."

Ira went over to the hearse and saw the keys in the ignition.

"Are any of his instruments in the back of his hearse?" June asked Ira.

"No, it's empty."

June finally got some news on the radio. They learned there was a manhunt out for their son, and he was spotted heading north in a stolen car. June started crying, and Ira hugged her, and he began to cry.

"Our poor boy," Ira said. The only thing he could really do was play his guitar. I don't want the hearse. I left the keys in it. I'll leave a note on the front seat and thirty dollars, so Mrs. Lambert can call a local junkyard to come and get it. These people don't want us here, June."

Ira wrote a note and placed it in the hearse along with the money. He got in their car and sighed with sadness.

"Will we ever see him again?" June asked him.

"I don't know," he said as he started up their car and drove back onto County Road.

❖

It was fifteen minutes to ten, and Grandma, Mom, and the girls were getting in the station wagon to drive down their old lane, past the old house and barn, to the field road. Mom drove to where Henry had plowed his truck through the corn. She drove right through the field to the edge of the woods. They got out of the car and started down the path to the waterfall.

When they got to the waterfall, Clive was sitting on a tree stump. He seemed very calm and quiet.

As they walked up to him, he started crying and said, "Help me. Help me."

The fairies began to twirl around all of them. Euphemia flew up to Molly and said, "We have to hurry. His parents are here to get him and take him home. Hurry, touch the ring, and hold Clive's hand. Mary, hold Molly's other hand. Joanna and Anna, put your hands on Molly's shoulders. Molly, repeat what I say. Heal Clive's fractured skull and burns. Close the bullet wounds."

Molly repeated it, and Clive moaned and almost passed out.

"Hurry now, and say, break Sarah's curse. Bring back Clive."

Molly repeated it, and as she did, a golden glow burst around them, and Clive passed out.

"Keep his hand, Molly. Don't anyone let go. Call Clive! Call him, and wake him up, Molly!"

When Molly called him, he woke up and asked where he was.

Euphemia said, "Clive, Run! Follow the fairies, and find your parents!"

A swirl of fairies led Clive through the woods and out onto County Road where his father had just finished changing a tire on the car.

"Clive!" his mother shouted as he ran into her arms. His father ran around the car and hugged him and June, and they cried together.

One of the fairies got up near Clive's ear and said, "Go home now! Go, hurry!"

"We have to go. Get in the car," Clive said as he got in the back seat. "Drive, Dad!"

They took off for home and were never heard from again.

As Molly was walking through the woods with the others, she said, "He even looked different after the curse was lifted and a lot younger."

"The evil left him. He won't even remember the time he was cursed," Grandma said.

Euphemia flew up to them and said, "He's with his mother and father on his way home. Bye for now, ladies."

Molly, Mary, and Grandma waved goodbye to Euphemia.

"I wish I could see fairies," Mom said.

"I could give you my beryl stone necklace," Molly said.

"I could try it."

"Sunshine!" Grandma said as they walked out of the woods. "Everyone, hold hands and form a circle. Raise your hands up and shout, "What a beautiful day!" Now, quickly, put your hands down. Raise them up again and laugh."

"Is this something, Grandma?" Molly asked.

"No. It's just fun."

"We all make such a good team!" Molly said with a big smile and a sparkle in her green eyes.

Back at the waterfall, a stone shook, and the fairies giggled.

COMING SOON

BOOK TWO

MOLLY O'NEAL

Caskets, Cupcakes, and
Bedroom Windows

An excerpt from Chapter One

"Oh, here he comes. I forgot to tell you, Mother Theresa got sick, so we have a substitute. He's awful," Paula said as the girls lined up.

"Line up quietly, children," said Mother Rachael. She blew her whistle, and the children from all the grades became silent. They lined up behind the number of their grade painted on the asphalt, and walked single file to their classrooms.

"His name is Mr. Burn," Paula whispered.

"You two, get to the end of the line, and stop outside the classroom door," Mr. Burn sneered.

The other children filed into the classroom and sat at their desks.

"What did you say to her, Paula?"

"I told Molly your name was Mr. Burn, since she wasn't here yesterday."

"Get in the room, Paula."

"Yes, Molly. I am Mr. Burn," he said as he twitched. "Don't I know you from somewhere? Did your family ever have a funeral at Cole Funeral Parlor?" he said as he got so close to Molly's face, she almost gagged on his coffee and cigarette breath.

"Oh, I remember now," he said as he backed up a couple of feet. "Just forget I said anything. Get in the room."

Mr. Burn was about five feet six inches tall and skinny. He had greasy black hair with visible dandruff. He wore a plain black suit, white shirt, and black tie. He looked like an undertaker.

"Oh, I collected the weekly milk money yesterday and the order was put in, so you, Milly, don't get any milk this week," he said as he glared at Molly.

"My name is Molly, not Milly," she said.

"Milly, Molly, what's the difference?"

Molly could feel her face burning. She forgot to get her milk money that morning anyway, and she was sure Mary forgot hers too.

"Line up for, Mass," he said. "And be quiet!"

No one wanted to be first in line behind Mr. Burn. Molly was at the back of the line with Paula and Diana McKinney.

"Don't worry, Molly. I'll loan you my thermos to take home," Diana whispered.

"Quiet," hissed Mr. Burn.

Mr. Burn stopped at the side entrance to the church, which was in the school hallway. Molly noticed he wouldn't even put a foot in the door of the church.

"I'll be waiting at this door after Mass. I'll be watching you," he said as he waved them in.

When they got to their pews, they knelt down.

"My father said the school was in a bind, since Mother Therese became ill so quickly. They called my mother to see if she could come in to substitute, but she was busy, so I guess Mr. Burn was the only teacher available at such short notice," Diana said. Everyone stood for Mass to begin.

During lunch, Mr. Burn took a sack out of his desk

drawer and began to eat a braunschweiger sandwich and a hard-boiled egg. His dessert was three cupcake packages with two full-size cupcakes in each. He also took the one leftover chocolate milk from the basket and drank it. He was a messy eater, and he twitched a lot.

Whether the children remembered to bring their milk money or not, the same amount of milk was ordered and delivered every day. The milk was for Molly, but he drank it along with the coffee in one of his two thermoses.

Molly ate her bologna sandwich and one of the boys sitting next to her gave her some of his potato chips. She was grateful, even though they made her even thirstier.

"Line up for recess children," Mr. Burn said.

Diana walked by and put her thermos on Molly's desk, and Molly put it in her satchel.

"Go straight out to the playground. No drinks or bathroom breaks," he said. He let them go out alone, so he could go out another door and smoke.

Molly and Paula ducked in the bathroom, and the rest of the children went outside.

"I'm thirsty," Molly said.

"Let me look out and see if he's gone," said Paula as she peeked around the corner. "Okay, he's gone."

Molly went out in the hallway and got a big drink from the water fountain.

"Hurry let's get outside before he comes back," Paula said.

At recess, Molly and Paula were jumping rope when Diana walked up to them and said, "Did you see the car Mr. Burn drove to school. It's in the parking lot over there," she said.

"It looks like a black station wagon. It's real shiny," Paula said.

"It's a hearse. His family owns the big funeral parlor

about three blocks from here. I'm sure you've seen it. It's called Cole Funeral Parlor," Diana said.

"I know where it is. Creepy place," Paula said.

"Well, I think he's mean, and he gives me the creeps," Molly said. "Why isn't it called Burn Funeral Parlor?"

"He's a nephew of the owners, Mr. and Mrs. Cole. They took him and his brothers in when they were kids. Can I take a turn jumping?" Diana asked.

"Sure," Molly said. Paula held one end of the rope and Molly held the other.

When the bell rang for recess to be over, Mr. Burn walked from the back of the church blowing smoke out of his mouth and nose and tossing his cigarette to the side.

Made in the USA
Monee, IL
02 January 2023